KU-441-964

THE LETTER

Tina Craig longs to escape her violent husband. She works all the hours God sends to save up enough money to leave him, also volunteering in a charity shop to avoid her unhappy home. Whilst going through the pockets of a second-hand suit, she comes across an old, sealed letter. The letter will alter the course of her life forever. This is the story of two women, born decades apart, whose paths are destined to cross and how one woman's devastation leads to the other's salvation.

THE LETTER

THE LETTER

by

Kathryn Hughes

Magna Large Print Books
Long Preston, North Yorkshire,
BD23 4ND, England.

British Library Cataloguing in Publication Data.

Hughes, Kathryn
    The letter.

       A catalogue record of this book is
       available from the British Library

       ISBN   978-0-7505-4348-4

First published in Great Britain in 2015 by Headline Review,
an imprint of Headline Publishing Group

Copyright © Kathryn Hughes 2013

Cover illustration © Jarek Blaminsky by arrangement with
Arcangel Images Ltd.

The right of Kathryn Hughes to be identified as the author of this
work has been asserted by her in accordance with the Copyright,
Designs and Patents Act, 1988.

Published in Large Print 2016 by arrangement with
Hodder & Stoughton Ltd.

All Rights reserved. No part of this publication may be reproduced,
stored in a retrieval system, or transmitted in any form or by any
means, electronic, mechanical, photocopying, recording or otherwise
without the prior permission of the Copyright owner.

Magna Large Print is an imprint of Library Magna Books Ltd.

Printed and bound in Great Britain by
T.J. (International) Ltd., Cornwall, PL28 8RW

Extract from 'All Through the Night' copyright
© 1884 Harold Boulton, translated from
'Ar Hyd y Nos' copyright © 1784
John Ceiriog Hughes.

All characters in this publication are fictitious
and any resemblance to real persons,
living or dead, is purely coincidental.

For Rob, Cameron and Ellen.

Prologue

Present day

It was the small things she took pleasure in. The faint hum of a huge furry bumble bee busily flitting from one flower to another, oblivious to the fact that it was completing a task on which the entire human race depended. The heady scent and glorious abundance of colour provided by the sweet peas that she grew in the vegetable patch, despite the fact that the space could be given over to their more edible cousins. Then there was the sight of her husband rubbing his aching back as he dug fertiliser into the rose bed without complaint when there were a thousand things he would prefer to be doing.

As she knelt down to pull up a few weeds, she felt her granddaughter's hand slip into hers, so tiny, warm and trusting. It was another small thing, the one that gave her the most pleasure of all, that always brought a smile to her face and made her heart lurch.

'What are you doing, Grandma?'

She turned and looked at her beloved grand-daughter. The little girl's cheeks were tinged pink with the afternoon sun and she had smudges of soil across her button nose. She took out her handkerchief and gently wiped them away. 'I'm just pulling up these weeds.'

'Why?'

She thought about this for a second. 'Well, they don't belong here.'

'Oh. Where do they belong, then?'

'They're just weeds, love, they don't belong anywhere.'

Her granddaughter stuck out her bottom lip and furrowed her brow. 'That doesn't seem very nice. Everything belongs somewhere.'

She smiled and planted a light kiss on the top of the child's head as she glanced across towards her husband. Although his once-dark hair was now smattered with grey and his face was more heavily lined, the years had not diminished him too much and she was thankful every day that she had found him. Against the odds their paths had crossed, and now they belonged together.

She turned back to her granddaughter. 'You're right. Let's put them back.'

As she dug a little hole, she marvelled at how much could be learnt from children, how much their wisdom was underestimated or even dismissed.

'Grandma?'

She was shaken out of her reverie. 'Yes, love.'

'How did you and Grandpa meet?'

She stood up and took hold of her granddaughter's hand. She brushed away a strand of golden hair from her little face. 'Well, let's see now. That *is* a long story...'

PART ONE

PART ONE

1

March 1973

This time she was going to die, of that she was certain. She knew she must only have a few seconds left and she silently prayed for the end to come quickly. She could feel the warm, sticky blood as it ran down the back of her neck. She had heard the sickening sound of her skull cracking as her husband slammed her head into the wall. There was something in her mouth that felt like a piece of gravel; she knew it was a tooth and she desperately tried to spit it out. His hands were gripped so tightly around her throat that it was impossible for her to draw breath or make any kind of sound. Her lungs screamed out for oxygen and the pressure on the back of her eyeballs was so intense she was sure they were going to pop out. Her head began to swim, and then, mercifully, she started to black out.

She heard the long-forgotten sound of the school bell and suddenly she was five years old again. The chatter of the other children was almost drowned out by the incessant ringing. As she screamed at them to stop, she realised she had a voice after all.

She stared up at the bedroom ceiling for a second and then squinted at the alarm clock that had just roused her from her sleep. Cold sweat trickled down her spine and she tugged at the bedclothes, pulling them up to her chin in an effort to savour the warmth for a few seconds longer. Her heart was still pounding after the nightmare and she blew out gently through her mouth. Her warm breath hung in the frigid air of the bedroom. With an enormous effort she heaved herself out of bed and winced as her bare feet found the icy roughness of the wooden floor. She glanced over at Rick, who thankfully was still sound asleep, snoring off the effects of the bottle of whisky he had drunk the night before. She checked that his cigarettes were still on the bedside table where she had carefully positioned them. If there was one thing guaranteed to put Rick in a foul mood, it was not being able to find his fags in the morning.

She crept quietly into the bathroom and eased the door shut. It would probably take an explosion not seen since Hiroshima to wake him, but Tina wasn't taking any chances. She ran a basin for a wash, the water freezing as usual. Sometimes it was a choice between feeding themselves and feeding the meter. Rick had lost his job on the buses, so there was little money for heat. Enough to drink, smoke and gamble, though, she noted in the silence of her brain.

She went downstairs, filled the kettle and placed it on the stove. The paper boy had been and she absently pulled the newspapers through the letter box: *The Sun* for her and *The Sporting Life* for Rick. The headline caught her attention. It was Grand National day. Her shoulders sagged and she shuddered at the thought of all the money Rick would squander on the race. There was little doubt he would be too drunk by lunchtime to

18

venture out to the bookmaker's, and it would be left to Tina to put the bet on. The betting shop was next door to the charity shop where she helped out on Saturdays, and the bookie, Graham, had become a close friend over the years. Despite working all week as a shorthand typist in an insurance office, Tina looked forward to her day in the charity shop. Rick had told her it was ridiculous for her to spend the day voluntarily sorting through dead people's clothes when she could work in a proper shop and contribute even more to the family coffers. For Tina, it was an excuse to spend the day out of Rick's way, and she enjoyed chatting to the customers and having normal conversations where she didn't have to watch every word she said.

She switched on the radio and turned the volume down a touch. Tony Blackburn always managed to make her smile with his corny jokes. He was just announcing Donny Osmond's new single, 'The Twelfth of Never', when the kettle began to give its hollow whistle. She snatched it up before the noise became too shrill, and put two spoonfuls of tea leaves into the old stained pot. She sat down at the kitchen table while she waited for the tea to brew, and opened her paper. She held her breath as the toilet flushed upstairs. She heard the floorboards creak as Rick padded back to bed, and exhaled with relief. Then she froze as he called:

'Tina! Where are my fags?'

Jesus. He smokes like a beagle.

She jumped up immediately and belted up the stairs two at a time.

'On your bedside table where I put them last

night,' she replied, arriving breathlessly at his side.

She ran her hand over the table in the gloom but could not feel them. She swallowed her rising panic.

'I'll have to pull the curtains a little. I can't see.'

'For God's sake, woman! Is it too much to ask for a man to be able to have a fag when he wakes up? I'm gagging here.'

His sour morning breath stank of stale whisky.

She finally found the cigarettes on the floor between the bed and the table.

'Here they are. You must have knocked them off in your sleep.'

Rick stared at her for a moment before he reached up and snatched the packet from her. She flinched and instinctively covered her face with her hands. He grabbed her wrist and their eyes met for a second before Tina closed hers and fought back the tears.

She could recall the first time Rick had hit her like it had happened only yesterday. Even the memory of it caused her cheek to sting and burn. It wasn't just the physical pain, though, but the sudden stark reality that things were never going to be the same again. The fact that it was also their wedding night made it harder to take. Up until that moment the day had been perfect. Rick looked so handsome in his new brown suit, cream shirt and silk tie. The white carnation in his buttonhole confirmed him as the groom and Tina thought it was impossible to love anybody more than she loved him. Everyone had told her she looked stunning... Her long dark hair was swept up into a loose bun and woven through with tiny flowers. Her pale blue eyes shone out from beneath thick false eyelashes and her complexion radiated a natural beauty that needed no help from cosmetics. The party after the wedding was a lively affair at an inexpensive local hotel, and the happy couple and their guests had danced the night away.

As they were preparing for bed that night in their hotel room, Tina noticed that Rick was unusually quiet.

'Are you all right, love?' she asked. She put her arms around his neck. 'It was a wonderful day, wasn't it? I can't believe I'm Mrs Craig at last.' She pulled away from him suddenly. 'Hey, I'll have to practise my new signature.' She picked up a pen and paper from the bedside table and wrote *Mrs Tina Craig* with a flourish.

Still Rick said nothing; just stared at her. He lit a cigarette and poured himself a glass of cheap champagne. He swigged it down in one gulp and walked over to where Tina was sitting on the bed.

'Stand up,' he commanded.

Tina was puzzled by his tone but did as she was asked.

Rick raised his hand and whipped it sharply across her face.

'Don't ever make a fool of me again.' With that he stormed out of the bedroom.

He spent the night slumped in the hotel lounge surrounded by empty glasses, and it was days before he would tell Tina exactly what her transgression had been. Apparently he hadn't liked the way she had danced with one of his work colleagues.

She had looked at him too provocatively and flirted with him in front of their guests. Tina couldn't even remember the guy, let alone the incident, but it was the start of Rick's paranoid fixation that she was coming on to every man she met. She often wondered if she should have left him the very next day. But she was a romantic at heart and wanted to give her fledgling marriage every chance to succeed. She was sure the incident was a one-off, and Rick allayed any niggling doubts when he presented her with a bouquet by way of an apology. Such was his remorse and contrition that Tina had no hesitation in forgiving him immediately. It was only a few days later that she noticed a card buried amongst the flowers. She smiled to herself as she pulled it out. *With fond memories of our beloved Nan,* she read. The bugger had stolen the flowers from a grave in the church-yard!

Now, four years later, they stared at each other for a second longer before Rick released his grip.

'Thanks, love.' He smiled. 'Now be a good girl and fetch me a brew.'

Tina exhaled with relief and rubbed her crimson wrist. Ever since that wedding night incident, she had vowed she was not going to be a victim. No way was she going to be one of those battered wives who made excuses for their husbands' vile behaviour. There had been many times when she had threatened to leave, but she always backed out at the last minute. Rick was so repentant and humble and, of course, promised never to raise his hand to her again. These days, though, he was drinking a lot more heavily and his outbursts were more frequent. The time had finally come when she could stand it no longer.

The problem was, she had nowhere to go. She had no family, and although she did have a couple of close friends, she could never impose on them to the extent of asking them to take her in. It was her wages that paid the rent, but there was no way Rick would leave voluntarily. So she had started an escape fund. She needed enough money for a deposit and a month's rent on a new place, and then she would be free. That was a lot more diffi-cult than it sounded. She rarely had any spare money left to save, but no matter how long it took, she was determined to leave. The old coffee jar she kept hidden at the back of the kitchen cupboard was filling up nicely, and she now had just over fifty pounds. But with rent on even the most basic bedsit commanding eight pounds per week, plus a deposit of at least thirty, she would need to save a lot more before she could make the break. For the time being she would make the best of it, staying out of Rick's way as much as possible and trying not to get him riled.

She carried Rick's tea upstairs, together with *The Sporting Life* tucked under her arm.

'Here you are,' she said, trying to sound breezy.

There was no reply. He was fast asleep again, propped up on the pillow, mouth open, a cigarette balanced precariously on his dry, cracked bottom lip. Tina picked it off and stubbed it out.

'For Christ's sake! You'll kill us both,' she mut-tered.

23

She set the mug down and pondered what to do. Should she wake him and incur his wrath? Or should she just leave the tea on the bedside table? When he woke up it would no doubt be stone cold, which would be sure to send him into a rage, but by then she would hopefully be at the shop and out of harm's way. The decision was taken out of her hands as he stirred and forced his eyes open.

'Your tea's there,' she said. 'I'm going to the shop now. Will you be OK?'

Rick pushed himself up on to his elbows.

'My mouth's as dry as a camel's,' he sniffed. 'Thanks for the tea, love.'

He patted the quilt, indicating for her to sit down.

'Come here.'

That was what life was like with Rick. He was an evil, spiteful bully one minute and an angelic choirboy the next.

'Sorry about before. You know, about the ciggies? I wouldn't hurt you, Tina, you know that.'

Tina could scarcely believe her ears, but it was, never a good idea to contradict Rick so she merely nodded.

'Look,' he continued. 'Could you do me a favour?'

She let out a small, inaudible sigh and raised her eyes to the ceiling. *Here we go.*

'Could you put a bet on for me?'

She could bite her tongue no longer.

'Do you think that's a good idea, Rick? You know how tight things are. With only me earning, there's not much spare cash for things like gambling.'

'*With only me earning*,' Rick mimicked. 'You never miss a chance to get that in, do you, you sanctimonious cow?' Tina was momentarily startled by his vicious reaction, but he was not finished. 'It's the Grand National, for Christ's sake! Everybody has a bet today.'

He reached down to the floor, picked up his trousers from where he had discarded them the night before and pulled out a roll of banknotes.

'There's fifty quid here.' He tore off the lid of his cigarette packet and wrote the name of a horse on the back. 'Fifty pounds to win.'

He handed her the money and the scrap of cardboard. Tina was stunned.

'Where did you get this?' She held up the roll of notes.

'Well it's not really any of your business, but since you ask, I won it on the horses. There, you see, who says it's a mug's game?'

Liar.

Her head was swirling and she felt her neck begin to flush.

'This is more than a week's wages for me, Rick.'

'I know. Aren't I clever?' he replied smugly.

She clasped her hands together as though in prayer and brought them up to her lips. She tried to remain calm as she blew gently through her fingers. 'But this money could pay our electricity bill or our food bill for a whole month.'

'Christ, Tina! You're so boring.'

She fanned out the notes in her trembling hands. She knew then that she was not physically capable of handing over such a large amount to a bookie.

'Can't you put it on?' she begged.

'You work next door to the bloody betting shop, I'm hardly putting you out.'

Tina could feel the tears starting to sting but she had made up her mind. She would take the money and discuss with Graham what to do. She had taken money from Rick before for a bet and not put it on. The horse had inevitably lost and he had been none the wiser. However, Tina felt she had aged about ten years during the course of that race, and this time it was different. The stakes were so much higher. *Fifty pounds, for heaven's sake.*

Suddenly and inexplicably she found herself in the grip of panic. She felt the heat rise from her toes to the back of her neck and she found it difficult to breathe. She backed out of the bedroom, muttering excuses about having left the toast under the grill, and ran downstairs to the kitchen. She climbed up on to a stool and reached into the back of the cupboard, feeling around for the coffee jar containing her escape fund. Her fingers found the familiar shape and she pulled the jar out and clutched it to her chest. Her hands shook as she tried to unscrew the lid. Her sweaty palms could not get the grip she needed and she groped around for the tea towel. Finally the lid yielded and she peered inside. There was nothing but a few coppers left. She shook the jar and looked again, as though her eyes had deceived her the first time.

'Bastard!' she cried out. 'Bastard, bastard, bastard!'

She started to weep, the huge sobs making her shoulders heave.

'Thought you could pull the wool over my eyes, did you?'

She jumped and spun round to see Rick leaning in the doorway, another cigarette hanging from his lips and wearing only his greying tea-stained vest and grubby underpants.

'You took it! How could you? I've worked all hours to save that money. It's taken me months.'

She slumped down on to the floor and rocked back and forth, still clutching the almost-empty jar. Rick strode over and dragged her roughly to her feet.

'Pull yourself together. What do you expect when you hide money from your own husband? What are you saving for anyway?'

To get away from you, you drunken, manipulative waste of space.

'It was supposed to be a ... surprise, you know, a little holiday for us. I thought a break would do us both good.'

Rick pondered this for a second and then relaxed his grip on Tina's arm. He frowned doubtfully.

'A nice idea. Tell you what, when that horse romps home, we'll have a belting holiday, maybe even go abroad.'

Tina nodded miserably and wiped her eyes.

'Go and get yourself cleaned up. You're going to be late for work. I'm off back to bed. I'm knackered.'

He dropped a kiss on the top of her head and headed back upstairs.

Tina stood alone in the middle of the kitchen.

27

She had never felt so wretched or desperate in her life, but she was determined she was not going to put that bet on. That fifty pounds was hers, and no way was it going to be wasted on a horse race, Grand National or not. She took the money and stuffed it into her purse, then took a cursory look at the name Rick had written on the cigarette packet.

Red Rum.

You'd better not win, you bugger.

Tina arrived at the shop and fished in her handbag for the keys. In spite of the notice on the shop door asking people not to, someone had left a sack of old clothes on the doorstep. It was inconceivable to Tina that anyone would actually steal clothes that had been donated to charity, but it had happened on several occasions. Even in these gloomy economic times of strikes and power cuts, it was still surprising how low some people would stoop. She hoisted the bag over her shoulder, unlocked the door and went inside. After two years of working here, the smell of the place still caused her to wrinkle her nose. Second-hand clothing had an odour all of is own and was the same in every charity shop or jumble sale you went to. Mothballs mixed with stale sweat and biscuits.

Tina put the kettle on for the second time that morning and opened the sack. She pulled out an old suit and held it up to give it the once-over. It was very old but incredibly well made and of a quality the likes of which she had not encountered before. It was an unusual greenish colour, with a very faint gold stripe, and made entirely of wool.

28

The bell rang on the shop door, causing her to halt her examination.

'Nice suit, er ... lovely colour. No wonder they wanted rid of it!'

It was Graham from the bookmaker's next door.

'Morning. I'm surprised you've got time for idle chit-chat today,' Tina teased.

'Yeah, busiest day of the year for me, but I'm not complaining,' he replied, rubbing his hands together. 'Nigel's opening up so I've got a couple of minutes.'

Tina gave him a warm hug.

'Well it's nice to see you.'

'How are you today, then?'

It was a loaded question. Graham knew full well the circumstances of her domestic situation. He had commented on her bruises or split lip on more than one occasion. He was always so kind and Tina could feel herself beginning to wobble. Graham took her elbow and guided her to a chair.

'What's he done this time?' he asked, tilting her chin and scrutinising her face.

'I hate him sometimes, Graham, I really do.'

He pulled her into his arms and smoothed her hair. 'You deserve so much more, Tina. You're twenty-eight years old. You should be settled in a loving marriage by now, perhaps a couple of kids...'

She pulled away, her mascara-smudged eyes searching his. 'You didn't come to help, then.'

'I'm sorry.' Graham cradled her head again. 'Tell me what's happened.'

'You haven't got time for this, today of all days.'

But Tina knew Graham would always have time

29

for her. He had been hopelessly in love with her since the day they met. Tina loved him too, but only as a dear friend and father figure. He was twenty years her senior, and besides, he already had a wife, and it just wasn't in her nature to steal another woman's husband.

'He wants me to put a bet on.' She sniffed, and Graham pulled out a crisp starched handkerchief and handed it to her.

'Nothing new there,' he said. 'He's one of my best customers. And it is Grand National day.'

'That's what he said. But this is different, Graham. He's talking about fifty pounds!'

Even Graham baulked at the amount.

'Where on earth did he get that kind of money?'

'He stole it from me,' Tina sobbed.

Graham looked confused, as well he might. 'From you?' he asked. 'I don't understand.'

'I've been saving up, Graham. Saving for my esc–' She stopped abruptly. She didn't want to go down that road with Graham right now. He had offered her money in the past, but she had refused. She still had some pride and self-esteem left. 'It doesn't matter what I've been saving for; the fact is it's my money and he wants me to put it on a horse in the Grand National.' Her voice rose with incredulity at it all.

Graham wasn't sure how to respond, but it was the bookie in him that spoke first.

'Which horse?'

Tina glared at him in disbelief.

'Does it matter? I'm not doing it.'

'Sorry, Tina. I was just curious, that's all.' He hesitated. 'What if it wins?'

'It won't.'

'What's its name?' Graham insisted.

Tina sighed and rooted in her handbag for the cigarette packet, which she handed to Graham. He read the name and exhaled gently.

'Red Rum!' He nodded his head slowly. 'He's got a chance, Tina, I have to be honest. It is his first National, but he may yet start as favourite. There's a big Australian horse though, Crisp. I think he's likely to be up there too.' He put his arm around Tina's shoulders. 'He's got a chance, Tina, but there are no guarantees in the National.'

She leant against him, welcoming the comfort of his arms.

'I'm not doing it, Graham,' she said quietly.

There was a steeliness in her voice that told Graham arguing would be futile.

'It's your choice, Tina. I'll be here for you whatever happens.'

She smiled and kissed him on the cheek.

'You're a good mate, Graham. Thanks.'

Graham looked away, slightly embarrassed.

'Anyway,' he said brightly, 'you never know, you might find a fifty-pound note in the pocket of that old suit.'

Tina scoffed. 'Do fifty-pound notes actually exist? I've never seen one.'

Graham managed a laugh. 'I'd better get back,' he said. 'Nigel will be wondering where I've got to.'

'Of course. I won't keep you any longer. What time's the race?'

'Three fifteen.'

Tina glanced at her watch. Only six hours to go.

31

'Let me know if you change your mind about the bet.'

'I won't, but thanks.'

When Graham had gone, Tina turned her attention back to the bag of clothes that had been left outside the shop. She held up the jacket of the suit once again, and remembering Graham's words, she slipped her hand into the inside pocket. She suddenly felt a bit foolish, but then her hand touched what appeared to be paper and her heart skipped a beat. She pulled it out and turned it over. It wasn't a fifty-pound note, but an old, yellowing envelope.

2

Tina smoothed out the creamy envelope and regarded it curiously. She pressed it to her face and inhaled its musty smell. It was addressed to Miss C. Skinner, 33 Wood Gardens, Manchester. In the corner was an unfamiliar postage stamp, bearing not the picture of Queen Elizabeth II as expected, but that of a man Tina presumed to be King George VI. She turned the envelope over and noticed it was still firmly sealed. Looking again at the stamp, she was surprised to see there was no postmark. For some reason this letter had never been posted. To open it seemed a terrible intrusion somehow, as though she was prying into someone else's business, and yet she couldn't simply discard it. The bell on the shop door rang again, making her jump, and she felt her face inexplicably redden as she stuffed the envelope into her handbag and greeted her first customer of the day.

'Morning, Mrs Greensides.'

'Morning, Tina love. Just come for my usual root round. Anything new?'

Tina regarded the bag of clothes that had been left on the doorstep and eased it round the back of the counter with her foot.

'Erm, later maybe. I've got some to sort out.'

She wanted to have a good look through the bag for any clues as to where it might have come from before putting the clothes out on the racks.

A steady stream of customers throughout the morning managed to take Tina's mind off the forthcoming race, but at three o'clock she turned on the black-and-white portable television set that was kept in the back room. The horses were making their way down to the start and Tina looked for the one that was going to seal her fate. He was easy to spot with his big furry noseband, and the jockey had a huge diamond on the front of his jersey that the commentator said was yellow. The horses lined up behind the tape, dancing on the spot, eager to get away. Finally, at 3.15, the flag went up and the commentator shouted, 'They're off!'

Tina could hardly bear to watch as they approached the first fence. So far, Red Rum hadn't even been mentioned by the commentator. There was a faller at the first and she desperately tried to make out if it was him, but no, he was safely over. Another faller at the second, but Red Rum was over again, although a long way behind. She could imagine Rick at home now, shouting at the television, urging him on, riding the armchair as though he himself were the jockey, can of lager in one hand, cigarette in the other. He probably wasn't even dressed. As they headed towards Becher's Brook for the first time, she covered her eyes with her fingers. She didn't know much about horse racing, but even she knew that this fence was notoriously difficult and had claimed many victims over the years. Julian Wilson was commentating now.

'Over Becher's, Grey Sombrero's over from Crisp in second, Black Secret third, Endless Folly fourth, fifth is Sunny Lad, sixth is Autumn Rouge, seventh is Beggar's Way, and he's down. Beggar's Way has fallen at Becher's.'

Tina let out a huge sigh. She hadn't realised she had been holding her breath and she felt a little dizzy. Red Rum had not even warranted a mention and she dared to relax a little. Rick couldn't pick the winner in a one-horse race.

The door in the shop opened and Tina cursed to herself as she went to serve the new arrival. To her immense frustration, it was old Mrs Boothman. The elderly woman loved to stay and chat, and on any other day Tina would have been more than happy to oblige. Mrs Boothman lived a lonely existence since she'd been widowed, and her two sons didn't bother to visit her much. A cup of tea and a natter with Tina was the highlight of her week.

'Hello, Mrs Boothman,' Tina greeted her. 'I'm just busy in the back at the moment. I won't be

34

long. You have a good look round.'

Mrs Boothman looked perplexed and Tina knew why. She didn't need to look round. Not once in all the time she had been visiting the shop had she ever bought a single thing.

'No problem, love. I'll just perch here until you're ready.'

She pulled up a stool and plonked her bag on the counter.

'Is that the TV on in the back?'

'Er, yes,' Tina said guiltily. 'I was just watching the Grand National.'

Mrs Boothman looked surprised.

'I didn't know you were interested in horse racing.'

'I'm not, it's just that–'

'Have you put a bet on?' Mrs Boothman interrupted.

'No! God no,' Tina spluttered. She wasn't sure how she found herself in the position of having to make excuses to Mrs Boothman.

'I've never gambled in my life,' Mrs Boothman continued. 'My Jack always said it was for fools. Why waste your hard-earned money like that?'

'I haven't put a bet on, Mrs B,' said Tina patiently. 'I'm just interested, that's all.'

She stood in the doorway between the shop and the back room so she could still hear the television. Peter O'Sullevan had taken up the commentary.

'It's Crisp in the lead from Red Rum, but Red Rum's making ground on him.'

He was second! How on earth had that happened? Tina felt as though the breath had been knocked out of her.

'Are you OK, Tina? You look a bit peaky all of a sudden,' said Mrs Boothman.

'I'm f-fine.'

'Here, you'll never guess what's happened,' whispered Mrs Boothman conspiratorially. 'Her from number nine – you know, that little strumpet, what's her name?'

'Trudy,' replied Tina absently, straining to hear the television.

'That's the one. Been caught shoplifting in Woolies, she has.' She folded her arms under her ample bosom and pursed her lips, waiting for Tina's reaction.

'Oh, really?'

'Is that all you can say?' exclaimed Mrs Boothman. She didn't seem pleased that this juicy piece of gossip was being received so casually.

Tina ignored the elderly woman's indignation and concentrated on Peter O'Sullevan.

'Crisp is still well clear with two fences to jump in the 1973 Grand National. He's got twelve stone on his back and there's ten stone five on the back of Red Rum who's chasing him and then look to have it absolutely to themselves. At the second last, Crisp is over and clear of Red Rum, who's jumping it a long way back.'

Tina gripped the door frame and breathed deeply.

'Are you sure you're OK, Tina?'

Peter O'Sullevan's voice carried on relentlessly in the background.

'Coming to the final fence in the National now and it's Crisp still going in great style. He jumps it well. Red Rum is about fifteen lengths behind him as he

36

jumps. Crisp is coming to the elbow and he's got two hundred and fifty yards to run.'

Tina was sure she had made the right decision not to put the bet on. Red Rum looked beaten, with far too much ground to make up now. She cheered up a little.

'I'm fine. Let's have a cup of tea, shall we?'

This gave her an excuse to go into the back, where she could see the television. She put the kettle on and picked up two cups and saucers, then froze in front of the screen. Peter O'Sullevan's tone had changed.

'Crisp is beginning to lose concentration. He's been out there on his own for so long and Red Rum is making ground on him. They have a furlong to run now, two hundred yards for Crisp, and Red Rum is making ground on him.'

The cups began to rattle in their saucers as Tina stared in horror and disbelief at the television.

'No! No!' It was a hoarse whisper. 'Please God, no.'

'Crisp is getting very tired now and Red Rum is pounding after him, and Red Rum is the one who finishes strongest. Red Rum is going to win the National. At the line, Red Rum has just snatched it from Crisp and Red Rum is the winner.'

Tina felt the blood drain from her face and her bowels turned to water as she dropped to her knees, the teacups shattering into a thousand pieces. Holding her throbbing head in her hands, she was trembling like a cornered stray dog. Tears burnt their way down her cheeks as Mrs Boothman came through uninvited to the back.

'Whatever's going on? You did have a bet on,

37

didn't you?' she exclaimed. 'What did I tell you? Nothing good ever comes of gambling. My Jack always–'

'Please, Mrs Boothman. I just need to be left alone.'

She ushered the elderly woman out of the back room, through the shop and on to the street. Mrs Boothman could hardly get her words out as Tina slammed the door shut, bolted it and turned the sign around to read *Closed*. Then she pressed her forehead against the glass in the door, welcoming its coolness. She felt as though she was going to vomit and could actually feel the bile rising and the juices flooding her mouth. She swallowed hard and rubbed her face. Overcome with despair, she crept into the back room and turned out all the lights. She needed to think what to do next. Rick would be expecting her home with God knows how much money. She didn't even know the starting price, hadn't thought she would need to know, and now this. There was no way he was going to let her off this one.

Tina didn't know how long she had sat there in the dark when she was startled by a tapping on the shop door. Her eyes widened with fright at the thought that it might be Rick.

'We're closed,' she called wearily.

'Tina? It's Graham. Let me in.'

That's all I need, she thought. Graham's sympathy and kindness were sure to tip her over the edge.

She heaved herself up and unbolted the door.

'I'm sorry I couldn't get round any earlier. It's

been manic in there today.'

'It's OK, Graham.'

He stared at her tear-stained face.

'You watched it, then?'

'He's going to kill me,' she said simply. 'I mean, I actually think he's going to kill me.'

Graham reached into his back pocket and pulled out a wad of notes.

'What's that?' asked Tina.

'Four hundred and fifty quid. Here.' He pressed the money into her hand.

'I don't understand.'

'Sshh.' Graham put his finger to her lips. 'I placed the bet for you.'

'You?' She couldn't take it in. 'But you're the bookie, Graham. You can't have a bet with yourself.' There was no fooling Tina.

'I know. I sent Nigel down to Ladbrokes.'

Tina could feel her chin beginning to wobble.

'You did that for me?'

'I just had a feeling about that horse. I couldn't risk it. There was so much money going on him, he started as 9/1 favourite.'

'But it was so close, Graham. He nearly lost.'

Graham shrugged. 'Look, you've got four hundred and fifty quid there to give his lordship, *and* you've still got your fifty quid, so everybody's happy.'

'If he'd lost, you would never have told me about this, would you?'

Graham shook his head. 'But he didn't. Let's not dwell on what might have been.'

'I honestly don't know what to say, Graham. I think you may have actually saved my life.'

39

'Now, now, don't be so dramatic.'

Tina cupped Graham's face in her hands and, pulling him towards her, planted a kiss firmly on his lips.

'Thank you,' she said simply.

Graham blushed. 'You're welcome.' Then, more seriously, 'I'd do anything for you, Tina, you remember that.'

'I won't forget this, Graham,' Tina said as she stuffed the money into her handbag. 'I'd better go, he'll be waiting. At least he'll be in a good mood for once.'

3

When Tina put the key in the lock of the front door, her head was pounding, her mouth was dry and her hands were trembling so much she could hardly turn the key. As she entered the dark hallway she could hear the television. Dickie Davies was just wrapping up *World of Sport* and Rick was no doubt slumped on the settee, probably asleep, certainly drunk. She peered into the lounge but it was empty.

'Rick, I'm home.'

'Upstairs,' he answered.

She rummaged in her handbag and pulled out the wad of notes as she climbed the stairs.

'In the bathroom,' Rick called.

Tina pushed the bathroom door open and gasped. He had run a lovely deep bubble bath, with gallons of piping-hot water. He had even lit a couple of candles. Condensation ran down the windows and Tina struggled to see through all the steam.

He bent over the bath and swirled his hand around in the bubbles. 'I've had the immersion on,' he explained.

'The immersion? But that costs–'

Rick put his finger to her lips to silence her.

'Haven't you got something for me?'

Tina handed over the money.

'I've kept the fifty pounds if it's all the same to you.' She sounded bolder than she felt.

Rick ignored her tone and pressed the banknotes to his nose. He took a deep breath and inhaled their inky smell before stuffing them into his back pocket.

'Everything's going to be different now, Tina, I promise. Look at me.'

Tina had to admit he had scrubbed up well. He was dressed, which was by no means a foregone conclusion for a Saturday teatime, clean-shaven, and he'd been liberal with the Old Spice. She couldn't be sure, but he might even have washed his hair. Admittedly there was the lingering smell of alcohol on his breath, but he seemed quite sober.

'I was way out of order this morning, Tina. I know that. Can you forgive me? I'm so sorry.'

He pulled her closer and buried his face in her long dark hair. Tina stood there rigid. They had been through this so many times before. He was a complete bastard, she got upset, he was filled with remorse and asked for forgiveness. She

41

pushed him away gently.

'You need help, Rick. With the drinking, I mean.'

'I'm fine, Tina. I can stop whenever I like. Look ... I've stopped now, that's it.'

Tina sighed and indicated the bath.

'Is this for me?'

'Of course. Come on, let me help you.'

He slid her jacket off her shoulders and let it fall to the floor. He slowly unbuttoned her blouse and let that slide too as he began to kiss her neck. Tina closed her eyes as he pushed her gently against the wall, his mouth finding hers. He kissed her eagerly.

'The water's getting cold,' she said, ducking out from under him.

Rick tried to hide his disappointment.

'OK, love, sorry. Look, you have a long soak and I'll make tea.' Tina eyed him suspiciously. 'What? I can make tea, you know. I promise you, Tina, I've changed. Winning this money is the new start we need.' He sounded so plausible, and had Tina not heard it all before, she might have been taken in. But Rick was a master manipulator of women, a skill he had learnt from a very early age, and Tina knew exactly who was to blame.

Richard Craig was a war baby, the only son of George and Molly Craig. Whilst his father was away fighting for his country, his mother took him to live in the countryside with her sister, where he would be safe. Little Ricky was adored by his mother and his childless aunt and had an idyllic childhood. Every whim was catered for by the two women, so it was a shock to the three-year-old boy when one day he was refused a wooden train he had seen in a toy shop.

'It's a lot of money, darling,' reasoned his mother.

'I want it,' demanded Ricky.

'Maybe you could have it for your birthday.'

'Want it now.' Ricky folded his arms across his chest and scowled.

His aunt interjected. 'Your birthday is only a few months away; it's not that long to wait.'

Ricky didn't reply but glared at the two helpless women. Then he took a deep breath and held it.

'What are you doing?' demanded his mother.

Ricky ignored her and closed his eyes. As the two women watched in horror, his face went a bright scarlet and slowly his mouth turned blue. Then he passed out.

'Do something!' his mother screamed.

His aunt picked up the wooden train and brandished it at the startled shop assistant.

'We'll take it.'

When Ricky came round a few moments later, the first thing his eyes focused on was the little wooden train. He smiled to himself. He knew that from now on his mother and aunt would be putty in his hands.

When he was five years old, the war ended and his father returned home. Rick started school and predictably did not enjoy it one bit. He had a problem with discipline and was expelled from several establishments. When he finally left for good at the age of fifteen, he trained as a bus conductor before eventually qualifying as a driver. His dark, swarthy good looks meant he was never short of female attention, and he had a friendly rapport with all his passengers, especially the women. His only other interests were the horses and the dogs. He accompanied his father to the bookmaker's every Saturday morning, followed by a couple of pints in the pub. Thursday nights were always spent at the Belle Vue dog track. This tread-mill existence ended the day Tina boarded his bus. His eyes met hers and they held each other's gaze for a second longer than was necessary. Rick had told her many times that from that moment on, he knew he was going to have her and never let her go.

Tina felt marginally better after her soak in the bath. The day had drained her physically and emotionally. Her eyelids were heavy with exhaus-tion and her limbs felt like lead. She could hear the chip pan in the kitchen bubbling away furiously. Not quite a gourmet meal, but at least Rick was trying. As she entered the kitchen, he was frying a couple of eggs.

'Sit down, love,' he said, pulling out a kitchen chair. 'It won't be long. I've opened a tin of peaches for afters. We can have them with some Carnation milk.'

'Lovely, thanks.'

'How was your day in the shop? Did you manage to watch the race?'

'Er, I caught a bit of it, yes.'

'Bloody brilliant, wasn't it? I thought he was beaten but he came through right at the end. I bet Graham was miffed. I love it when the bookie gets stiffed.'

'Well he's had plenty of your money over the years.'

'Tina, don't start...'

'I wasn't.'

'Look, we've hit the jackpot today. Four hundred and fifty quid. I was only earning three grand a year on the buses. You know, we should celebrate. You take over here and I'll nip to Manny's for a bottle of champagne.'

'Champagne? Where do you think you are, Rick? I doubt Manny even stocks it. Not much call for it round here.'

Rick bounced on the balls of his feet and ran his fingers through his hair. 'Well, that other stuff then, Pomagne or Babycham or whatever they call it.'

'Rick, there's no need. I don't really drink and you've given up, remember?'

He hesitated for a moment.

'Well, when I said I'd given up, I didn't mean totally. I can still have the odd drink on special occasions, and they don't come much more special than this.'

'You're an alcoholic, Rick. You can't just have the odd drink.'

'You're an expert now, are you?'

'Actually, yes, living with you has made me an expert on the effects of alcoholism.'

'Don't keep saying that word. Who are you to diagnose me as an alc– you know, one of those.' He slipped his jacket on. 'I'll be back in five minutes.'

Tina shook her head. He was never going to change. He couldn't even say the word, let alone actually get professional help. He would drag her down with him if she let him.

Tina's early life had shown a lot more promise, which made the situation she was in now all the more heartbreaking. An only child, she excelled at school, passing the eleven-plus exam and going to a state grammar. Her exam results were among the best the school had ever produced, and both she and her headmistress thought a university education beckoned. Tina had hoped to study English and pursue a career in journalism. Fate, however, had other ideas. Her father, Jack Maynard, died suddenly at the age of forty-five, and despite the protestations of both the school and her mother, Tina didn't hesitate. She left school immediately and found work in a small insurance office to help support the family. Her duties were menial, with wages to match, but she attended night school, where she learned how to type and take shorthand. Her doggedness and fortitude paid off and she rose through the ranks, eventually becoming the best shorthand typist in the company. The job, however, was boring and the hours were long. The highlight of Tina's day was the bus journey home. The driver of the 192 was incredibly good-looking and always greeted her with a smile and a wink. One day he plucked up the courage to ask her out for a drink, and from that day on they were inseparable. Tina might have had to abandon her dreams of a career in journalism, but Richard Craig would more than make up for it.

They retired to the lounge, where Rick had put one bar of the electric fire on. With no central heating, the house was always freezing. Rick was now on his third glass of cheap fizzy wine and was beginning to slur his words. That was the trouble with him. He never completely sobered up, so it didn't take that much for him to be incoherent again. Tina was still nursing her first glass. She didn't even like the taste of sparkling wine, and it gave her a headache.

Rick was sprawled on the settee watching *The Generation Game.*

'Have you ever seen such crap prizes? What in Christ's name is a fondue set anyway?'

'It's a little pot that heats up a cheesy sauce and you dip chunks of bread in it.'

'Sounds vile.'

'It's supposed to be the height of sophistication.'

Rick patted the sofa next to him. 'Turn the telly off and come and sit here, love.'

Tina put down her glass and shuffled over to join him.

'Is there any more bubbly left?' he asked.

'A little, yes, but don't you think you've—'

'Had enough? No, I don't. I'm fine, Tina. Please don't be such a nag. You'll spoil everything. Come here.'

He pulled her into his arms and tried to kiss her. Tina pursed her lips instinctively and stiffened.

'What's the matter now?' Rick demanded.

'Nothing.' She pushed him away gently. 'I'll get you that drink.'

He grabbed both her wrists and held her firmly.

47

'It'll wait.'

He pushed her back on to the settee and pressed himself down on top of her. He forced his tongue into her mouth and she nearly retched. She pleaded with him to stop but she was no match for his strength and she could not stop him from yanking down her pants and spreading her legs apart.

'Rick, wait,' she reasoned, trying to buy herself some time. 'Let's go upstairs where it's more comfortable.'

He slapped her hard across the face.

'You must think I was born yesterday. Now shut up and enjoy it, you frigid cow.'

Tina turned her head to one side and closed her eyes. It wasn't the first time he had forced himself on her, but she vowed it would be the last. She had let this go on long enough. She needed to get out. Her life depended on it.

Sundays were the worst day of the week for Tina and she was always looking for excuses to leave the house. Rick had spent the night on the settee, too drunk to even stagger up the stairs, for which she was grateful. She sat in the kitchen warming her hands on a mug of tea and surveying the mess. The place stank of greasy food and the frying pan was congealing in the bowl of icy water where Rick had left it. He appeared in the doorway, his hair stuck up at wild angles and his eyelids drooping with sleep. He was still dressed in yesterday's clothes.

'Where are my fags?' His voice was gravelly and he gave a disgusting snort, thumping his chest as he did so.

Tina grimaced. 'Morning. I'm fine, thanks, how are you?'

'What?' He paused. 'Oh, look, is this about last night?'

Tina shoved the packet of cigarettes across the table.

'Here.'

He pulled up a chair and joined her at the table.

'Any chance of a brew?'

Tina nodded. 'Kettle's over there.'

Rick took a long drag on his cigarette. 'You're right. I am a complete bastard, you deserve better. Now *please* make me a brew.'

'Finally the penny's dropped.'

'It's not all my fault, though,' Rick countered defensively. 'I mean, you have to take some of the blame.'

Tina put her mug down and shook her head.

'In what way is this my fault? I told you not to buy booze last night after you promised me you wouldn't drink again, but no, you knew best. Said one or two wouldn't hurt, it was a special occasion, blah blah blah...'

Rick blew a cloud of grey smoke in her face.

'I also recall you telling me yesterday not to put that bet on. Hmm? Who knew best then?'

'That money was mine,' Tina said calmly.

'What's yours is mine. We're a partnership.'

'OK, give me half the winnings, then.'

Rick sneered. 'That's mine. You don't approve of gambling, remember?'

He was impossible to reason with and Tina didn't have the energy any more. When she spoke,

49

she sounded braver than she felt.

'I'm leaving you.'

Rick looked as though he'd had the wind knocked out of him. He took hold of her hand.

'Christ, Tina. I know I was a little, er, enthusiastic last night, but that's no reason to be hasty. I love you, you know that.' She could sense his desperation. She had seen it all before. He would do and say anything at this stage in order to placate her. The cycle was so familiar.

'You don't get it, do you? I'm scared of you, Rick. Scared of what you're going to do to me next. I'm sick of turning up at work and having to lie about my bruises, sick of treading on eggshells around the house, sick of living in this freezing cold pigsty and having to work all hours to pay the bills.'

'But–'

Tina held up her hand.

'I haven't finished. Have you any idea what it's like to live in fear? And why should I? I'm the one who supports us. You don't contribute one penny; you're just a drain on our finances and a drain on my emotions.'

'That's charming, that is! I cooked tea for you last night.'

'A plate of egg and chips?' Tina scoffed. 'If that's your idea of pulling your weight, you're more deluded than I thought.'

Rick was breathing hard now and his fists were clenched, but Tina ploughed on. She had never stood up to him like this before and she suddenly felt empowered.

'You need the sort of help that I can't give you.'

Without warning he stood up, reached across the table and grabbed her hair.

'There's someone else, isn't there? Who is he? I'll kill him, and then I'll kill you.'

Tina stared defiantly into his eyes.

'There's no one else, Rick. Can't you just accept that I'm leaving you because of *you?* This is nobody's fault but yours.'

He released his grip on her hair.

'Why do you make me do these things to you?' he said softly. 'Please, Tina, don't go. I need you.'

Tina reached for her coat and picked up her little suitcase.

'You've packed? You bitch. How long have you been planning this?'

'Oh, I don't know. Since the day you hit me so hard across the face I needed stitches over my eye.'

'That wasn't my fault, my ring caught you–'

'Since the day you punched me and split my lip, since the day you stubbed your cigarette out on my arm, since the day you first *raped* me, since the day you stole my money to put a bet on. Since our bloody wedding day. Should I carry on?'

As she voiced all this out loud for the first time, she found a long-buried inner strength, and with it a conviction that her sanity and indeed her very survival depended on her walking away.

She was in the hallway now, and as she opened the front door, she held her head high and marched away without a single backwards glance.

'Tina, come back. I'm sorry.' Rick's knees gave way and he crumpled to the floor.

51

It was all Tina could do not to break into a run as she made her way down the terraced street. She felt like she could run and run forever. And she would need to when Rick discovered that she had raided his back pocket whilst he was asleep and taken all his winnings.

Later that day, Tina knocked on the door of the smart semi and waited nervously for an answer. An attractive blonde woman, fully made-up and sporting masses of gold jewellery, opened it.

'Can I help you?'

'You must be Sheila. I'm Tina.'

She held out her hand, which Sheila ignored.

'Er ... is Graham in?'

'Does he know you?'

'Yes, I'm a friend. I work in the shop next door to his on Saturdays.'

'Who is it, Sheila?' Graham called from somewhere in the house.

Sheila opened the door a little further and beckoned Tina in.

'Says she's a friend of yours.'

'Tina!' exclaimed Graham, arriving in the hallway. 'What's happened, love?'

Seeing Graham's caring, concerned face made Tina's voice wobble. 'I've left him, Graham.'

'Oh God. Come here.' He took her in his arms and embraced her firmly.

Sheila looked on with bemusement and Graham turned to her.

'Sheila, put the kettle on, would you?'

Tina pulled herself together. 'It's all right, Sheila, I'm not stopping. I just wanted to let Graham know what's going on. He's been a good friend to me, and if it wasn't for what he did for me yesterday, I wouldn't have been able to leave.'

'You took his money?' Graham asked incredulously.

Tina managed a smile. 'Every penny. I've found a small bedsit to rent. I spotted it a few weeks ago but couldn't afford it then. Anyway, it's still available so I'm going there. It's not too bad really. The furniture's ancient and the walls are so thin I can hear the bloke next door change his mind, but at least it's all mine.'

'He'll come looking for you, you know,' Graham said gravely.

'I've no doubt he will. He knows where I work, he may turn up at the shop too, but I don't care. He won't lay a finger on me in public. He's way too clever for that.'

'He could follow you, though.'

'Please, Graham. Don't you think I know all this? Why do you think it's taken me so long to make the break?'

'Sorry. Do you need a hand moving in?'

'I only left with a small suitcase so there wasn't much to move in really, but thanks anyway. Look, I'd better get going. I've a few things to do.'

'If you're sure. I'll pop into the shop next Saturday. Take care of yourself now.'

As Tina settled down later that evening with a cup of cocoa, she began to relax a little. She was exhausted, so she allowed her head to loll back on the settee and closed her eyes. She felt strangely empty as she reflected on her disastrous four-year marriage. She didn't know what the future would hold and this filled her with both fear and excitement. She fumbled in her handbag for a tissue, and when she couldn't find one, she tipped the contents of the bag out on to the floor. Lying on top of all the clutter was the letter she had found in the pocket of that old suit. Feeling incredibly intrusive, she picked it up and carefully opened the sealed envelope, trying not to damage it in any way. The writing was neat enough but strangely childlike, as though the writer was not used to using a pen. Tina tucked her legs beneath her and began to read.

180 Gillbent Road
Manchester
4th September 1939
My darling Christina
I'm not very good at this sort of thing, as you know, but right now my heart is breaking and this is spurring me on. The way I treated you yesterday was unforgivable, but please know that it was just the shock and no reflection on my feelings towards you. These past few months have been the happiest of my life. I know I've never told you this before, but I love you, Chrissie, and if you let me I want to spend every day we have left together proving it to you. Your father tells me you don't want to see me anymore and I don't blame you, but it is not about us now – there is the baby to consider. I want to be a good father and a good husband. Yes, Chrissie, that is my clumsy way of proposing. Please say you will be my wife so we can raise our child together. The war may separate us physically, but our emotional bond will be unbreakable.

54

I need you to forgive me, Chrissie. I love you
Forever yours
Billy xxx

She finished reading and shivered involuntarily. Although she never used her full name, she had been christened Christina herself and she felt an instant bond with this Chrissie. It was all so sad. Why had Billy not posted his letter? What became of Chrissie and their baby? Maybe she could try to find out who these people were and deliver the letter to its rightful recipient. At the very least it would be a welcome distraction from all her other problems.

4

Spring 1939

Billy Stirling had always known he was handsome, because his mother never tired of telling him so. It came as no surprise to anyone that at the age of twenty-one, he was never short of female attention. His black hair, worn a little too long, was swept back with Brylcreem, his clean-shaven face revealed a dark, almost swarthy complexion, and amazingly, given the number of cigarettes he smoked, his teeth were a brilliant white and perfectly straight. When he laughed, his smile illuminated his face and his cheeks revealed dimples that made him look like an audacious schoolboy. The deep scar over his left eyebrow only added to his exotic looks, and there were always gasps of sympathy from adoring girls when he told the story of how he had acquired it. Not that he could remember anything about the incident, but his mother had told him the tale many times.

Alice Stirling loved her son with a fierce intensity and was extremely protective of him. Her husband, Henry, thought she thoroughly spoiled him, and was even a little jealous of the amount of love and attention she lavished on the boy. When their first-born son, Edward, died in infancy from consumption, Alice had been inconsolable and blamed herself. Nothing Henry said or did could reassure her that she was not at fault. If only he had managed to sound convincing, she might have believed him. All Henry knew was that he had returned at the end of the Great War and his son was dead. He never even got to hold him.

Edward was only five months old when he died and his little body was too fragile to sustain the relentless coughing up of blood, night sweats and fever so typical of the disease. Even though consumption was associated with poor hygiene conditions, Alice had cared for her son in the best way she could. She knew that they were poor. Food was scarce since rationing had started in January 1918, but this was the case with the majority of families during the war and their, babies hadn't died. The flat they rented was a one-room hovel, but Alice had done her best to keep it clean. It was damp and clammy and the moisture clung to everything. Edward had been a sickly baby from birth and the smell of his regularly regurgitated milk hung in the air. At bed time, Alice swaddled him in blankets and took him into her bed, where she held him close all night, waking frequently to check he was still breathing. However, in spite of all her efforts, Edward had died anyway and the guilt had gnawed away at her, slowly sapping her belief in herself as a mother. After he came home from the trenches, Henry withdrew into himself and Alice found it increasingly difficult to reach him. They rarely spoke to each other and this miserable existence seemed set to define their marriage. Even though she doubted herself as a mother, Alice longed for another baby. There was an emptiness in her that could only be filled by nurturing a new life. However, the chances of her falling pregnant were non-existent given the distance that had grown between her and Henry.

One day not long after little Edward had passed away, Alice overheard two women gossiping in the corner shop. Her ears pricked up and she sidled closer so she could hear what was being said. When she had heard enough, she left the shop with her heart racing and hurried home. To her relief, Henry was not there. She quickly changed into her Sunday best, complete with fur hat and gloves. The hat smelled musty and dank but it would have to do. She gave it a quick brush and arranged it carefully on her head, then regarded herself in the tiny square mirror over the kitchen sink, which also doubled as their bathroom, and added a smear of pink lipstick. She knew she should really wear flat shoes for the long walk ahead, but heels looked so much more elegant with her suit. With one final look in the mirror, her face a picture of determination, Alice closed the front door and set off at a brisk, purposeful pace.

The grey facade of the orphanage was ingrained with decades of dirt, and weeds grew in abundance in the gutters. The black paint on the front door had long since lost its lustre and was now cracked and peeling. The whole place looked austere and most unwelcoming. Nevertheless, Alice swallowed her apprehension and climbed the stone steps to the entrance porch. She wafted away a cobweb that had caught in her hat. The huge brass knocker was stiff and she fumbled with it clumsily before managing to coax the iron ring into producing a satisfactory rap. After what seemed like an eternity, the heavy door opened and a woman in a starched nurse's uniform looked Alice up and down.

'Yes? Can I help you?'

It was at this point that Alice realised she had not rehearsed what she was going to say.

'Hello... Er... I... My name is Alice Stirling,' she stumbled. 'May I come in?'

The nurse folded her arms across her chest and stared down at her. 'Do you have an appointment?'

'No, I'm afraid not. Is that a problem?'

The nurse shook her head and sighed but opened the door wider and beckoned Alice inside.

'Wait here. I'll get Matron.'

Alice watched as she disappeared down the hall. The smell of disinfectant and over-boiled cabbage pervaded the air, a combination that made her feel nauseous. Her mouth was dry and perspiration beaded on the back of her neck. She was beginning to regret wearing the hat.

'How can I help you?'

She spun round. The matron had a kind, expressive face that did not fit with her voice, and Alice was momentarily taken aback.

'My name is Alice Stirling and I'm here about the baby.'

'What baby? We have lots of babies here.'

'Of course,' Alice apologised. 'I'm sorry, I don't know his name.'

'You'll need to be more specific, I'm afraid.'

A baby began to cry in the distance and Alice suddenly felt her throat constrict and her eyes fill with tears. She wiped them away with her gloved hand.

'Are you all right?' asked Matron, her tone softening somewhat.

'Not really. I lost my baby, you see.'

'And you think he might be here?'

Alice was confused for a second.

'Oh no, of course not. He's dead.'

The matron's eyes widened at the bluntness of Alice's response. She took her by the arm and led her to her office, and closed the door.

'Now, why don't you tell me what all this is about?'

Alice felt an overwhelming desire to unburden herself.

'My baby, my beautiful son Edward, died when he was only five months old. Consumption, they said. There was nothing I could do, but I know that Henry–'

'Henry?' interrupted Matron.

'My husband,' explained Alice. 'I know he

blames me. He says he doesn't, of course, but I couldn't even keep Edward alive until his father returned from the war. What sort of a mother am I? He never got to see his own son. Now we barely speak. He drinks too much and never shows me any affection. He thinks his grief is worse than mine because at least I got to spend five precious months with Edward.'

The matron handed her a handkerchief.

'Now, now. Don't blame yourself. Lots of babies die from consumption. It's very common, you know. I'm sure you did everything you could.'

Alice blew her nose noisily.

'It wasn't enough, though, was it?' She didn't know how much longer she could endure this misery.

Matron glanced at the clock on the wall.

'We're about to have tea now and I need to go and supervise. Why don't you join us?'

'You're very kind. I will, thank you.'

'Then you can tell me what brings you here. You mentioned a baby…'

Alice followed the matron to the dining room, where the children were already seated at long wooden tables. Tea was simple, just thick slices of bread and butter and a watery stew.

She knew it was him the moment she saw him. It was the heavy gash over his left eyebrow that confirmed it. She went up to him as he sat in his high chair banging his spoon. As soon as she approached, he stopped, beamed a toothless smile and held his arms aloft, asking to be picked up. She scooped him up and breathed in his milky scent. He wore a little paper wristband bearing his name and date of birth. *William Edwards. 20th March 1918.*

'It's all right,' Alice whispered in his ear. 'Mama's here now.'

Later, in Matron's office, she learnt the full story of how little Billy had ended up in the orphanage. Like Alice, Billy's mother, Frances Edwards, had given birth during the war, but tragically his father, Albert, had been killed in action just a month before the end of hostilities. On Armistice Day, 11 November 1918, as church bells around the country rang out in celebration, Frances cradled her precious baby and held him tight as she leapt off a railway bridge. She was killed instantly, but miraculously, Billy survived with only a deep cut over his left eyebrow. It seemed his mother's body had cushioned his fall. Despite various pleas, no relatives had come forward to claim him, so he had been placed in the orphanage by the authorities.

Alice wiped a tear from the corner of her eye.

'So what will happen to him now?'

Matron shrugged. 'We'll look after him here. He'll be well cared for.'

'I'll take him,' Alice declared. 'He's a baby without a mother and I'm a mother without a baby. Please, Matron.'

Matron looked doubtful. 'We don't have a formal adoption policy, but there will be some checks and paperwork to go through.' She looked at Alice's pleading expression. 'I'll see what I can do.'

Alice gave a thin smile. 'Thank you. I'll talk to my husband.'

Billy had left the orphanage one week later with

only two possessions: his late mother's engagement ring, and a Flanders poppy, which Albert had pressed and sent to Frances from the trenches. With it was a letter.

12th October 1918
My darling Frances,
 I wish you could see these poppies in the fields. They are even more stunning when they are blowing in the wind. I saved this one from the Flanders mud. Look after our boy. I can't wait to meet him.
 All my love and affection for ever.
 Albert xx

He was killed in action two days later.

Now, in the spring of 1939, at the age of twenty-one, Billy was devoted to his adoptive mother. His relationship with his father, however, was a little complicated, to say the least. He found that the best way to deal with the situation was to keep his distance. Henry Stirling spent an awful lot of time in the pub or just wandering the streets, so this wasn't difficult. He had never really accepted Billy as his son, and the amount of love and attention Alice lavished on the boy only served to compound his feelings of resentment.

One night, Billy and his best friend Clark were propping up the bar of their local pub.

'I feel sorry for you,' announced Clark.

Billy took a long drag on his cigarette and regarded his friend.

'Why's that then?'

'Well, you never experience the thrill of the

chase, do you? I mean, girls just fall at your feet. All you have to do is walk into a room and the eyes of every girl in the place are on you. Where's the challenge in that?'

Billy shrugged and clicked his fingers at the barman.

'Two more rums when you have a minute, please, mate.'

He turned to Clark. 'Is that what you really think? Has it ever occurred to you that girls who are obsessed by a bloke's looks are completely shallow? They have no substance at all, and whilst they might be fun for a one-night stand, after that I'm bored with them. I want a serious, steady relationship as much as the next man.'

He passed a glass over to Clark.

'Cheers!'

Clark did not sound convinced. 'I don't stand a chance hanging around with you, do I?' he grumbled.

This was true. Girls flocked around the two of them at the dance hall, but it was Billy they wanted to talk to, Billy they wanted to twirl them round the dance floor and Billy they wanted to walk them home at the end of the night.

'You're my best mate, Clark. We've been friends since we were kids in short trousers, with scabby knees and dirty faces. Are you suggesting we stop hanging round together in order to give you a better chance with the girls?'

Clark sighed. 'No, of course I'm not saying that. I just feel like I'm never going to meet anyone.'

Billy slapped him on the back. 'Snap out of it,

63

Clark, stop feeling sorry for yourself. No girl wants a bloke who's drowning in self-pity.'

Billy regarded his friend in the smoky atmosphere of the pub. Whilst it was true that Clark's ginger hair and freckles were not exactly a magnet for the girls, his piercing ice-blue eyes seemed to look directly into your soul as they shone out from what was essentially a very handsome face. His lack of height could be a drawback to girls in high heels, and his lingering Black Country accent was also out of place in Manchester and made him sound a little slow-witted when actually the opposite was true. But a more solid, dependable and thoroughly decent chap it would be hard to find.

'Sorry, Billy,' said Clark. 'D'you want another?'

Billy looked at his watch. 'Better not. Mum'll have my tea ready. I'll see you tomorrow at the Buck, yeah?'

The Buccaneer dance hall was their favourite Friday-night haunt. Clusters of girls giggled nervously at the edge of the dance floor, surreptitiously glancing around, hoping for an invitation to dance. There was a three-piece band and the lights were dim enough to create a romantic atmosphere should it be needed. This was in contrast to the dances at the local church hall, where the vicar insisted on acting as chaperone and would separate couples who, in his opinion, were getting rather too close to each other. One time Billy was literally thrown out for letting his hands stray too low down his dancing partner's back. Needless to say, Clark had found that episode hilarious.

There were no such restrictions at the Buccaneer, though, and after their conversation last night, Billy was determined to find Clark a lovely girl who would take him home to meet her mother, marry him and have his babies. Or, failing that, at least someone willing to dance with him. The band was in fine form and it was difficult to talk above the music. Billy cupped his hands and spoke directly into Clark's ear.

'Have you seen anybody you want to ask for a dance?'

Clark rubbed his ear. 'I'm not deaf!'

'What about those two over there?' Billy pointed to a couple of girls who had been glancing in their direction all evening. One was tall, rather loud and wore an awful lot of make-up. She tossed her long dark hair back provocatively as she caught Billy's eye. Her friend was obviously uncomfortable and gazed at the floor. Billy suddenly straightened up and nudged Clark.

'Bugger me, they're coming over.'

They both watched as the taller girl sashayed across the dance floor towards them, her friend scurrying behind trying not to slosh her drink all over the place.

'Hello, girls,' said Billy.

'Evening,' nodded Clark.

'We noticed you looking over,' said the taller girl, flicking her hair back again. 'I'm Sylvia, but you can call me Syl, and this is my friend Chrissie.'

'How do you do? I'm Billy, and this is Clark.'

Clark nodded again and wiped his sweaty palm down his trouser leg before shaking hands with the two girls.

Chrissie smiled sweetly, her blue eyes shining with amusement. Although much more reticent than her friend, she was by far the more attractive of the two. Her blonde hair was neatly curled, her skin glowed and she wore only the faintest smear of pink lipstick. Billy could hardly take his eyes off her, but Syl had other ideas. She pulled at his tie, forcing him to put down his drink.

'Come on, let's see what you're made of.'

Billy made to protest, but it was no use. Syl now had him firmly by the arm and was steering him towards the dance floor. He looked back to see Clark and Chrissie settling down at a table and felt an unexpected pang of jealousy.

Syl was a great dancer, but modesty was not one of her attributes.

'Hey, we make a dazzling couple, don't we?'

When they rejoined their friends at the table, Clark and Chrissie were so deep in conversation that they hardly noticed. The band had slowed the music down now and couples began to glide on to the dance floor for the slow numbers. Billy knew this was the part of the evening Clark always dreaded – but not tonight, it seemed. Without saying anything, he held out his hand to Chrissie, who took it shyly and stood up. Billy could only watch as Clark escorted her on to the dance floor and placed his hands around her waist. They swayed to the music as Billy and Syl looked on.

'Aww, they make a lovely couple, don't they?'

Billy couldn't answer. He had the terrible feeling that he had just lost something very precious. Something he had never owned but that nevertheless should have belonged to him. Clark held

Chrissie close and turned to look at him. He raised both thumbs behind her back and grinned. Billy forced a smile and lifted his glass to them. He could not explain it, but he felt as though his heart had been ripped out and replaced with a lump of lead, and he suddenly realised that Chrissie was meant to be the love of his life. Unfortunately, she was now in the arms of his best friend.

5

Spring 1939

Chrissie propped her bicycle against a wall and cursed to herself. The chain had come off, there was oil all over her white ankle socks and now she was going to have to walk the rest of the way. Fortunately, the spring day felt more like summer and she had nearly finished her round, so it could have been worse. As the daughter of a doctor and a midwife, she was used to being drafted in to help, and today she was making the daily deliveries of medicine to her father's patients.

Chrissie worked in the surgery in Wood Gardens in Manchester, where her duties varied from making up prescriptions to polishing the ornate mahogany medicine cabinets. Dr Skinner was a revered physician, and Chrissie was in awe of him and more than a little terrified. He was a strict disciplinarian, with his wife, his daughter and even his patients. He had no time for malingerers, and

67

persistent offenders were often given a concoction containing no more than a mixture of lactose and some other foul-tasting substance. This smelled malodorous enough to convince the patient that it would cure them of their imagined ailment, and had the added advantage of allowing the doctor to charge, three shillings and sixpence a bottle. Many a mother had regretted taking her child to see Dr Skinner about a sore throat. The next day the unfortunate boy or girl would be laid out on their own kitchen table, and with the merest whiff of chloroform, the doctor would remove their tonsils.

Such was the reverence with which the good doctor was regarded, nobody questioned these methods, and he had built up a reputation in the community of being able to cure anything. All the well-off people in the vicinity went to see Dr Skinner. They were permitted to use the front door of the surgery and allowed to wait in the pleasant surroundings of the family's dining room. Chrissie would even make them tea while they were waiting There was no appointments system as such, but it was accepted by everyone that front-door patients took precedence over those who had had to enter via the back. These were the less well-off people, who struggled to pay the doctor's bills and were considered a nuisance by him. Unfortunately, it seemed that these characters fell ill with more regularity than the good people of Manchester who had the wherewithal to pay him on time. Chrissie was frequently embarrassed by her father's harsh attitude, and on more than one occasion had let customers off without paying. She had become rather adept at hiding these bad debts when she worked on the accounts for the practice. Dr Skinner might have been a talented physician, but an accountant he was not.

She decided to leave the bicycle where it was for now and picked up the brown paper bag from the basket on the front. This contained four more medicine bottles that needed to be delivered. Chrissie had personally made up the concoctions herself and carefully applied the sealing wax and the white label detailing the name of the patient. She was relieved to find that two of the bottles were for the same person, so that meant just three more house calls and she was finished for the day.

It was important that she was home on time today, because tonight she was going to defy her parents' stringent rules and go to the Buccaneer dance hall with her friend Sylvia. They had known each other since their schooldays, when Sylvia had taken her under her wing, and had remained friends ever since. They were complete opposites in almost every respect, but somehow their friendship had endured all the obstacles, not the least of which was the disapproval of Chrissie's parents. They believed that Sylvia was a bad influence on their daughter, and did everything they could to discourage the closeness between the two girls. Tonight, however, Dr and Mrs Skinner were going out, and Chrissie had seized the opportunity to arrange a clandestine visit to the Buccaneer. As long as she was home before midnight, they would be none the wiser.

Once she had finished her deliveries, Chrissie collected her bicycle and pushed it the rest of the way home. Waiting at the garden gate was Leo, their ever-faithful Airedale terrier. He really was the most loyal, brave, intelligent creature Chrissie had ever known. Whenever she went out on her rounds, he would wait patiently at the gate for her return, greeting her with uncontained excitement. His whole body wiggled from side to side as he wagged his tail and his lips actually curled tip at the sides so that he looked as though he was smiling. If Dr. Skinner was out visiting patients and was required urgently back at the surgery, Leo would be dispatched into the neighbourhood with a note around his collar to find him.

'Hello, Leo,' greeted Chrissie, ruffling the dog's ears. She opened the squeaky garden gate for him, but he leapt over the wall instead and ran down the path to the front door. She could hear her parents talking in the kitchen and her heart sank a little. It was only teatime, but she needed to start getting ready for the dance. She wanted to set her hair in curlers, which would take at least an hour and could not be done with her parents still in the house.

She stepped into the kitchen, trying to appear casual.

'What time are you going out?'

'Good evening to you too, Chrissie,' replied Mrs Skinner. 'Everything all right with the deliveries?'

'What? Oh yes, fine, except my chain came off again.' She pointed to her oily socks.

'Your father will put it back on tomorrow, won't you, Samuel?'

Dr Skinner stubbed out his cigarette and lit up another. 'It's about time you learnt to take better care of that bike. If it's not the chain, it's a puncture or the damn brakes.'

'Father, it's not my fault–'

Mrs Skinner pressed her finger to her own lips and glared at Chrissie, who stopped abruptly.

She turned to her husband. 'Now, now, Samuel, don't be grumpy. Why don't you take a bath and I'll bring you up a whisky.'

'Good idea, I think I will. I'm so tired, I might give this dinner-dance a miss tonight.'

Chrissie felt a sudden rush of panic at this news and held her breath. Sylvia would be round to call for her in a couple of hours.

Mabel Skinner ushered her husband out of the kitchen and followed him upstairs. 'You'll feel much better after a bath, and anyway, I've bought that new dress now, haven't I? It would be a shame to waste it.'

Chrissie breathed a sigh of relief and called after her mother: 'What's for tea?'

Her mother's muffled reply floated down the stairs. 'Just get yourself some bread and jam, will you? Your father and I will be eating at the dance.'

Charming, thought Chrissie as she carved herself a thick slice of bread and spread it with butter, slipping a piece to the ever-patient Leo, who was drooling at her side.

At last her parents left for the evening, but not before issuing her with instructions. 'Don't forget to update the patients' records from today's surgery, make a list of all those who still owe money for medicine, and take Leo for a last walk around ten o'clock.' Chrissie was practically pushing them out of the door by the time they had finished.

'I won't. Have a good time.'

'Be good now,' warned Dr Skinner as he took his wife's arm and led her down the path. 'We'll be back around half past midnight, I expect.'

Chrissie watched until they were out of sight and then quickly closed the door and bounded up the stairs two at a time. By the time the doorbell went, she had bathed, set her hair and changed into the only decent dress she owned. She opened the front door just wide enough for Sylvia to slip inside.

'You weren't followed, were you?' she asked in hushed tones.

Sylvia rolled her eyes. 'We're going to a dance, not enrolling in the Secret Service. Now let's have a look at you.'

She looked her friend up and down, appraising her appearance.

'Not bad. You could do with a little rouge and some lipstick, though.'

'Oh, I'm not sure. I don't want to look like a clown.'

'Look at my face,' Sylvia commanded. 'Do I look like a clown?'

Chrissie scoured her friend's heavily made-up face. Her eyebrows were perfectly arched and blackened with kohl, her skin was pale and flawless, making her bright ruby lips the centre of attention. It was a look that Chrissie could never hope to carry off.

'Of course not, Syl, but you're so much more sophisticated than I am. You're tall, elegant, confident—'

Sylvia held up her hand. 'And you are pretty and sweet, like a little golden-haired doll.'

Chrissie wasn't sure this was such a great compliment, but she said thank you anyway.

'Maybe I'd better have some lipstick, then.'

'Good girl,' said Sylvia, opening her handbag.

'Oh no, not yours. It's too ... you know... Well, it's not me. I'll just run upstairs and see what my mother has.'

She returned moments later, her lips shining with a pale pink lipstick that seemed to garner Sylvia's approval.

'Much better,' she proclaimed. 'Now come on, we have got some serious dancing to do.' She opened the door and trotted off down the path. Chrissie hurried after her.

The hall was only half full when the girls arrived, and people hadn't really begun to dance. Regardless of this fact, the band continued to play, and Sylvia suggested they buy themselves a drink while the place filled up. After only a couple of minutes, she nudged Chrissie rather painfully in the ribs.

'Ow, what was that for?'

'Shh. Look at those two, just walked in.'

Chrissie turned her head to see a couple of young men striding over to the bar.

'The tall one is absolutely gorgeous, don't you think? He's mine.'

Chrissie had to agree. He was rather exotic-looking and she knew he wouldn't look once, let alone twice, at her. 'Great,' she said. 'I prefer the look of his friend anyway. He has a kind face, but he seems so nervous and unsure of himself, just like me!'

'Shall I ask them to join us?'

Chrissie was horrified. 'But shouldn't we wait for

them to ask us? I mean, it would be so forward.'

'All right,' conceded Sylvia. 'I'll give them half an hour and then I'm going over.'

She crossed her long legs and pulled up her skirt a little as the pair walked past. Chrissie shook her head and stared intently at her drink. Her friend really was incorrigible.

The dance floor began to fill up and Sylvia noticed that the two young men had not strayed from their position near the bar. Suddenly the taller one pointed over in their direction. Sylvia wasted not one second as she caught his eye.

'Come on, Chrissie,' she said. 'It's time.' She sashayed across the room with Chrissie trailing in her wake.

The young men introduced themselves as Billy and Clark, and Sylvia immediately dragged Billy on to the dance floor.

'Shall we sit down?' ventured Clark, pulling a chair out for Chrissie. 'Can I get you another drink?'

'No thanks, I still have this one,' replied Chrissie.

'Your friend's a great dancer,' said Clark.

'So's yours.'

'What, Billy? Yeah, he's had plenty of practice. I don't think any girl has ever refused him a dance.'

Chrissie noticed the melancholy in Clark's eyes. 'Never mind about Billy, tell me about you.'

'Me?' Clark looked astonished. 'Well, what do you want to know?'

Chrissie realised that he was actually more nervous than she was, and this relaxed her a little.

74

She shrugged. 'Well, where are you from? Not from round here by the sound of it.'

'You're right. I was born in Birmingham but we came to live in Manchester when I was seven. I met Billy at school and we've been friends ever since. I used to get teased because I spoke differently to everybody else, but Billy stuck up for me, and as he was the most popular lad in the class, they all listened to him. My schooldays would have been awful without him. In turn I'd sometimes do his homework for him. Not that he's thick or anything, you understand, he was just always so busy with his sport and everything that he never really gave much thought to his studies. His mother spoils him rotten too. That lad can run rings round anyone.'

Chrissie glanced at Billy and Syl on the dance floor. Billy seemed distracted and kept looking over at their table. When he saw Chrissie watching, he gave her a small smile and she felt her neck flush. She turned away in embarrassment.

'It looks like he's met his match with Syl.'

'Oh, he'll be all right. She's gorgeous, isn't she? Billy always gets the best-looking ones.'

Chrissie stared into Clark's blue eyes and waited for him to realise what he had just said. He looked mortified. 'Oh, I'm sorry. I didn't mean... You're very pretty, in a much less obvious way,' he floundered. 'I mean, you don't need all that make-up and stuff, you're naturally pretty and–'

Chrissie held up her hand and smiled. 'Enough! I forgive you.'

She sneaked a peek at her watch.

'I'm not keeping you, am I?' asked Clark.

'Not at all. It's just that I have to be back by midnight, which means leaving for the walk home about eleven thirty.'

'Plenty of time,' said Clark, relaxing a little. 'Would you like a cigarette?'

'No thanks, I don't smoke, but you go ahead.'

'If you're sure?'

Clark opened his packet of Capstan and took out a cigarette. 'Tell me about yourself.'

'Not much to tell really. I work for my father, Dr Skinner, in the surgery. My mother's the local midwife so I sometimes help her as well, but I'm a bit squeamish. I've seen enough births to put me off sex for good.'

Immediately the words were out, Chrissie wanted the ground to swallow her up. She could feel her face flushing a bright scarlet. She couldn't imagine what on earth had possessed her to say such a thing. Clark choked on his drink and spluttered the amber liquid down his chin.

'I'm sorry, I didn't mean...' Chrissie apologised.

Clark began to laugh, and Chrissie joined in until they were both helpless.

By the time Billy and Syl returned to the table, they were deep in conversation again. The band had slowed the music right down, and Clark silently stood up and held out his hand. Chrissie took it and allowed herself to be guided on to the dance floor. They were timid and awkward at first, with Clark treading clumsily on her toes, but as they got used to the feel of each other's bodies, they both began to enjoy the experience. Clark was not much taller than Chrissie, so it was easy for her to look into his eyes. He smiled back and pulled her closer, allowing her to catch the scent of his skin, a fresh, citrusy smell, only slightly masked by tobacco. She wondered suddenly if he would attempt to kiss her, and that caused panic to rise inside her. She took deep breaths and forced herself to calm down. She was nineteen years old, for goodness' sake.

Her arms were around Clark's neck now, and she pulled him closer to steal another look at her watch behind his head. He bowed into her neck and his arms tightened around her waist. She was astonished to see that it was almost eleven thirty already. She needed to be making a move, but she was reluctant to break the spell. She silently cursed her father.

When the music eventually stopped, they gently parted.

'I'm sorry, but I really need to be going now.'

'I understand. Would you like me to walk you home?'

Chrissie glanced over at Billy and Sylvia. She was gently caressing his face, running her fingers over his scar. He looked decidedly uncomfortable.

'That would be lovely, thank you. I'll just have to see if Syl minds.'

Of course Syl didn't mind. She was entranced by Billy and was glad Clark and Chrissie were leaving so they could have time to themselves.

Clark sidled over to Billy.

'I can't believe it. She's lovely,' he enthused. 'I've offered to walk her home. You don't mind, do you? Looks like you've got your hands full here anyway.'

'No, mate. You go ahead. Good luck!'

Chrissie joined Clark and Billy. 'Are you ready

to go?' she asked.

'Yes, I am,' replied Clark, taking hold of her hand.

'Goodbye, Billy. It was nice to meet you.' She held out her other hand to Billy, and as he took it, their eyes met for a second. Chrissie felt muddled by what she saw. It was a mixture of incredible sadness and longing. His eyes were such a deep brown you could hardly see his pupils.

'Goodbye, Chrissie. You look after Clark now.' He winked as he said it, and she flushed again, grabbing on to Clark's arm to steady herself, heady with confusion.

'Er ... I will. Bye now,' she managed.

Billy held her gaze and her hand for a second longer, until Sylvia pulled him to his feet.

'Come on, we've got time for another dance.'

Clark and Chrissie made their way to the exit, hand in hand. Clark opened the door for her and Chrissie fought the urge to look back. Clark was lovely and she felt totally relaxed in his company, so why did she feel she was leaving with the wrong man?

Although the April evening was somewhat chilly, by the time Chrissie and Clark arrived back at her house, the brisk walk had warmed them through and Chrissie was slightly out of breath. Clark looked at his watch;

'Five past twelve. I think we did pretty well.'

Chrissie was relieved. The house was in darkness so her parents were obviously not yet home. Now came the awkward bit.

'I can't ask you in, I'm afraid. My parents will

be back soon, and–'

Clark put his fingers to her lips. 'It's not a problem, but I'd really like to see you again.'

She hesitated as she thought of Billy and the dejection she had seen in his eyes. She imagined him and Sylvia swaying together in the soporific gloom of the dance hall. He could never be interested in a naïve, innocent girl like her anyway. She suddenly became aware of Clark's expectant face. She nodded. 'I'd like that too.'

'Really?' Clark sounded astonished.

Chrissie laughed. 'Yes, really. I have Sunday free. Perhaps we could go for a walk.'

'Perfect,' said Clark. 'I'll call round about one o'clock.'

Chrissie felt momentary panic. 'Er, no. I'll meet you in the park, at the bandstand. I'll bring some sandwiches and a flask if you like.'

'I shall look forward to it.' He raised her hand and softly kissed the back of it. Then, without another word, he turned and walked away.

As Chrissie opened the garden gate, she froze in absolute horror. Sitting on the doorstep, shivering and whimpering, was Leo. She knew she had left him in the house, so this could only mean one thing. Her parents were already home.

6

Chrissie fumbled in her handbag for her key. In her frenzied haste, she went through the contents twice before realising that it had actually been in her coat pocket all the time. Leo was circling round her ankles demanding to be fussed.

'Stop it, Leo, please. I need to get in the house.'

She held her breath as she entered the hall. All was quiet and in darkness. That was very strange indeed. Maybe her parents weren't home after all. Perhaps she had left the back door open and Leo had escaped that way. She felt along the hallway to the kitchen and flicked on the light, causing her to squint in the sudden brightness. Leo had followed her through and was now lapping thirstily at his water. The back door was locked and there were two used coffee cups on the table.

Chrissie's heart sank as she heard a creaking on the staircase. Panic turned to sheer terror as she swung round to see her father standing in the doorway. He was absolutely incandescent with rage, crimson-faced and taking deep breaths, obviously having difficulty in finding the words that would adequately convey his wrath. As Chrissie stood there shaking, Leo cowering behind her, Dr Skinner took one step further, raised his hand and hit her hard across the face. She reeled backwards, fell over Leo and hit her head on the stone floor. Still without uttering a word, Dr Skinner turned abruptly on his heel and stomped back upstairs.

Chrissie could taste blood in her mouth and felt herself beginning to retch. She sat up, but that made the room spin, so she lay back down again and began to weep. Leo licked her face, then curled up beside her, and they spent the rest of the night in fitful slumber on the hard, unforgiving floor.

On Saturday lunchtime, Billy and Clark met in the pub for a pint.

'I can't wait, Bill,' Clark said, passing a drink over to his friend.

'So, where are you meeting her?' asked Billy. He knew he should be pleased for Clark, as he'd waited so long for a date, but he was jealous and finding it difficult to hide.

'In the park, by the bandstand. She's bringing a picnic.'

'That's nice. Did you kiss her?'

Clark was taken aback by the sudden question. 'Er, no, only on the hand.'

Billy was relieved. 'Maybe you will tomorrow then?'

'I'm not rushing it, Billy. I don't want to spoil things. I think she could be the one.'

'You've only met her once.'

'I know, it's ridiculous, but she's just so warm and friendly and–'

'Like a Labrador?'

Clark snorted into his pint. 'Bugger off, Billy.' He laughed. 'You know what I mean.'

That was the trouble. Billy did know, because

81

he felt exactly the same way.

The next day, Clark waited anxiously by the band-stand. It was ten past one already and there was no sign of Chrissie. There was no need to panic just yet, he reasoned to himself as he checked his watch again. The spring day was unseasonably warm and he was regretting wearing his suit and tie. His stomach was in knots and he felt like he needed to use the toilet yet again. There were some public conveniences within his sight, but he didn't dare go in case Chrissie arrived in his absence and assumed he had not turned up. He bounced from one foot to the other, nervously pulling his cuffs and smoothing his tie. He stared at the park gates, willing Chrissie to skip through them. He imagined her looking all fresh-faced and glowing, carrying a brown wicker picnic basket and a tartan rug, apologising profusely for her tardiness. He would politely kiss her on the cheek and insist that no, she wasn't that late, and tell her how beautiful she looked. She would be slightly out of breath through hurrying and they would collapse on the rug together, where they would lie with fingers interlocking as though they had known each other all their lives.

By half past one, Clark knew with absolute certainty that Chrissie wasn't coming. How could he have been so stupid as to believe she ever would? Girls like Chrissie had always been out of his reach and nothing had changed. He slumped down on the grass and savagely pulled the head off a daffodil. Its petals were crusty now and past their best, soon to wither completely and become an eyesore instead of the dazzling display of hope and happiness they had once been.

Alone in her bedroom, Chrissie peered at her reflection in the mirror on her dressing table. The cut on her lip had now congealed with blood, but it was still swollen, and her head pounded. Her heart ached as she looked at the clock and wondered how long Clark would wait by the bandstand before giving up. She boiled with silent rage. Her father had no right to keep her prisoner like this. She had spent the whole of Saturday locked in her room with little to eat or drink. Now it was Sunday and there didn't seem to be any hope of a release.

On Saturday morning she had faced a grilling from both parents about the previous evening's escapade.

'I only went with Syl to the dance hall,' she protested.

'Which one?' demanded her father, as if it would make any difference.

'The Buccaneer.'

'That den of iniquity?' He turned to his wife. 'I told you, Mabel, this girl's out of control.'

Chrissie couldn't help herself and actually laughed out loud.

'Samuel, don't exaggerate,' Mabel admonished.

She turned to her daughter. 'You should have asked us if you wanted to go out. It's the deceit we find intolerable, you see.'

'I knew you wouldn't agree to it.'

'Who was that boy you were with?' Samuel Skinner suddenly demanded. He must have been looking out of the window. Thank God they hadn't kissed, thought Chrissie. He would have been incensed.

'His name is Clark,' she said defiantly. 'He is a decent chap, very polite, and he saw that I got home safely.'

'What happened to Sylvia?' asked Mabel.

'I left her at the dance hall with Clark's friend Billy.'

'That girl is a bad influence, always has been,' muttered Samuel.

Chrissie started to defend her friend, but she opened her mouth too wide, which caused her lip to start bleeding again. She dabbed at it with a tissue. Her father averted his gaze and had the decency to look a little ashamed.

'Look, I'm sorry I hit you,' he admitted. 'We just worry about you, that's all. We can come to some arrangement about letting you go out a bit more if you like, but you overstepped the mark last night and for that you need to be punished.'

As if a slap in the face and a night on the kitchen floor wasn't punishment enough, thought Chrissie bitterly.

'You will spend the rest of the day in your room,' said Mabel. She stared at the floor so she wouldn't have to see the look of resentment on her daughter's face.

'The rest of the weekend,' insisted Samuel.

Mabel glared at her husband before continuing.

'You will spend the rest of the *weekend* in your room.'

Chrissie thought about her meeting with Clark

and began to protest. Her father raised his hand to silence her, and Chrissie actually flinched.

'Enough! Go to your room at once.'

She stood up miserably and started to climb the stairs.

Mabel called after her: 'I'll bring you a little something to eat later.'

'Don't forget to take Leo out, then,' Chrissie retorted. 'And the returned medicine bottles have to be washed before Monday. Oh, and the surgery instruments need disinfecting.' She felt this was a minor victory, and a wry smile played across her lips as she closed her bedroom door.

Now she felt terrible for letting Clark down, though she prayed silently that he wouldn't come to call for her. That would incur such wrath from her father that she feared she would never see beyond the four walls of her bedroom again. She had no way of contacting him, as she didn't even know his surname, let alone where he lived. She was desperate to explain, and the helplessness and guilt she felt left her breathless. Clark would believe he had been stood up, and he did not deserve that. He seemed such a kind and considerate person, but beset with self-doubt and an utter lack of confidence. Chrissie recalled the expression on his face when she had agreed to meet him. A look of total disbelief, followed by elation as he realised she wanted to see him again. Now he would be simply crushed.

When Billy entered the pub that evening for last orders, the barman immediately nodded over to the corner of the room. There, slumped in a chair, surrounded by empty glasses and overflowing ashtrays, was Clark.

'Been there since opening,' informed the barman. 'Banging on the door he was. Made a terrible racket.'

Billy walked over and pulled up a stool. Clark's tie was askew and he had his sleeves rolled up. His eyelids drooped over his bloodshot eyes as he gazed into yet another pint.

'All right there, mate?' ventured Billy. 'I take it this means it didn't go well with Chrissie.'

'It didn't go at all.'

Billy's heart quickened. 'How do you mean?'

'Didn't show up, did she.'

Clark could not keep the bitterness out of his voice. He lit up another cigarette and coughed violently.

'Look at the state of you,' said Billy. 'Don't you think you've had enough?'

'Enough of what? Cigarettes, alcohol or yet more disappointment?'

'Come on, pull yourself together and tell me what happened.'

Clark leant back in his chair and rubbed his face.

'Like I said, she never showed up. Left me standing there like an idiot. I really liked her, Billy. Why did she do this to me?'

'I'm sure there must be a good reason,' Billy said, hoping he was wrong. 'She seemed keen the other night. She can't have just changed her mind, surely?'

'I'm finished with girls. More trouble than they're worth,' said Clark.

On Monday morning, Billy stood outside the surgery in Wood Gardens. Clark had told him Chrissie's surname and that she was a doctor's daughter, so it hadn't needed Sherlock Holmes's powers of deduction to work out where she lived. He wasn't even sure why he was here, let alone what he was going to say, but he felt compelled to see her again. She had awakened something in him on Friday night that was difficult to explain. Maybe it was because she'd seemed more interested in Clark than him, a situation that had never occurred before. All the time he was lumbered with the beautiful but ghastly Sylvia, he could not stop thinking about Chrissie. Every time he glanced over to where she and Clark were sitting, he had felt a stabbing pang of jealousy.

Billy knew that Clark had always felt inferior to him because of his popularity at school, but in truth it was Billy who was in awe of Clark. While Billy worked at the local bakery in a job that was not exactly stimulating or well paid, Clark was employed by the Manchester Co-Operative Society collecting cash for goods that had been bought on credit. He had once showed Billy the huge leather-bound ledger, explaining that all the payments needed to be entered into it and then balanced. Billy had shaken his head in wonder and wished he had concentrated harder at school. His job at the bakery consisted of shift work, and he often toiled through the night and then slept all the next day. On the plus side, however, he did receive his fair share of free custard tarts.

He suddenly heard a dog barking, and a large

curly-coated black-and-tan dog appeared from the ginnel at the side of the house, followed by Chrissie pushing her bicycle. Billy watched from behind a bush as she struggled to turn the bicycle upside down and cursed out loud as it toppled over. He hesitated slightly before coming out from his hiding place and opening the garden gate.

'Need any help?' he asked.

The dog rushed to greet him as though he was a long-lost friend. Chrissie looked up and raised her eyebrows. Billy could see she recognised him instantly.

'Thank you, that's very kind.'

He strode over and settled the bike on its seat and handlebars. He noticed immediately the cut on her lip and a yellow bruise on her cheek.

'The chain came off. My father was supposed to have fixed it but he forgot,' explained Chrissie.

'Would you like me to do it?'

'If you don't mind, that would be very helpful.'

Billy removed his jacket and rolled up his shirt sleeves. In a matter of seconds he had put the chain on and turned the bike back up the right way.

'All done,' he said, rubbing his hands together in an effort to get rid of the oil.

He'd noticed Chrissie looking around nervously, as he worked. Now she seemed anxious to be gone.

'Are you all right, Chrissie?' he asked gently.

'Please, come with me,' she said.

She wheeled the bicycle down the path and Billy held the gate open for her. They walked in silence for a couple of minutes, until they reached the square patch of greenery from which Wood Gardens acquired its name. Chrissie propped the bicycle against the railings, and they found a bench and sat there side by side.

Billy stared directly ahead as he asked, 'What happened to your face?'

He listened in horror as she recounted the tale.

'Your father did this to you?'

'It's nothing really. It was my own fault. I shouldn't have sneaked out like that. My parents are very strict, you see. They worry about me.'

Billy was silently fuming at the thought of Dr Skinner raising his hand to Chrissie and then keeping her locked up all weekend. He turned to face her and gently cupped her face in his hands, letting his thumb graze over her split lip. It was a bold move for a near-stranger, and one that he had not planned; Chrissie looked stunned, but seemed more than content to let Billy gaze into her eyes.

After a while, she spoke.

'How's Clark?'

The question completely broke the bond between them and Billy dropped his hands and looked away.

'I'm sorry,' Chrissie continued. 'But I feel terrible about letting him down yesterday.'

'You had good reason,' said Billy. 'A prisoner in your own home...'

'Have you seen him? I feel I ought to explain, but I have no idea how to contact him.'

'I've seen him, yeah,' admitted Billy. 'He was pretty fed up, to be honest, but he'll get over it, I expect.'

'Especially when I tell him the reason,' said Chrissie.

'Do you have to tell him?' implored Billy.

'Why ever not?'

Billy knew he was being unreasonable, spiteful even, but he couldn't help himself. He was ashamed to admit it, but he wanted this girl even at the cost of his friend's happiness.

'Chrissie, look. When I met you on Friday night, I couldn't take my eyes off you. It was you I wanted to talk to, dance with, but that bloody Sylvia practically kidnapped me, and then you and Clark seemed to be getting along so well. I was devastated when he said he was walking you home.'

Chrissie looked pained. 'I felt the same way too, but I never dreamed anyone so ... so ... well, you know ... so *handsome* would ever look at me.'

Billy took hold of her hand and squeezed it gently. 'You are beautiful, Chrissie. You have poise, grace, and elegance. Sylvia cannot hold a candle to you.'

She blushed and gave him a coy smile.

'What happened with you and Sylvia?'

'Nothing.' Billy shrugged. 'I walked her home out of politeness but said I couldn't see her again because there was someone else in my life.'

'Is there?' asked Chrissie nervously.

He winked. 'Not yet.'

Chrissie jumped to her feet, a look of alarm on her face.

'I really need to get on.'

'Can I see you again?' asked Billy.

'I'd like that, but what about Clark?'

90

Billy was ashamed to admit he had forgotten all about his friend.

'I'll talk to him,' he assured her.

Billy had considered keeping his fledgling romance with Chrissie a secret from Clark, but he realised that wouldn't be possible, and in any event it was the coward's way out. A filthy, duplicitous little scumbag he might be, but a coward he was not. The conversation could have gone better.

'What do you mean, you're taking Chrissie out?' Clark asked incredulously.

'I'm sorry, Clark, really I am, but Chrissie and I just clicked. We both feel the, same way and–'

Billy was unable to finish his sentence as Clark grabbed him by the throat.

'You just can't bear to see me happy, can you? What is it with you? You know I was so excited about seeing her, you know how long I've waited for a girl like Chrissie, or any girl for that matter, but you have to spoil everything. You are fucking unbelievable, Billy!' Clark's eyes blazed with fury and spit gathered at the corners of his mouth as he shoved Billy hard against the wall.

'Calm down, mate...' Billy was completely taken aback by his friend's uncharacteristic outburst.

'I am not your mate. I never want to set eyes on you again. Ever.'

Clark stormed off, leaving Billy gaping after him. So that was it. A boyhood friendship severed for the sake of a girl. It must have happened countless times, in places all around the globe, but the thought did nothing to console Billy. Now he was determined to make Chrissie happy at whatever cost. Unfortunately, two men, neither of whom Billy had met, would conspire against him. One was Chrissie's father, Dr Skinner, and the other was busy, marauding his way through Europe, hell-bent on expanding his empire.

7

The summer of 1939 was the happiest of Billy's life. Even with the constant threat of war hanging over the nation, he was in a permanent state of euphoria. His relationship with Chrissie had matured into something real and tangible despite the disapproval of her father. As could have been predicted by anybody, Samuel Skinner had a profound dislike of Billy and only barely tolerated him. In his eyes, Billy was nowhere near a match for his daughter. He was an orphaned nuisance in a dead-end job, idolised by his deluded mother and practically ignored by his alcoholic father. Dr Skinner remembered the family well. Alice Stirling was a worrier and after the death of her first-born son, she had brought the adopted Billy to his surgery with tedious regularity. Now his daughter was smitten with Billy Stirling and that riled the good doctor no end.

At least Chrissie had had the good sense to approach her father about Billy and not go behind his back. Dr Skinner in turn had assumed the relationship would be shallow and short-lived, but his judgement had turned out to be wrong. His only hope was that Billy would be called up to serve his National Service in the not-too-distant future and that that would herald the end of the matter.

The first meeting between the two of them had not gone well. Dr Skinner had not seen Billy since he was a boy, but he recognised the name and knew him instantly. The scar over his left eyebrow was still as visible as ever.

'Good evening, Dr Skinner,' said Billy, holding out his hand.

The doctor ignored it and turned to Chrissie.

'I want you home by ten o'clock.'

Mabel Skinner appeared from the kitchen, still in her midwife's uniform.

'You must be Billy,' she said. 'I'm very pleased to meet you.'

Samuel glared at his wife as she and Billy shook hands. It had taken Mabel all her persuasive powers to convince her husband that they should allow Chrissie a little more freedom.

'Thank you, Mrs Skinner. I'll take good care of your daughter.'

'Come on, Billy, let's go,' urged Chrissie.

Mabel disappeared back into the kitchen and Chrissie and Billy started down the front path as Samuel Skinner watched from the door.

Billy suddenly caught Chrissie's arm. 'Wait here for a second, will you?'

He retreated up the path and arrived at the front door just as Samuel Skinner was closing it. He slipped his foot inside and pushed his face close to the doctor's.

'If you ever lay one more finger on your daughter, I swear to you I will kill you with my bare hands.'

Dr Skinner was not usually lost for words, but he watched in stunned disbelief as Billy strode off, placing his arm protectively around Chrissie's waist.

Billy had never had a significant romantic relationship before, and he cherished the feelings it aroused in him. He knew he was falling in love, and not even the vile Dr Skinner could dampen his ardour. However, he was terrified that war would soon be declared and he would be sent off to some far-flung battlefield to take part in a conflict he barely understood. Billy had only been a baby at the end of the Great War, but he knew it had taken the life of his father, and indirectly that of his mother too. It all seemed so senseless, and now another war was threatening to scupper his burgeoning relationship with Chrissie.

The two of them were strolling hand in hand along a quiet stream. The weather was bright and sunny, the sky a deep azure, and the birds – yellowhammers, skylarks and song thrushes – seemed to be competing to see who could sing loudest and sweetest. The scent of wild garlic hung in the air and watercress grew in abundance in the water. Chrissie was wearing her favourite summer dress: pale blue with little yellow polka dots and a white belt that nipped in her narrow waist. Billy had taken his jacket off and carried it over his shoulder with one hand, a bulging picnic basket in the other. Leo bounded ahead of them, chasing every rabbit in sight but catching none.

'Where would you like to stop?' Billy asked.

Chrissie surveyed the riverbank. 'Over there, under that oak tree. It will be nice and cool.'

Together they spread the picnic rug on the long grass and sat down. Chrissie opened the basket and took out hard-boiled eggs, potted meat sandwiches, ripe tomatoes and home-made fruit cake. Leo sat between them and put his cute face on. He never took his eyes off the sandwiches, and eventually a long sliver of drool escaped his mouth and landed on the rug.

'For goodness' sake, Leo,' cried Chrissie. 'Shoo.'

The dog tucked his tail between his legs and slunk away.

'It's so peaceful here, isn't it?' said Chrissie. 'Surely there can't be another war.'

Billy looked at the gas masks they were all now required to carry.

'I don't know, Chrissie,' he replied solemnly. 'But fretting about it won't make any difference. We might as well enjoy the time we have left together.'

Chrissie looked alarmed. 'You make it sound as if war has already been declared!'

Billy took her hands in his and gazed into her pale eyes.

'I hope it won't come to that, but we need to be realistic. At the very least I will have to serve my military training.'

He took a stray curl and tucked it behind her ear. Her eyes filled with tears and she bowed her head. Billy jumped up. 'Come on, let's go for a paddle.'

What? That water's freezing.' She laughed.

Billy was already removing his shoes and socks and rolling up his trouser legs. Leo perked up and bounded into the water. Chrissie took off her shoes and ankle socks too, and hand in hand they skipped down to the water's edge.

Billy was the first to dip his toe in.

'Christ, this water's freezing!'

Chrissie laughed. 'I told you.'

'I'm sure it never used to be this cold when we were kids.'

Chrissie sat down at the edge of the water. 'You've been here before?'

Billy was immersed in the stream up to his ankles, and his feet ached with the cold.

He stared into the distance. 'Yeah, me and Clark. We used to come here after school. Sometimes instead of school,' he admitted. 'Stony Brook we called it. Not sure if that's its real name or whether we just made it up. We used to fish for minnows with pieces of cotton tied to a cork float. The little blighters swallowed the cotton and we would fish them out.' He smiled at the memory. 'Squirrels too,' he continued. 'Forestry Commission used to pay tuppence ha'penny for every squirrel tail brought in. Considered a pest, see; grey ones only, mind, not the red ones. Tree rats, we called them. We spent hours with our home-made catapults trying to bag one, but we never did.' He turned to Chrissie, a look of sadness on his face.

'You miss him, don't you?' said Chrissie.

Billy waded through the water and joined her on the bank. 'More than you'll ever know. I called round there again last week but his mum said he was out. I know he wasn't, though. I'd just seen

96

him go inside.'

He pulled Chrissie to her feet.

'Come on. Let's go and eat lunch.'

Chrissie grabbed a bunch of watercress from the stream and shook off the excess water. Billy frowned.

'To liven up the potted meat,' she explained.

As they lay side by side in the shade of the oak, the sandwiches and fruit cake heavy in their stomachs, Billy closed his eyes. He was truly happy with Chrissie, in spite of her father. She was a dear, sweet girl who would make the perfect wife. She was pretty, intelligent and such a kind soul, she found it difficult to say a bad word against anyone. It was no wonder Clark had been so smitten with her, and then so crushed by their duplicity.

He propped himself up and gazed at her face. She seemed to be dozing, and he marvelled at her long, sweeping eyelashes, her full rosy lips and her cheeks now tinged pink by the sun and with a smattering of freckles. He picked a long blade of grass and traced it gently down her cheek. She stirred and flapped her hands about.

'Oooh, what was that? Something was on me.' She sat up and took in Billy's impish grin.

'You!' She laughed and lay back on the rug with her hand behind her head.

Billy leant over and kissed her gently on the lips. She opened her eyes and cupped his face in her hands, pulling him closer. He kissed her again, deeper this time and more urgently. Chrissie responded, and Billy rolled himself on top of her. He tried to part her legs with his own but was stopped in his tracks by a low rumbling sound close to his ear. He looked up to see Leo growling softly, not quite baring his teeth. Chrissie giggled as Billy rolled on to his back.

'Bugger off, dog,' he said, waving his hand at Leo. 'A bloody passion-killer, that creature is.'

He ruffled Leo's head and the dog wagged its tail enthusiastically.

'Bloody hell, he thinks that's an invitation to join in!'

Chrissie loved Billy with all her heart, of that she was certain. The situation with her father was trying, to say the least, but she hoped that he would come round eventually and grow to accept Billy. He was her first boyfriend, however, and she was nervous about the physical side of their relationship. She need not have worried. Billy was a perfect gentleman and never forced her to go further than she was comfortable with. That day by the river, though, had it not been for Leo... Chrissie found herself aroused by the thought, and felt embarrassed. After all, hadn't she been brought up better than that? Her father would be incensed if he knew the extent of their physical relationship.

As the weeks passed, the days grew longer and hotter and Billy and Chrissie spent many hours down by Stony Brook. The babbling sound of the water running over the gleaming pebbles was soothing; the sight of the cattle grazing contentedly in the pastures was reassuring, and most importantly, they could find solace together away from the disapproving glare of Chrissie's father.

This was a special place, a quiet haven in the suburbs of Manchester, a world away from that huge, sprawling city with its billowing, belching chimneys and noisy motor vehicles.

On this particular day, the sky had an ominous look to it. Although it was stiflingly warm, the sky was a myriad of colours, mostly grey, black and purple, a landscape artist's dream. Thunder was in the air. As Billy and Chrissie approached their favourite spot under the oak tree, they both stopped in their tracks at the same time. The figure was unmistakable. There, crouched down in the stream with his back to them, was Clark.

'What shall we do?' whispered Chrissie.

'I'm not sure,' replied Billy. 'He hasn't seen us yet.'

'Go and talk to him,' urged Chrissie. 'I'll wait here.'

Billy hesitated for only a second before creeping up to Clark. His heart was pounding as though it was trying to escape the confines of his ribcage.

'All right there, mate?'

Clark jumped and turned round. He straightened up and looked at Billy, recognition taking a few seconds. Billy's hair was shorter now, and his face was tanned.

'Christ, you startled me,' he said.

'What have you got there?'

Clark held up the jar by a piece of tatty string. 'Sticklebacks!'

For a moment his blue eyes shone with excitement, then they clouded over. He ran a wet hand through his red hair and swept it off his face. His freckles were more pronounced than usual, and for a moment Billy saw him as an eleven-year-old again. He felt his throat constrict, which made his next sentence a strangled croak.

'We had fun, didn't we, Clark?'

Clark snorted and set the jar of fish down on a large stone. He waded out of the water and sat down heavily on the bank. Billy edged closer and then tentatively sat down next to him.

'Don't get too comfortable,' said Clark.

'Look, Clark. Can't we be friends again?'

'Can't we be friends again?' mimicked Clark. 'We're not in the school playground now, Billy.'

'Why did you come here?' asked Billy.

Clark thought for a moment. 'To reflect.' He reached inside his jacket and pulled out a brown envelope. 'Here,' he said, thrusting it into Billy's hands.

Billy opened the envelope and stared at the contents. 'You've been called up?'

'Military training,' explained Clark.

Billy knew it was only a matter of time. Since Parliament had passed the Act in April, all men aged twenty and twenty-one were required to undertake six months' military training.

He didn't know what to say. 'Clark, look...' He passed the envelope back.

'How's Chrissie?' asked Clark, looking Billy directly in the eye.

Billy was taken by surprise at the sudden mention of her name and picked at a blade of grass.

'She's fine, thanks. In fact she's with me now, over there.'

Clark looked in the direction of Billy's finger and Chrissie slid out sheepishly from behind a tree. Billy motioned with his head for her to join them. It was the first time she had seen Clark since the night of the dance.

'Clark,' she began. 'How nice to see you again.'

Clark stood up and nodded. He paused awkwardly.

'I'd better be going. It looks like rain.'

Right on cue, a huge swollen raindrop landed on the envelope, staining it a darker brown. Clark put his jacket on and pulled up his collar.

'I'll see you around.' He set off up the bank, quickening his pace with each falling raindrop.

Chrissie looked at Billy, a look of hopelessness on her face. Billy called after his friend: 'Clark, wait!'

Clark stopped, turned round and waited. Billy jogged his way over. He stopped a yard in front of Clark and the two men stared at each other. Billy was the first to speak. 'Good luck, mate.'

He held out his hand, and Clark stared at it for a moment. Then, very slowly, he pulled his own hand out of his pocket and took hold of Billy's. He shook it firmly, looking Billy directly in the eye, and gave a faint smile. No further words were exchanged, but they both knew a hatchet had been buried.

Clark turned and never looked back as he made his way home in the pouring rain. Billy sprinted back to where Chrissie was sheltering under the tree.

'Everything all right?' she enquired anxiously.

Billy stared at Clark's jar. The two fish were swimming round in circles, banging into the glass in a desperate attempt at freedom. He picked up the jar and tipped it into the stream. In a flash of silver, the fish wriggled off in separate directions. He looked up at Chrissie and smiled. 'Everything's fine now.'

Despite the shelter of the old oak, raindrops dripped off the leaves and on to the rug where Billy and Chrissie lay. The lightning lit up the sky and the thunder rumbled like the stomach of a starving elephant.

'I'm not sure this is the safest place to shelter,' said Chrissie.

Billy looked around. 'It's not the tallest tree around, so I think it will be all right.'

He looked at Chrissie's anxious face. Her hair was soaked, and curls of it clung to her face. He pulled her to her feet. 'Come on, it's drier by the trunk.'

They leant against the trunk of the mighty tree, waiting for the storm to pass. The cows in the field were now all huddled against the hedge and the stream had become swollen and rapid as it tried to cope with the sudden influx of water.

'Our shoes!' cried Chrissie, as a surge of water engulfed them where they had been abandoned. 'We shall have to walk home barefoot.'

Billy dashed out, picked up the shoes and poured the water out of them. He stood in the open for a few seconds and turned his face to the skies. The water ran down his neck and he shivered involuntarily. He remembered an incident from his childhood when he and Clark had been caught in a storm in this very spot. The bank had become slippery and Billy had fallen down and ripped his shorts on a rock. He'd known he would be in big trouble with his mother and was afraid to return home. When Clark suggested they swap shorts, Billy had never been more grateful. Once again his friend had bailed him out. It wasn't until months later that Billy learned about the scolding Clark had received from his own mother when she saw the state of the shorts.

'Billy, come back here,' called Chrissie. 'You're soaked.'

Her voice jolted him back to the present and he joined her under the tree. 'Sorry, I was miles away.'

'You look awful,' exclaimed Chrissie. 'What's the matter?'

'I was just thinking about Clark. I can't believe he's going away. I still think of him as a little boy sometimes, and now he's going off to fight. I'm not sure how he'll cope.'

'Billy, he is not going off to fight. He's only been called up for military training. We are not at war, remember.'

'I know, you're right, but he'll be away for six months and by then we might be.'

Chrissie clamped her hand over his mouth.

'Don't say it. There isn't going to be a war. I don't want to lose you now.'

Billy gazed into Chrissie's blue eyes, glistening with tears, then took her into his arms and held her tightly.

'Your shirt is drenched,' said Chrissie. 'Here, let me.'

Without taking her eyes off his face, she slowly unbuttoned Billy's shirt and let it fall to the floor. He was breathing harder now and he kissed her urgently. She opened her mouth as his tongue probed between her lips, and he pressed her body against the trunk of the tree. The roughness of the bark caused her to gasp out loud. Billy closed his eyes and thought of Clark. It should be Clark here now with Chrissie up against this tree trunk. All Billy had ever done was take from his friend. In school he had passed his homework over to Clark to complete and he had done it all, grateful for the fact that Billy had deigned to be his friend when nobody else cared. At that moment, Billy hated himself and his mind became clouded. He pressed himself harder against Chrissie and she emitted a muffled squeal. He lifted her arms over her head and pinned them together at the wrist against the tree. With his other hand he lifted her skirt. Chrissie caught her breath but she did not pull away, so he let go of her arms and unbuttoned his trousers. He buried his face in her neck, his own breath coming in short, hot bursts.

It was not how Chrissie had planned to lose her virginity, but she was at least grateful that it was not possible to get pregnant whilst standing up.

8

September 1939

Chrissie had been up for around two hours, unable to sleep. She sat at the kitchen table and poured herself a third cup of tea. She dunked yet another ginger biscuit and sucked on it miserably. It was supposed to cure you of the feeling of nausea, but that had to be an old wives' tale, as she still felt wretched. She heard the letter box flap in the hallway as the paper boy shoved the *Daily Telegraph* through, thrusting yet more unwelcome news into her life. She reluctantly heaved herself up and retrieved it. The headline screamed out at her: BRITAIN'S LAST WARNING. Yesterday, Adolf Hider had invaded Poland, and war now seemed inevitable. Air-raid shelters had been erected and thousands of children had already been evacuated.

Chrissie cupped her stomach with both hands and sighed. She was harbouring a secret that would bring more disruption and upset to this household than the declaration of war ever could. She was startled by the urgent ringing of the doorbell and glanced at the clock on the wall. Who on earth could be here at six thirty in the morning? Whoever it was now banged on the door as well.

'All right, I'm coming,' called Chrissie irritably. She opened the door to Mr Cutler, a neighbour and one of their patients.

'Where's your mother?' he demanded. 'Maud's gone into labour, screaming the place down she is.' He pushed his way into the hall. 'Where is she?' He called up the stairs. 'Mrs Skinner?'

'She's in bed asleep, or at least she was until you started banging the door down.'

Mabel Skinner appeared on the landing, hurriedly tying the cord of her dressing gown.

'Mr Cutler,' she exclaimed. 'What is it?'

'Maud's having the baby, please come quick.'

Chrissie and her mother exchanged worried glances. Maud Cutler's baby wasn't due for another four weeks.

'Chrissie,' barked Mabel. 'Get dressed and get my bag ready, will you. I'll have to drive Maud to the hospital.'

Mr Cutler looked alarmed. 'Can't you deliver the baby at home, Mrs Skinner? You know she wanted to give birth in her own bed.'

'No, Mr Cutler, I can't,' explained Mabel. 'The baby isn't due for another month; there may be complications. Given Maud's age, I think it would be better to go to hospital. Now go home and wait for me there.'

Chrissie stood rooted to the spot. In just a few short months she would be in this position, screaming in pain, legs akimbo in stirrups, suffering the disapproving stares of the midwives, the wrath of her father, the disappointment of her mother. She began to have difficulty breathing and tried to tell herself it would be all right. Billy would be with her, and as long as she had him, she could get through anything. She gripped the door frame to steady herself. Her mother's sharp voice made her jump.

'Chrissie! Move!'

The next day, Sunday 3 September, was gloriously sunny. It seemed unthinkable that war could be declared on such a beautiful day. The Skinners sat around the kitchen table with the wireless in the middle, each nursing a mug of tea, lost in their own thoughts. Chrissie was thinking about her unborn baby, because she never thought about anything else. Mabel was thinking about the Cutlers' baby, born yesterday, too soon, too small, and willing him to live. Dr Skinner was already thinking about how to celebrate the fact that Billy Stirling would soon be out of his daughter's life for good. His call-up papers would surely arrive in the next few weeks.

The silence was broken by a tap on the back door. Dr Skinner rose and opened it cautiously. It was the last person on earth he wanted to see right now.

'What do you want?' he demanded.

'I wanted to listen to the broadcast with Chrissie. Is she in?'

Chrissie heard Billy's voice and jumped up.

'Come in, Billy, have a seat.'

He kissed her on the cheek and took his place at the table. He took hold of Chrissie's hand and stared Dr Skinner in the eye. The doctor looked away and fiddled with a knob on the wireless.

At 11.15, the Prime Minister, Neville Chamberlain, addressed the nation, struggling to keep the anguish from his voice.

'This morning the British Ambassador in Berlin handed the German Government a formal note stating that, unless we heard from them by eleven o'clock this morning that they were prepared at once to withdraw their troops from Poland, a state of war would exist between us. I have to tell you now that no such undertaking has been received, and that consequently this country is at war with Germany.'

Chrissie had been holding her breath, but let out a huge sob. Billy wrapped his arms around her and she turned and clung to him. Dr Skinner calmly lit a cigarette and blew the smoke across the table.

'Well that's that then,' he declared. 'Better get your bags packed, Billy.'

'Samuel!' shouted Mabel. 'Stop it. Can't you see Chrissie's upset?'

Billy stood up. 'It's all right, Mrs Skinner. Come on, Chrissie, let's go for a walk.'

As they wandered down the path, Chrissie gazed up at the sky. 'Do you think it will be safe?'

Billy laughed. 'I don't think the Luftwaffe will get here that quickly.'

The streets were almost empty, save for a few mothers clutching their babies tightly. They were off to church to have their infants baptised immediately. The panic in the air was tangible, and Chrissie clung to Billy's arm.

'I'm sorry about my father.'

'You've been apologising for him since the day we met. He's never going to accept us as a couple, so we might as well get used to it. Anyway, he's right. I will have to go away.'

Chrissie stopped in her tracks and covered her face with her hands.

Billy put his arm around her shoulders and pulled her close. 'I don't know what to say, Chrissie. It's terrible, I know, but there is nothing I can do.'

They had reached the park, and Chrissie plonked herself down on a bench.

'It's worse than you think,' she said miserably. Her hands trembled in her lap. 'Can I have a cigarette, please?'

Billy widened his eyes in astonishment as he held out a packet of Woodbine. She pulled one from the pack, but her shaking hands couldn't keep hold of it.

'Can you light it for me?'

'Of course.' He expertly lit the cigarette and took a long drag before handing it to Chrissie.

She placed it between her lips and sucked.

'You're not doing it right. Breathe from your lungs.'

Chrissie took a deep breath and felt the smoke fill her chest. She immediately spluttered and coughed violently as the smoke travelled down her nose, making her eyes water.

'Thanks,' she managed, handing the cigarette back to Billy. 'I feel better for that.'

Billy laughed and kissed her forehead lightly. 'We'll get through it, you know.'

Chrissie fell silent and gazed at the children running round the park. She wondered if they had understood what had happened that morning. War probably seemed like the most exciting adventure in the world to them. They would soon be evacuated, though, separated from their families for months, even years. She shuddered at the thought.

Billy lay back on the bench with his hands

clasped behind his head, face up to the sun, eyes closed. She laid her head on his chest. She could hear his heart beating gently, and she welcomed the warmth of him, the scent of his freshly laundered shirt and the feel of the tight muscles in his stomach. She didn't know if she could endure being parted from him.

'Billy?' she whispered eventually.

'What?' he replied, without opening his eyes.

'I'm pregnant.'

He froze for a second, and Chrissie felt the change in his heartbeat. He pushed her away slightly so he could look into her eyes.

'What? How? I mean, you can't be. It's not possible.'

She watched the blood slowly drain from his face as he waited for an explanation.

'Well it obviously is possible,' she replied, somewhat indignantly. 'Because I am.'

'But the only time we've ever made love was under the oak tree during the storm.' He stood up and put his hands on his hips. 'How could you let this happen?'

Chrissie recoiled as though she had been slapped. 'Me? I think you'll find it takes two people to make a baby.'

'A baby?' Billy repeated. 'I can't believe this. How long have you known?'

'I'm two months gone.'

'And you've never said anything until now. Are you sure?'

'I'm the daughter of a doctor and a midwife. Of course I'm sure.'

'This is a disaster,' proclaimed Billy. 'How could

you be so, so...'

'So what, Billy?'

He slumped back down on the bench and held his head in his hands.

'Have you told your parents?'

Chrissie snorted. 'What do you think?'

'Can you give me a minute? I can't... Look, I need to be on my own while I take this in. I'm sorry. This has come as a complete shock.'

He rose from the bench and strode off without a backward glance. Chrissie watched him as he broke into a run and disappeared round the corner. She had never felt so abandoned and alone in her entire life. Fear washed over her and then abruptly turned to anger. How could Billy *do* this to her? She looked around the park, expecting someone to come to her aid, but they were all engrossed in their own lives. She might as well be invisible. She clutched her stomach and sank to her knees. Her whole body heaved as she sobbed uncontrollably.

Alice Stirling looked up from her sewing as her son burst through the door. Her fingers were sore from pushing the needle through the heavy blackout fabric, but she had nearly finished the curtains for their tiny house. He looked a dreadful mess with his tousled hair and profusely sweating brow.

'Billy!' exclaimed Alice. 'Oh come in, sit down. It's dreadful news, isn't it?' She ushered her son to his place at the kitchen table and massaged his broad shoulders. 'What a terrible shock. I know some people have been expecting it, but nevertheless—'

Billy turned to look at his mother, perplexed. 'How do you know?'

'What do you mean, how do I know? I heard it on the wireless. I went next door and Reg let me listen with him.'

'Oh the war, yes, it's terrible. But like you say, we've been expecting it. It was only a matter of time.'

He glanced around the kitchen. 'Where's Dad?'

Alice scoffed. 'I don't know. He went out early this morning.'

Billy hugged his mother tightly. She deserved so much better.

There was a pot roast in the oven, and despite his turmoil, Billy felt comforted by its delicious aromas. It was only a cheap cut of meat, but by the time Alice Stirling had finished with it, it would have the taste and texture of the finest fillet steak. The thought of the rich gravy bubbling away inside the oven made his mouth water. His mother was a wonderful cook. Her roast potatoes were legendary, the best in the world, sweet and fluffy in the middle, crisp and dark on the outside. She had made his favourite apple pie too, and it was sitting on the side waiting to be cooked.

'Are you making custard as well?' asked Billy.

'When have I ever served apple pie without it?'

Billy stared up at his mother and his eyes filled with tears. What would have become of him if she had not marched into that orphanage all those years ago and scooped him up out of his high chair, creating that instant bond between them? He knew that the war would separate them and his heart ached for the pain his mother would have to endure. He watched her at the sink now, her back shaking as she vigorously scrubbed the potatoes.

'I love you, Mum.'

Alice stopped scrubbing and gripped the edge of the sink, trying to compose herself. She wiped her hands on her apron and turned round to face her son.

'I love you too, Billy. Never forget that.' She crossed the kitchen and kissed him on the forehead. She didn't mention the tear that had escaped his eye and run down his cheek. 'Now then, would you set the table please?'

'Of course I will. For how many?'

Alice sighed and began work on the potatoes again. 'Three. One of these days your father may remember where he lives and grace us with his presence for lunch. Better to be prepared. Oh, and put some wine glasses out too.'

'Wine?'

'Yes,' continued Alice. 'And some serviettes as well. We've had bad news today and a proper Sunday lunch will perk us all up. There's a bottle of red in the back of that cupboard. I can't even remember where it came from, but I'm sure it will be all right.'

'Blimey, it must be well hidden if Dad hasn't found it!'

'Now, now, Billy. Show some respect to your father.'

'Sure. Sorry, Mum.'

How she could be so loyal to his feckless father was beyond him.

After they had finished eating, Billy pushed his plate away and leant back in his chair.

'Mum, I've got some news.'

Alice stood up to clear the table.

'Have you? What news?'

He caught hold of her hand. It was rough and calloused from years of domestic chores and he was amazed he had not noticed this before. 'Sit down, please. Leave the pots for now.'

Alice pulled up a chair and a worried look clouded her face. 'What is it, love?'

'Chrissie's pregnant.'

Her hands flew to her mouth. 'Oh God, Billy, how could you have been so stupid?'

Billy stood up and paced the room. 'You're right. I'm an idiot. What am I going to do?'

Alice stood up and hugged him tightly. 'It'll be all right. We'll work something out.' She glanced anxiously towards the door. 'Best not tell your father just yet, though.'

Billy nodded his agreement. 'Poor Chrissie. It was such a shock when she told me that I couldn't take it in. I just ran off and left her. She will be utterly distraught. I can't believe I behaved so selfishly.'

His mother was horrified. 'Billy! You need to talk to her. She'll be in turmoil. Oh God, what a mess, what a day!'

'You're right, I need to see her again. My behaviour was appalling.' He grabbed his jacket off the back of his chair and kissed his mother on the cheek. 'I'll see you later.'

Billy jogged the two miles to Chrissie's house, his

Sunday lunch lying heavily in his stomach. By the time he arrived, he was breathless and his damp shirt stuck to his skin. He started to make his way round the back of the surgery, but changed his mind and used the front door instead. He pushed his finger on to the doorbell and held it there. He suddenly felt incredibly antagonistic towards Dr Skinner and didn't care if he annoyed him. He could hear Leo barking excitedly and silently prayed that Chrissie would answer the door. Alas, it was her father's gruff tones he could hear coming down the hallway.

Dr Skinner opened the door and looked down from his vantage point on the porch step.

'Dr Skinner, is Chrissie in, please?'

'No.'

This took Billy by surprise.

'Oh. Well do you know where she is?'

'No.'

'Do you know how long she will be, then?'

'No.'

How Billy hated this man. He struggled to speak calmly. 'Well could you give her a message? No, actually, on second thoughts, don't bother. I'll wait.'

Without another word, Dr Skinner closed the door and put the chain on.

Chrissie sat on the top stair and smiled to herself. She had known for sure he would come back, but he had behaved monstrously and she needed some time to gather her emotions. She thought it would do him no harm to reflect on his abominable behaviour. She would leave it for half an hour and then go out to him.

Billy sat on the pavement, chain-smoking as he contemplated his future. However he looked at it, it didn't promise much. His girlfriend was pregnant out of wedlock, her father hated the very sight of him, and war had just been declared, a war that he was going to have to fight in whether he wanted to or not. He jumped at the sound of footsteps close behind him. Samuel Skinner crouched down and spoke menacingly into his ear.

'She is in but she doesn't want to see you.'

Billy spun round. 'What? I don't believe you.'

'Suit yourself, but I'm telling you, you're wasting your time. You've obviously had some sort of row. She won't tell me what it's about, but I suggest you go home and forget all about her.'

Billy stood up now and faced his nemesis.

'You'd like that, wouldn't you, but unfortunately you are not in possession of all the facts.' He snatched up his jacket. 'Tell Chrissie I'll be back tomorrow.'

Dr Skinner turned and went back into the house. He called up the stairs.

'Chrissie, he's gone. Said he was fed up of waiting. Didn't think you were worth the bother, and anyway, he'll be going away soon. He said not to wait for him but to move on with your life. You know, I'm not sure we'll be seeing that young man again.'

Chrissie stood shocked and rigid at the top of the stairs, steadying herself on the banister. She could not believe it. She had only meant to keep him waiting for a little while, and now he had left her. This couldn't be happening. She ran to the bathroom and retched into the toilet, the nausea this time having nothing to do with the baby growing inside her.

9

By the time Billy arrived back home, his mother had tidied away all the pots and was sitting by the fireside knitting. His father had returned and was asleep in the chair opposite her. Alice Stirling put her finger to her lips as Billy entered the kitchen.

'Did you speak to her?' she whispered.

Billy motioned for his mother to follow him into the front parlour.

'Don't switch the light on; I've not put the black-out curtain up yet. I know it's not quite dark, but I'm not taking any chances.'

They stood facing each other in the gloom as Billy told her of his encounter with Dr Skinner.

'That man is so vile. How he ever entered such a caring profession is beyond me. Do you think it was true what he was saying, about Chrissie not wanting to see you?'

'I'm not sure, Mum. It might be. I was pretty vile myself.'

'She'll come round, she has to. She's carrying your baby. Just give her a little more time. Her hormones are all over the place too, don't forget. She knows you came to see her and she'll be grateful for that. She'll talk to you when she's ready. In the meantime, why don't you write her a letter?'

'A letter? Oh, I don't know.'

'Think about it, Billy. It's much easier to say what you mean if you write it down. You can apologise to her and let her know your feelings without worrying about saying the wrong thing. You could post it. That would be a nice touch, shows you've made the effort. Hmm? What do you think?'

'OK, I'll do it tomorrow. I'm too tired to think about it now. It's been a horrible day.'

'One we'll remember for the rest of our lives, I expect. Now come on, why don't you help me put up the rest of these curtains.'

'Sure, I need something to do.'

By the time they had finished putting up the curtains, darkness had fallen outside and the streets were eerily quiet.

Billy peeled back the curtain slightly and squinted into the shadows. Already the blackout was strictly enforced.

'You can't see a thing out there.'

His mother crept up behind him and peered out. 'I know. All the street lamps have been turned off. Apparently, if you do ever need to venture outside after dark, you have to use a torch covered with brown paper. Drivers aren't even allowed to put their headlamps on.'

'That's for our own safety, is it?' Billy shook his head.

'You have to trust the people in charge, Billy. They know what they're doing.'

'Let's hope so.' He stepped back and kissed his

mother on the cheek. 'I think I'll turn in now, Mum, if you don't mind.'

'Of course. Night, son, sleep well. Everything will seem different in the morning.'

Chrissie sat on the bathroom floor facing the toilet, her arms coiled round the seat. She could not imagine anything less dignified. Her boyfriend did not want anything more to do with her, and now she would have to endure the shame and humiliation all by herself. The thought of telling her parents made her heave into the bowl again. The back of her nose and throat were sore from the stinging bile and her stomach muscles ached. She could hear her parents downstairs in the kitchen, talking in soft tones. It was impossible to tell what they were saying, but Chrissie could guess. Dr Skinner would be jubilant that Billy had left her and that he had been proved right about him. She froze as she heard footsteps coming up the stairs. She strained to listen and was relieved that they sounded soft and cautious, more like her mother's than her father's. There came a hesitant tap on the bathroom door.

'Chrissie? whispered Mabel. 'How much longer are you going to stay in there? You've been there for hours.'

She waited for a reply, and when none was forthcoming, she tried again.

'Chrissie, love, you can't stay in there all night. Let me in and we can talk about it.'

Still Chrissie stayed silent.

'All right then,' insisted Mabel. 'I'm just going to sit here until you are ready to come out. Your

119

father is not happy, by the way. He's had to use the toilet in the back yard.'

This piece of news brought a faint smile to Chrissie's lips. Her father hated having to go outside to use the toilet. She tried to stand up but found her legs had locked into position and she was so stiff she could barely move. Slowly she clambered to her feet and stood shakily, like a newborn foal taking its first steps. Her fingers trembled as she fumbled with the lock on the bathroom door and slowly slid it back. She opened the door to her mother's startled face.

'My God! What happened to you? You look dreadful.'

Chrissie's mouth was too dry to speak, so she simply pushed past her mother and threw herself on to her bed. Mabel followed her into the bedroom, where Chrissie lay face down, her head buried in her pillow. She sat on the edge of the bed and rubbed Chrissie's back.

'Come on,' she encouraged. 'It's not that bad. It's not as if Billy was the one. I mean, he's a nice enough chap, but we always knew you could do so much better.'

Chrissie sat up and faced her mother. Her face was shiny with sweat and tears and her eyes were swollen and red-rimmed. 'I love him, Mother,' she said simply.

Mabel hesitated. 'I know you think you do, but do you really know what love feels like? He was your first boyfriend, after all.'

'Will you stop talking about him in the past tense,' interrupted Chrissie. 'He's not dead.'

She felt the bile rising again and swallowed

hard. She began to shake and lay back on the bed once more. Mabel stared intently at her, and then the colour drained from her face and she too began to tremble. Despite her consternation, her words were perfectly enunciated.

'You slut!'

'There's no fooling you, is there, Mother?'

'Is that all you can say? How far gone are you? I take it Billy is the father. My God, is this why he left you?'

Chrissie sat up again. Her mother's reaction had made her defiant. 'Which question do you want me to answer first?'

Mabel stood up and paced the room. 'I can't believe this, you stupid little girl. Your father was right all along about him.' Her voice rose with each word. 'Oh God, your father.' She hurriedly closed the bedroom door and leant against it, taking huge gulps of breath. Chrissie thought she might actually pass out, but all she said was 'I need to think.'

The next day, as the people of Great Britain tried to come to terms with the fact that they were now at war, Billy sat down and began his letter to Chrissie. 'What's the date, Mum?' he called.

'The fourth,' answered his mother from the kitchen.

He carefully wrote out the address at the top of the page and inserted the date underneath. Now came the difficult part. In different circumstances he would have enlisted Clark's help with this sort of task; in fact his friend would have ended up writing it for him, no doubt. Billy pushed all thoughts of Clark from his mind and tried to concentrate. With no idea of how he was going to finish, he began 'My darling Christina'. He felt the use of her full name would give the letter more sincerity. After that the words flowed surprisingly well, and he was happy with the result. He wrote Chrissie's address carefully on the envelope and added a stamp. Then, tucking the letter into his jacket pocket, he called to his mother.

'I'm just off to post this.'

He'd thought about putting it through her door, but he was not ready yet for another encounter with Dr Skinner. No, he would take it to the post box, and would go round to see her after she'd had time to digest his words. He felt buoyant as he walked down the road, and suddenly had the feeling that he and Chrissie were going to be fine after all. His spirits lifted as he patted the envelope in his pocket. Yes, he had been a complete fool, but this letter was going to make everything all right again.

10

1973

Tina read Billy's letter three times before she finally folded it up and laid it on the coffee table. She picked up her mug of cocoa and took a sip. It was stone cold. The emotional day had left her feeling exhausted, but the clammy grey sheets on the single bed were not exactly inviting. Billy's letter had taken her mind off Rick for a while, but now she felt sick when she considered the enormity of what she had done. She was completely on her own, but instead of feeling free, she felt isolated. Deep down she knew that leaving her abusive husband was the right thing to do, but she was scared of what lay ahead.

She lay back on the small, worn sofa and closed her eyes as she tried to put Rick out of her mind. She imagined Billy writing his letter to Chrissie thirty-four years earlier. War had been declared the day before, so there must have been an air of uncertainty, but why had he not posted it? Perhaps he had changed his mind and called round in person instead. Maybe he had been killed on his way to the postbox. Tina shuddered and chastised herself for being so dramatic.

It was almost midnight when she crawled into bed, and she tossed and turned on the unfamiliar lumpy mattress in an attempt to get comfortable. Right then, she would have given anything to be snuggled up in her own bed, even with Rick snoring beside her, for there was something comforting in his presence as they slept. She felt desperately lonely and afraid. She was not used to sleeping alone, and every little sound seemed to be magnified. She could hear footsteps out on the landing, which seemed to stop right outside her door. The fridge in the corner hummed loudly and the tap in the sink dripped rhythmically. She lay there wide-eyed and hardly daring to breathe as she forced herself to calm down. She thought about the song her mother had sung to her each night as she tucked her into bed.

Sleep my child and peace attend thee
All through the night
Guardian angels God will send thee
All through the night

The haunting lullaby had always been a comfort, convincing her that there were no monsters in the cupboard. It wasn't doing its job now, though, and she was ashamed to admit, even to herself, that if Rick had come knocking, she would have followed him right away, back to the familiarity of their own bed. *Like a lamb to the slaughter.*

The next morning, Tina's spirits had lifted a little. It was funny how everything seemed so much better in the daylight. She washed and dressed and caught the bus to work. As usual, she was the first to arrive in the office, so she put the kettle on and set out the cups.

'Morning, Tina,' called Linda, one of her closest colleagues. 'Good weekend?'

Tina regarded her friend as she hung her coat up.

'I've had better.'

Linda moved closer and searched her friend's face. 'Rick?'

Tina turned away and busied herself with the tea.

'I've left him.'

Linda placed her hands on Tina's shoulders and squeezed them. 'Well, about time. Where did you go?'

Tina told her about the events of the previous day, and how she had ended up in the shabby bedsit.

'You should have come to mine,' exclaimed Linda. 'What have I told you? There will always be a bed for you at my place.'

Tina embraced her. 'I know, and I'm grateful, but this was something I had to do by myself.'

Linda shook her head. 'You are so proud, and so stubborn. Have you heard from him?'

Tina glanced nervously at the door as though expecting Rick to barge in. She jumped as it opened, but it was only Anne arriving for work.

'Look at this,' she said, as she heaved in a sack of clothes behind her. 'Found it on the step.'

Tina and Linda crowded round to have a look. 'There's a note,' said Linda. She tore off the piece of paper and handed it to Tina. 'It's for you.'

You've taken my heart and all my money, you might as well have the clothes off my back too.

'Who's it from?' asked Anne.

Tina ran to the door and looked up and down the street. There, sauntering along, dressed only in a pair of shabby grey Y-fronts, was Rick. She could just make out the sound of him whistling as he pulled the leaves off a hedge further along the road.

She shook her head. *Jesus, this is all I need.*

A week passed, and then another, and Tina had had no further contact with Rick. In spite of herself, she was worried about him. The passage of time certainly dulled the memory. On Saturday she was in the charity shop pricing up some clothes. She looked up as the bell rang and was astonished to see her mother-in-law enter the shop. Molly Craig looked old beyond her years, despite her usual heavy make-up and neatly coiffured blonde hair.

'Molly,' greeted Tina. 'How nice to see you.' Inwardly she winced at the lie. There was no love lost between the two women.

'Save it, Tina,' snapped Molly. 'You know why I'm here.'

'Do I? Are you looking for a new outfit?'

'Don't be facetious. What's going on with you and Rick? I've just been round there and he's in a terrible state. Says you've left him and he doesn't know why.'

'He knows damn well why.'

'Well perhaps you could enlighten me then.'

Molly pulled up the stool and fished around in her oversized handbag for her cigarettes, her long red fingernails making the task more awkward than it should have been.

Tina sighed. 'Make yourself at home. Do you want a cup of tea?'

'Have you got anything stronger?'

Tina raised her eyebrows. 'Coffee?'

Molly ignored her daughter-in-law's offer.

'Look, I don't know what's happened between you, but I think you should at least go round and see him. I called there this morning and the place is a pigsty. There was a week's worth of milk on the step, post piled up behind the door, and there was a fetid smell about the place. I honestly thought he must have died. All the curtains were drawn and it took him about ten minutes to answer the door.

126

When he finally shuffled down the hall to open it, I was shocked. He looked about ninety and was wearing only his underpants. He's a broken man, Tina. Surely whatever has gone wrong between you can be put right.'

Tina finally managed to get a word in. 'Did he tell you that he hits me?'

Molly had the decency to look shocked for a moment, and then recovered herself. 'What man doesn't cuff his wife once in a while? You must have done something bad to get him so riled. He always did have a short fuse, you know that as well as anyone. You should know how to handle him by now.'

'You are unbelievable, Molly, do you know that? You are part of the problem. You've spoiled him all his life. It's you who has created this monster.'

'A monster? My little Ricky! Don't exaggerate.' Molly took a long drag on her cigarette and narrowed her eyes. 'Please, Tina. It pains me to say it, but you know he thinks the world of you.'

'Well he could have fooled me.'

Molly softened her tone. 'I know he can be a bit of a handful, but he loves you, Tina, he really does.'

Tina could feel herself beginning to weaken, and she silently chastised herself.

'I know he does, Molly, and there is a part of me that will always love him, but I can't go back, not now that I've made the break.' She knew she had to stay strong.

'Please, Tina, just go round and see him.'

Tina had known Molly Craig long enough to

127

know that this woman was not going to leave the shop until she had got what she came for.

'All right, I'll call round there on my way home this evening. I could do with picking up some more things anyway.'

Molly breathed a sigh of relief. 'Thank you.' She patted Tina's hand in a false gesture of solidarity, and Tina instinctively withdrew it. 'I'll tell him you'll stop by later.' She heaved herself off the stool and headed out of the shop, mission accomplished.

Tina was well aware she had just been manipulated, but she told herself she was only going round to collect some more things. She would make it clear to Rick that she was not coming back and there was no future for them as a couple.

Later that day, Tina stood nervously at her own garden gate while she plucked up the courage to enter. She noticed that the borders were weed-free and that the small patch of lawn had been neatly mowed. Even the stone bird bath had been filled with water and the two garden gnomes were positively gleaming. She made her way up the path and started to knock on the door with her knuckles, but then noticed that the doorbell, which had been hanging by its wire for years, was now firmly screwed back into position. Molly Craig had clearly been exaggerating her son's descent into squalor. She tentatively stuck out her finger and pressed the shiny black button. Even though she was expecting it, the loud buzzer made her jump violently.

Without leaving any time for her to compose

herself, Rick opened the door. Tina stared at him open-mouthed as she took in his appearance. He was wearing a pair of the latest flared jeans, which emphasised his narrow waist, and a checked cheesecloth shirt that Tina had not seen before. His hair had grown so that it now curled round his cheekbones. He was clean-shaven and smelled of citrus fruits.

'Hello, Rick.'

'Tina. It's lovely to see you. Please come in.'

'You too, thank you.'

They were acting like virtual strangers, not husband and wife.

The hallway carpet still bore the tram lines of the vacuum cleaner, and Tina caught the smell of a casserole cooking in the oven.

'Coq au vin,' explained Rick, 'but without the vin. That's French for wine.'

'I know,' said Tina. 'You haven't gone to all this trouble on my account, I hope.' She glanced down at the shiny kitchen floor and the gleaming Formica worktops.

'Well, when Mum said you were calling round, I decided to pull myself together. It doesn't matter if you haven't got time to stay for tea. I can heat it up again tomorrow.'

Tina put her bag on the kitchen table. 'Well, it does smell good and I am suddenly quite hungry.'

Rick breathed a sigh of relief and pulled out a chair. 'Can I get you a drink – a soft drink, I mean. I've got rid of all the booze.'

'Oh, I'll have orange cordial then, please.'

'Think I'll join you.'

Rick opened the bottle and made the drinks.

'So, how have you been?' he asked.

'Not bad, thanks. You?'

'About the same.'

An awkward silence descended as they both took a sip of their squash.

'How long is it since you've had a drink, then?' Tina said eventually. She hoped her tone sounded casual.

'Since you left, so a couple of weeks, although it seems longer.' He smiled, and Tina saw a flash of the man she had fallen in love with.

'That's great, Rick. I'm so pleased for you.'

He stood up. 'Shall I serve the casserole?'

'Yes, please. Do you want any help?'

'No, you just sit there.'

The chicken was tender and flavoursome and the dish was not compromised at all by the absence of the red wine. After they had finished eating, Rick cleared away the dishes as Tina sat waiting for him in the lounge. He returned still clutching the tea towel. 'All done. Would you like a cup of tea?'

She glanced at the clock on the mantelpiece. It was showing the right time, indicating that Rick had remembered to wind it up.

'No thanks, I'd better get going.'

Rick looked disappointed but did not protest.

'Well thanks for coming, Tina. It's been great to see you, it really has.'

'It's been great to see you too, Rick.' And she was surprised to find she meant it...

It was only when she arrived back at the bedsit that she realised she had forgotten to pick up some more clothes. Never mind, she would call

130

round again tomorrow. This time he would be off his guard, and then she would know if he really had changed.

Sunday was Tina's only day off, and today, besides collecting some more clothes from her old home, she had something special to do. She was going to go to Chrissie Skinner's house and deliver the letter that should rightfully have been hers all those years ago. Of course she was not expecting it to be that simple. The chances of Chrissie still living at 33 Wood Gardens all these years later were slim to say the least, but it was a starting point. She had borrowed Graham's battered A–Z and found the address. It was only one bus ride away, and she felt a huge sense of excitement as she boarded the bus. She was reading the letter again as the bus conductor approached her, brandishing his ticket machine.

'Where to, love?'

She recognised the voice and looked up.

'Stan, how are you?' Stan was an old colleague of Rick's.

'Bloody hell! Tina Craig. You don't normally ride my route. How are you?'

She hesitated. 'Yeah, not bad, not bad.'

'Your old man was in the depot the other day. Looking for work again.'

Tina was astonished at this news. 'Rick?'

'Yeah, didn't he tell you?'

'Well, no, we're separated now.'

'Oh, I'm sorry to hear that. He didn't mention anything to the lads.'

'Well it's only just happened. It's a bit, you

131

know, raw.'

'I understand. Give him my regards if you see him, though.'

'I will. Wood Gardens, please.'

Stan punched some buttons, cranked the handle and the machine spat out Tina's ticket.

'See you around, love. Take care now.'

Wood Gardens was situated on the opposite side of Manchester to where Tina lived, and she was not familiar with the area. The road was laid out in a square, and in the middle was a grassy area surrounded by metal railings. Tina pushed open a rusted gate and went inside. The gardens were rather overgrown and there was a park bench covered with graffiti. There didn't seem to be any old houses around, only a row of modern-looking maisonette-type dwellings that could not possibly have been around in the 1930s. She was beginning to think she had had a wasted journey when she noticed an old lady shuffling along the path, using her walking stick to clear away the brambles obstructing her way. She huffed and puffed as she sat down heavily next to Tina on the bench.

'Morning,' she said.

'Morning.'

'Not seen you round here before. Have you just moved in?' The old lady nodded towards the maisonettes.

'Oh no. I just came here looking for someone. She used to live here many years ago. Number 33.'

'Well I've lived round here all my life. I've spent many happy hours here in these gardens and I still come every day. I like to sit down and reflect you see. If I close my eyes and concentrate I can hear the sound of the kiddies playing. I like that. Got a good memory for names from way back too. Can't remember what happened yesterday, mind!' The old lady laughed at her own joke, revealing a row of stained yellow teeth. 'Now who are you looking for?'

'Chrissie Skinner, she used to live at–'

The old lady raised her hand. 'I know where she used to live.' She dabbed at her eyes with her woolly sleeve. 'I knew the family well. Chrissie's father was the local doctor and her mother was the midwife. Chrissie used to help her out. The two of them delivered my baby.'

Tina was taken aback by this news. 'Oh my goodness! Well do you know what happened to Chrissie? I have something for her.'

'Why don't we get a cup of tea? There's a greasy spoon round the corner, we can have a proper chat.'

'I'd like that.' She held out her hand to the old woman. 'Tina Craig, pleased to meet you.'

The old woman struggled to her feet and took hold of Tina's hand.

'Maud Cutler,' she said.

Seated in the café with a mug of strong tea cupped in her hands, Maud Cutler began to talk.

'I'm eighty years old now, but it seems like only yesterday. It was the day before war broke out and I'd gone into labour with our Tommy. He wasn't due for another month, so I was naturally concerned. My husband, Jamie, ran round to the surgery to get Mrs Skinner. He was in a right panic, he was. It was very early in the morning and he was worried about waking the doctor. He had a fearful temper, that man. Chrissie answered the door, and even in his panic, Jamie noticed that she looked terrible. She was such a pretty little thing normally, but that morning she looked grey and tired. Anyway, because the baby was too early, we had to go to the hospital, and Chrissie came along with her mother. Poor Jamie, he was so scared of losing me and the baby. I was forty-six then, and he was only thirty, and he was convinced we were both going to die.'

Maud paused to take a sip of her tea, and Tina did the same.

'Anyway, when Tommy was born, Mrs Skinner took him away to revive him. He was blue, you see, not breathing. Jamie went with her and the baby and Chrissie stayed with me. The nurse had to fetch her a bedpan to throw up in. I couldn't understand it, because she had seen lots of births, but then I guessed and of course I was right. She was pregnant herself. Now this would be bad news in 1939 for anyone out of wedlock, but for someone with a father like Dr Samuel Skinner, it was disastrous. She was absolutely terrified of her father. He hated her boyfriend with a passion too. Poor Chrissie, she was literally shaking with nerves and I ended up looking after her instead of the other way round. She hadn't even told the baby's father.'

'Do you know what happened to Chrissie and her baby?' asked Tina.

Maud gazed off into the distance, as though she

was actually looking at the past.

'Tragic, it was. Poor Mabel Skinner was killed in the blackout. Hit by a car travelling without headlights. She just didn't see it. Lights weren't allowed, see?'

'That's awful. And Chrissie?'

'Sent away by her father. I think he lost his mind when his wife died. Sent Chrissie to stay in Ireland with his sister-in-law. He couldn't live with the shame. For a man of his standing it was a disgrace. Nobody saw her again.'

'Did you know her boyfriend?'

'Billy? No, not really. He was a couple of years older than her, so I guess he must have gone off to war. Why do you want to know all this anyway?'

Tina showed Maud the letter. The old lady's gnarled hands shook as she read it. 'She must have told him then. Looks like he didn't take it too well. How did you come by this?'

'I found it in the pocket of a suit that had been left on the doorstep of my charity shop. It was never posted and I just thought Chrissie ought to have it.'

'I'm sorry I can't be of more help,' apologised Maud.

'Not at all. You have been more than helpful and I have taken up far too much of your time already.'

'I've enjoyed your company, Tina. It's been a pleasure to talk to you.'

Tina hardly dared ask the next question. 'And your baby? Little Tommy?'

'He owes his life to Mabel Skinner. It was her skill as a midwife and the care she gave him after he was born that enabled him to survive. Every year on the anniversary of her death we put flowers on her grave. She's buried in St Vincent's churchyard. A wonderful woman she was. I do hope you find her daughter.'

A lump unexpectedly formed in Tina's throat. 'Thank you, Maud. I hope so too.'

11

Seated at her desk the next morning, Tina made a note of what she knew about Chrissie and Billy. She knew that Billy had lived at 180 Gillbent Road, Manchester, but did not know his surname. She knew where Chrissie had lived and the names of her parents, and that her mother had been killed in the blackout. If she visited Mabel Skinner's grave, she would be able to find out her date of birth. Maud Cutler had said that Chrissie had been sent to live with Dr Skinner's sister-in-law in Ireland – that must be Mabel's sister. Tina felt an unexpected rush of excitement at the thought of playing detective. It was a welcome diversion from her other problems.

'Morning, Tina, what are you up to?'

Linda's greeting made her jump and she spun round quickly, stuffing the notes she had made in her bag as she did so. She wasn't sure why, but she wanted to keep Chrissie's letter to herself.

'Nothing. Just jotting down my shopping list. How are you? Did you have a good weekend?'

Linda slumped down at the desk opposite Tina and pushed her typewriter back so she could lay her head down.

'I'm knackered. We went to Bob and Caroline's last night and he cracked open a Party 7. Didn't get home until two.'

'On a Sunday? Well you've only got yourself to blame then. Look out, here comes Mr Jennings.'

Linda sat up reluctantly and pulled her typewriter towards her as Mr Jennings stopped at her desk.

'Morning, Linda. You look terrible.'

'Thanks, Mr J.'

He dropped a sheaf of papers on her desk.

'I need that lot typing up by ten.'

Linda glanced at her watch. 'Ten? Aw, Mr J, please, that only gives me an hour.'

'Well you'd better get started then.'

He strode off and Linda pulled a face behind his back.

Tina laughed. 'Here, give some to me, I'll help you.'

'Are you sure? I mean, you've got loads of your own stuff to do.'

'Just give it here before I change my mind, and stop moaning.'

Tina's typing was legendary in the office. Her fingers flew over the keys and the bell indicating that she had finished yet another line rang out constantly. She could even hold a conversation at the same time.

'I called round to see Rick on Saturday.' She looked at Linda but her hands never left the keyboard.

Linda stopped fiddling with her typewriter ribbon and looked up. 'Can I say something?'

'Can I stop you?'

'I hope you're not thinking of going back.'

'Of course not. Molly called round at the shop and asked if I would check up on him, that's all. Said he was in a right state, but when I got there the place was immaculate and he even had a meal ready.'

'He knew you were coming, then?'

Tina grudgingly admitted that he had. 'Yes, Molly told him, but even so, he looked fantastic, and he's stopped drinking.'

'Hmm, how long for this time, I wonder.'

'Stop it, Linda. He really is trying, you know.'

'Oh, I know. Just be careful, that's all I'm saying.'

'I planned to call yesterday but ran out of time with one thing and another. I'm going tonight though. I need to pick up some more clothes. He doesn't know I'm coming so I'll be able to see if it's a one-off.'

'Prepare to be disappointed then, Tina.'

The typewriter bell rang again and Tina returned the carriage with a defiant sweep of her wrist.

As Tina approached her former home, she reached into her handbag and pulled out her compact. She dabbed a little powder on her nose and then puffed up her hair with her fingers.

Rick answered the door and opened it a crack.

'Hello, Rick. I'm sorry to drop by unannounced, but I forgot to pick up some more clothes on Saturday. Do you mind if I come in and collect them now?'

'Tina. Of course, no problem, come in.'

He looked furtively over his shoulder as he opened the door wider.

'I've got company actually. Just a friend.'

'Oh, I'm sorry. If it's inconvenient I can come back another time.' She turned to leave before he could see her flushed cheeks...

'Don't be daft, you're here now. This is still your home, Tina.'

'Well...'

A shrill voice rang out from the living room.

'Who is it, Rick?'

'Er, it's just Tina. She's come to collect some more clothes.'

He turned to Tina. 'That's Julie.' He hesitated before continuing. 'Like I said, a friend.'

Tina waved a dismissive hand. 'You don't have to explain yourself to me.'

'I know, but I don't want you to think I've jumped into bed with the first girl to come along.'

Tina found herself appalled at the thought. She couldn't imagine Rick with another woman, and the unexpected pang of jealousy made her neck and face flush even more.

'I'll just go upstairs and get my stuff.' In her haste, she tripped on the bottom stair and dropped her handbag. The contents spilled out on to the floor.

Rick bent down. 'Here, let me help you.'

'No, I can manage, you get back to Judy.'

'Julie,' he corrected with a small smile. Was he enjoying her discomfort or had paranoia completely taken her over?

139

When Tina entered the bedroom, she noticed that the bed was neatly made and nothing appeared out of place. No underpants on the floor, no overflowing ashtrays, no mugs with cold dregs of tea in them. She moved over to the bed, gently peeled back the eiderdown and picked up what used to be her pillow. She sniffed it deeply, like a wild animal trying to locate the scent of the enemy. It smelt familiar, comforting even, and the tears began to well. She pulled a tissue out of her sleeve and dabbed at the mascara which was already threatening to run. She composed herself with a few deep breaths, grabbed some more clothes from the wardrobe, and hurried down the stairs. She could hear voices in the lounge, so she stuck her head round the door. Rick and Julie were sitting on the sofa together. He had his arm draped casually around her shoulders and she had her big blonde head resting on his chest. Tina could barely breathe.

'I'm off now, Rick,' she managed.

He jumped up, pushing Julie away as he did so. 'I'll see you out.' He followed her into the hall. 'Have you got everything you need?'

Everything I need is right here. It was only a second or two before she came to her senses. Rick was a drunken bully who had belittled her, stolen from her, raped her, beaten her. She was determined to stay strong.

He leant forward and kissed her on the cheek. 'I'll see you around then.'

She turned and left without another word, not trusting herself to speak.

It was the metallic taste in her mouth that first alerted her. Then she went right off the taste of coffee and started feeling nauseous in the mornings, and when her period didn't arrive, her worst fears were confirmed. She had always wanted a baby and this news should have thrilled her, but to think it had been conceived in an atmosphere of hatred and brutality made her want to weep. She could imagine now how Chrissie must have felt when she found out she was pregnant, and she felt an enormous empathy with her. Although Billy and Chrissie had clearly loved each other, their baby had not been planned either, and she wondered if Rick would react in the same way Billy had. The thought filled her with panic, which was odd because she knew she would rather bring up a baby single-handedly than go back to Rick. It shouldn't matter to her what his reaction would be.

The baby was due around Christmas, and when Tina was about five months gone, she knew she had to tell Rick that he was going to be a father. They had seen each other only occasionally during the past few months, but had been getting along better. More importantly, not a drop of alcohol had passed his lips. He was working on the buses again now and earning a decent wage.

Tina contemplated her surroundings. Although the bedsit had brought her a degree of peace and solitude, she was desperately lonely. She pined for Rick and the brief but happy life they had once shared, before his drinking had ruined everything. She didn't belong in this place, with its dour, mouldy decoration and musty smells, where the highlight of the week was sticking her Green Shield stamps into books. From time to time she allowed herself to imagine a life with Rick again. Could he really have changed for good? She owed it to herself and the baby to find out. She made up her mind. It was time to tell him about the pregnancy.

He was in the kitchen ironing his work shirts when she called round that evening. He was dressed in his bus driver's uniform and Tina was immediately transported back to the giddy first days of their romance. He chatted away amiably while she put the kettle on.

'I need to be at work by six. I've got an evening shift.'

'Oh, right. That's great then.' She struggled to hide her disappointment. 'Well I have some news for you.'

He spat on the underside of the iron and pressed down hard on the collar of the shirt he was ironing.

'What news?' He picked up the shirt and arranged it on a hanger.

'Rick, could you please sit down for a minute?'

'OK, sure. That was my last shirt anyway.' He pulled up a chair and sat opposite Tina at the table. 'What is it?'

Her mouth was suddenly devoid of all saliva. She fiddled with the necklace at her throat. 'Well, it's best I just come out with it, I suppose.'

'I wish you would,' said Rick, glancing at his watch.

'Maybe I'd better come back another time.'

He reached across the table and took her hand. 'I'm sorry, Tina. Go on, what is it?'

She stood up and crossed the kitchen to stare out of the window. The back garden was neatly mowed and weed-free. A little stepping-stone path weaved its way down to the compost heap at the bottom. The apple tree had just started to bear fruit, and even though the bedding plants were past their best, the garden was a tranquil haven in the otherwise run-down back street. The brick wall surrounding the lawn ensured it was a safe environment for a child to play in, and Tina thought there might even be room for a little slide. She had to get out of that bedsit.

She turned round to face Rick.

'I'm pregnant.'

There was a long, weighted silence while neither of them moved, before Rick covered his face with his hands. Tina noticed his hands were trembling as he stood up and went over to the sink to splash cold water on his face.

'I can't believe it, Tina,' he finally managed. 'I feel as though I've been kicked in the teeth. I've tried so hard over the past few months. I haven't touched a drop, I've found a decent job, kept the house going, and not once have I put pressure on you to come back. Every time I see you, it's all I can do not to go down on bended knee and ask you to come back to me, and all the time you've been seeing someone else. Why didn't you tell me? Was it because you thought I would start drinking again if I knew there was no hope of you returning?'

Tina's brow furrowed as she tried to take in what

he was saying. 'Rick, I'm five months pregnant. The baby is yours.'

Slowly Rick's features lifted, his eyes cleared and his mouth pulled into a wide, disbelieving grin.

'What? Oh my God, Tina. Are you sure?'

He scooped her up, spun her round and then put her down as he remembered her condition.

'I'm sorry. I just can't believe it.' He pointed at her stomach. 'Can I have a feel?'

She smiled and nodded. He gently placed his hand on her middle and pressed gently.

'I can't feel anything.'

'Well, it's a bit early.'

He pulled out a kitchen chair and guided her into it. 'When's it due?'

'Christmas.'

'That's brilliant. I can't believe this,' he said again. He slid into the seat opposite her at the table and took her hands in his. 'What happens now?'

She shook her head and looked down. 'It can't be like it was before,' she whispered.

'It won't be,' he implored. 'I'm a different person now.' He squeezed her hands harder. 'You are my priority now, you and that baby. I promise you everything's going to be all right. I love you, Tina.'

She withdrew her hands and cupped them round her husband's face. 'I love you too, Rick.'

It was true. In spite of everything, she had never stopped loving him.

12

When Tina woke the next morning, it took her a few moments to realise where she was. She propped herself up on her elbows and blinked in the darkness. Then it all came flooding back. She was home. Rick was still soundly asleep beside her as she heaved herself out of bed and went downstairs. She was wearing one of Rick's shirts, which was far too big for her. As she gazed out of the window, she felt a flutter deep within her belly. She didn't know if it was the baby or the butterflies of sheer excitement because she was finally back home. She did not hear Rick approach until he wrapped his arms around her from behind.

'Gosh, you made me jump.' She turned round to face him and smiled. He leant forward and kissed her tenderly on the lips.

'Sleep well?' he asked as he moved his hands to the back of her neck underneath her long hair and kissed her more deeply. She responded hesitantly, but did not pull away. They had spent the night just lying in each other's arms and Rick had been content with that, but now it seemed he wanted something more. Just as she began to relax a little and enjoy her husband's sensitive touch for the first time in years, he pulled away and picked up the kettle.

'Do you want a brew?'

'Er, yes please.' She pulled the shirt tightly

round herself, folded her arms across it to keep it closed and sat down at the table.

Rick smiled. 'Don't be like that, Tina. We've both got to get to work. Now, do you want any help moving your stuff back tonight? I've volunteered to do an extra shift so I won't be finished until six, but after that I'm all yours.'

Tina tried to reconcile this new Rick, the one who volunteered to do extra shifts, with the lazy, work-shy one she had known before. 'No, it's all right. I've only got one small suitcase. I'll manage.' The truth was, she didn't want Rick to see the hovel in which she had been living.

Tina broke the news to Linda at the office. As she had feared, her friend was unsupportive.

'You are doing what?'

Tina carried on typing; she could not bring herself to look at Linda's face. 'He's changed, Linda, he really has.'

'He'll destroy you. Once a drunk, always a drunk.'

'You're not being fair. People can change, and besides, there's something else.'

'What?' demanded Linda.

'I'm pregnant.'

Linda leant back in her chair, her hands clasped behind her head. 'Jesus. He'll destroy both of you then.'

'Linda, how can you be so cruel? I want you to be happy for me.'

Linda began shuffling some papers on her desk. 'Look out, here comes Mr J.'

Both girls fell silent as he went by, glancing at

them to make sure they were hard at work.

'Look,' said Linda when he was safely out of earshot. 'Let's go for a drink, early doors, straight from here. We can talk about it properly then.'

'You won't make me change my mind.'

'Maybe not. But I couldn't live with myself if I didn't at least try.'

The pub was crowded with early drinkers and the air was already thick with smoke. They found a relatively quiet table in the corner and Linda brought over the drinks. Tina had already nipped back to the bedsit to collect her things and felt conspicuous carrying her little suitcase.

'Lager and black,' Linda said, putting the drink down in front of her. The bag of pork scratchings she was carrying between her clenched teeth muffled her words. She opened, her mouth and the packet fell on to the table.

'Lovely,' said Tina, pushing it back towards her. 'Just what I feel like, dried pieces of oily pig skin.'

'Give 'em here then, I'll have them.' Linda opened the packet and the salty, greasy aroma filled the air.

Tina covered her nose with her hands. 'I think I'm going to be sick.'

'Tina, you're so dramatic,' chastised Linda. 'Have a drink and stop moaning.'

Tina smiled at her friend's directness as she picked up her glass. 'I think I read somewhere that drinking alcohol while pregnant can harm the baby,' she mused, taking a sip. 'Do you think that's true?'

'I think that's the least of your worries. That

baby is going to be brought up with a brute for a father, a drunken, bullying brute who has clobbered you on numerous occasions, and each time you make excuses for him.'

'He's only ever hit me when he's been drinking.'

'There you go again. That makes it all right, does it?'

'Of course not, but I told you, he's not had a drink for months. I wouldn't be going back if I didn't believe he had changed. I have a baby to consider now.' She rubbed her stomach and smiled.

'And that's another thing. What if he hurts the baby?'

'God, Linda! You don't know me at all, do you? Do you think I would even consider going back to him if I thought for one second he would do that?'

'I'm just saying. When's it due, anyway?' asked Linda.

'Christmas.'

Linda counted on her fingers. 'So you're five months gone? I thought you were looking a bit podgy round the middle lately.'

Tina smiled. 'Be happy for me, Linda. I love him.'

Linda sighed. 'I'm sorry, but I can't be happy for you. I know love makes you blind, but I didn't know it made you stupid too.'

It was gone seven by the time Tina arrived home. She had missed the bus and had had to wait twenty minutes for another. Rick was already home, and she felt a flutter of excitement as she put the key in the door.

'Sorry I'm late,' she called, dragging her little suitcase into the hall. 'I missed the bus and–'

She stopped as she saw Rick standing in the kitchen doorway, a cigarette hanging from his lips.

'I thought you had changed your mind.' His tone was accusatory and more than a little menacing.

'Of course not.' She ran to him and wrapped her arms around his neck, deftly avoiding the cigarette. He didn't respond; merely stood there rigid. She pulled away and looked at him.

'I'm really sorry. I had a quick drink with Linda after work, and then–'

He pushed her away. 'You've been in the pub?'

Tina felt the first stirrings of panic in her stomach.

'Well, she wanted to talk to me. Mr Jennings doesn't like it when we gossip at our desks so she suggested a quick drink, and then I missed the bus.' She was aware that she sounded panicky and was talking too quickly.

'I didn't think it would be too much to ask for my wife to be on time for her tea on her first night back, but Linda obviously comes first.'

'Tea?' Tina squeezed past him and went into the kitchen.

The table was set for two, with candles and napkins and a jam jar of her favourite freesias in the middle.

'Well let's eat now, shall we. I'm starving.'

'It's in the bin.'

Rick turned and went into the lounge, leaving

Tina alone and speechless. She was only an hour late; surely he could have waited a little longer. She sat at the table and contemplated the effort he had gone to. Maybe she was being selfish: It was her first night back and he had gone to so much trouble. Perhaps he was right; she should have been home earlier, made more of an effort. Maybe it was she who should have cooked the meal, not him. Her heart pounding, she joined him in the living room and sat beside him on the sofa. He ignored her and continued to read the paper.

'Rick, I'm sorry. Can you forgive me?' she said gently.

He laid the paper down on his knee and looked at her.

'I'm disappointed in you, Tina, that's all. I thought this was what you wanted, but when you can't even be bothered to show up, I wonder if it really is what you want.'

'Of course it is, Rick. I want the three of us to be a family.' Her chin began to wobble and her voice cracked.

'Well you need to show some commitment, then, start putting me first for a change.'

'I will Rick, I'm sorry.'

In a second his mood changed and he smiled as he put his arm around her shoulders. 'Good girl. How about nipping down to the chippy, then? It's the least you can do.'

Tina exhaled with relief and kissed him on the cheek.

'Of course. I won't be long. You just put your feet up.'

Later, as she lay contentedly in his arms, she congratulated herself on making the right decision. In the old days, her turning up late would have sent Rick off into a violent rage and she would have paid for it with a split lip or a black eye. This time they had talked it over, remained calm and Rick had made her see the error of her ways. Linda was wrong: people could change.

'Tina?'

'Yes?'

'Tomorrow I want you to hand your notice in at work.'

She was taken aback. 'Why?'

'Well, you're going to have a baby in four months' time. I've got a good job now and presumably you still have some of the money left that you stole from me. You know, the money from the National.'

His use of the word 'stole' unnerved her but she admitted that most of the money was still in the bank. She had not been reckless with it and had only used it for the essentials like food and rent.

'That's settled, then. You can still work in the shop on Saturdays if you like. Be nice for you to get out and about a bit.'

Tina snuggled deeper into his arms and reflected on her husband's generosity. At last he was prepared to be the main breadwinner and support her and the baby. She would stay at home and cater to their every need. Everything would be perfect.

The next day, Tina stood in front of Mr Jennings' huge mahogany desk. It was the end of the day and she was eager to get home. She held the envelope in one hand and flapped it rhythmically against the other.

'What's this, Tina?'

'It's my notice, Mr J.' She held it out.

'I'm not taking that,' he replied, his hands still clasped in front of him.

'I'm afraid you're going to have to.' She dropped the letter on the desk.

'You're my best girl, Tina, you know that. You put the others to shame. What's brought this on?'

'Well, my husband now has a great job, we have a bit of money put by, and in any event, I'm pregnant.'

'I see.' Mr Jennings picked up the envelope and carefully opened it. 'And this is what you want?'

Tina wasn't sure how to answer. It had been Rick's idea, but she could see the sense in it. How could she look after a baby and work as well? Rick was right. Her place was in the home, looking after him and the baby.

'Yes, sir, it is,' she managed finally.

Linda was aghast at the news. 'You can't leave! I knew this would happen. You've only been back five minutes and already he's controlling you. You could at least stay until the baby is born.'

'This has nothing to do with Rick. It's my idea.' Tina was annoyed that Linda had jumped to this conclusion, and even more annoyed that she was right.

She hurriedly threw on her coat. 'Look, I've got to go. I don't want to be late home.'

'God forbid,' said Linda. 'Go on, I'll see you tomorrow.'

Tina was determined to be home before Rick and have a meal waiting for him. As it turned out, she had had time to make his favourite shepherd's pie, take a bath and tidy the house. When it got to eight o'clock, she began to worry. After the fuss he'd made yesterday, she had expected him to be on time. At nine o'clock she decided to ring the depot to see if he had been delayed at work. Marie on the switchboard told her that he had left around five o'clock. By the time the clock crawled round to ten, Tina was frantic. The shepherd's pie had dried up and her nerves were shredded. She could not bear the thought that something awful had happened to him, not now they were back together again with so much to look forward to. She peered through the brown velvet curtains for the hundredth time and her heart sank once more as she saw that the street was empty. She picked up the phone again to listen for the dialling tone, making sure it was still working. She could not sit still, and paced the room biting her fingernails, a habit she had managed to kick years ago. She froze as she heard a faint scraping on the front door and then ran to open it. Rick was poised with his key, trying to find the lock.

'Rick!' she exclaimed. 'Where have you been?' She flung her arms around him, allowing the relief to envelop her.

'Steady on. I told you I was going for a drink with the lads. Don't worry, I stuck to orange juice. Mitch's getting married next week.'

'Mitch?'

'Well, Mike. We call him Mitch because he looks like the Michelin Man.'

153

'Never mind about that. I've been worried sick here. You never said you were going out.'

'Didn't I? I'm sure I did. Anyway, where's my tea? I'm starving.'

He bent to kiss her on the lips and Tina was grateful her man had returned. If only his breath hadn't stunk of ale, everything would have been perfect.

13

Tina was perched on a stool behind the counter in the charity shop when Graham entered. A gust of wind blew in some crusty brown leaves and nearly took the door off its hinges. The late September weather had a distinctly chilly feel to it, and Tina shivered.

'Morning, Graham. How are you?'

He was calling in for his regular Saturday chat before his shop opened for business. He rubbed his hands together and blew on them. 'Morning, petal. By 'eck, it's nippy out there.'

He kissed her on the cheek and regarded her growing bump. 'Look at you!'

Tina slipped off the stool and sighed. 'Only three months to go now. I can't wait.'

'And how are things at home?' he asked warily.

'Graham, please stop worrying. Everything's fine, I told you.'

'You look tired.'

'That's because I'm six months pregnant. Im-

154

agine how tired I would be if Rick hadn't said I could give up work. He really is looking after me, you know.'

'And he still hasn't had a drink?'

Tina busied herself with making the tea.

'Tina?'

'Well I think he has the odd one – you know, down the pub with the lads from the depot – but you can hardly blame him for that. He only goes once a week, on a Friday night, and I think that's fair enough. He works hard for it. It's not like before.'

'Are you trying to convince me or yourself?'

'You're as bad as Linda. I trust him and that's all that matters.'

Graham relented. 'OK, I'm sorry.' He pointed to the envelope on the counter. 'Who's that from? It looks old.'

Instinctively Tina snatched it up and held it to her chest. She had told no one except Maud Cutler about Billy's letter to Chrissie, and she wanted to keep it that way. She couldn't explain why, but it was something she wanted to do by herself. She had deliberated long and hard about whether to take it any further. Maybe Chrissie and Billy were both happily married to other people now with families of their own and this letter could cause untold upset. Perhaps one or both of them had died and it would only open old wounds.

'It's nothing. Nothing to do with you, anyway.'

Graham looked hurt. 'Sorry.'

She instantly regretted her sharp tone. Graham was only making conversation.

'No, *I'm* sorry, Graham. I shouldn't have been

sharp with you. You're a good friend, really, but I'm fine, honestly. Now let's just have our tea and talk about something other than me, shall we?'

It was a blustery Friday afternoon late in October when Tina finally stood outside the terraced house in Gillbent Road. She had Billy's letter tucked firmly into her pocket. In spite of her reservations she was compelled to find out what had happened to the young lovers. As she tapped on the door, she noticed that the blue paintwork was peeling off and the knocker was stiff through lack of use. This house clearly didn't get many visitors. She knocked again, and was about to give up when she heard a noise from inside.

'Who is it?' called an elderly voice.

'Er, my name is Tina Craig. I'm looking for someone who used to live here.' She crouched down to the letter box and pushed it open with her finger so she could make herself heard. 'His name was Billy. Do you know him?'

There was a long silence and Tina was unsure what to do next. Then she heard a bolt slide across the door and it opened slightly to reveal a man well into his eighties. His face was heavily lined, and although he had a full head of hair, it was as white as snow. His bulbous nose was tinged purple and his teeth and fingers were heavily stained with nicotine.

Tina straightened up.

'Oh, hello. As I just said, I'm looking for a chap by the name of Billy. I think he used to live here many years ago and I was wondering if you knew him.'

The old man pushed his thick glasses up his nose.

'Never heard of him.' His voice was gravelly but determined and he closed the door in Tina's face, leaving her standing there wondering what to do next. She pulled her coat tightly round her growing stomach to keep out the chill and rubbed her aching back. She suddenly felt very foolish standing there on the pavement outside the stranger's home.

She looked around and noticed an old lady inching her way along the street pushing a tartan shopping trolley. She was staring at Tina and tried to quicken her pace, but her ancient bones were not built for speed so she raised her hand and indicated for Tina to wait. By the time she drew level, she was considerably out of breath.

'Can I ... can I ... help you?' she puffed.

Tina indicated the blue front door. 'Is this your house?'

'Indeed it is. I've lived here since 1923: fifty years.'

Tina was taken aback. 'Oh, is that your husband inside?'

The old lady pushed her key into the lock and edged the door open.

'Henry, I'm home.' She turned to Tina. 'Yes, he's my husband. Now what can I do for you?'

'It's OK, your husband has already answered my question. I was looking for someone who I thought used to live here, but if you've been here for fifty years then I must have the wrong address.'

The old lady's eyes ran with the cold and she pulled out a handkerchief to wipe them. 'Who were you looking for?'

'Well, like I said, your husband has already confirmed that he doesn't know–'

'The name?' insisted the old lady.

Tina looked into the eyes of her determined inquisitor. 'Well I only know his first name... Billy.'

The old lady's papery hands gripped the handle of her shopping trolley harder. The blue veins stood out and the knuckles turned white. Slowly she released one hand and held it out to Tina. 'Alice Stirling, pleased to meet you.'

Tina sat at the kitchen table opposite Alice, a steaming cup of strong tea in her hand. Henry was in an armchair by the fireside, gazing absently out of the window.

'He never accepted Billy,' began Alice, nodding towards her husband.

'He was not my son.' Henry's voice was surprisingly strong given his frail appearance.

'Shut up, Henry!' spat Alice. She turned to Tina. We adopted Billy when he was ten months old. Both his parents had been killed and he was living in an orphanage. He was well cared for, but he needed a proper home, you know, a mother and father. We had just lost our own baby, Edward, and the grief was...' She swallowed hard, trying to steady her voice. 'The grief was almost too much to bear, but then little Billy came into our lives and–'

'Took his place,' interrupted Henry. 'She never gave Edward another thought after he arrived.'

'Wash your mouth out, you vicious old fool.' Alice looked at Tina. 'Ignore him.'

Tina was beginning to feel uncomfortable. She reached into her pocket and pulled out Billy's letter. She passed it over to Alice, who carefully extracted it from the envelope and began to read. Tina stared at her, noticing the change in her breathing, which had become shallower.

When Alice had finished reading, she folded the letter in half and addressed Tina evenly. 'Where did you get this?'

Tina explained and Alice shook her head.

'I don't understand it,' she said slowly. 'Billy sat where you are now at this very table and wrote that letter. It was my idea – he was never very good at that sort of thing – but when he was finished he was pleased with it. He was glad he was able to express himself, tell Chrissie how he really felt. Then he went out and posted it.'

Tina turned the envelope over. 'He didn't post it, though. Look.'

Alice peered at the unfranked stamp. 'It's all such a long time ago. I get muddled. I thought he said he posted it but he mustn't have done. I know he called round and spoke with Chrissie's mother, but she knew nothing of the letter. She told him that Chrissie had been shipped off to Ireland to stay with her sister and have the baby over there. Billy pleaded with Mrs Skinner to let him have her address, and she said she would contact Chrissie herself to find out if that was what she wanted.'

'So they did get in touch then? Billy and Chrissie were reunited?'

Alice bowed her head and took a deep breath. 'Sadly, no. He never heard from Chrissie again. Mrs Skinner was knocked down by a car that night. She died without regaining consciousness.'

'Did Billy ever manage to find out what happened to Chrissie and their baby?'

Alice slowly shook her head. 'My Billy was killed in action in 1940. He was twenty-two years old.'

Tina sat open-mouthed. She glanced across at Henry. He had nodded off in the chair. Alice dabbed at her eyes with a handkerchief. Tina finally found her voice.

'I'm so sorry to have opened up old wounds.'

'You haven't. The death of my Billy is a wound that has never closed. I miss him every single day. I know I'm biased, but he really was the perfect son. I may not have given birth to him, but as far as I was concerned he was as much my flesh and blood as Edward was. Dr Skinner thought he wasn't good enough for his precious daughter, but the truth is he was too good.' Alice nodded at Tina's stomach. 'Life is precious, Mrs Craig. You cherish every moment you have with that baby of yours. You will never know another love like it.'

Tears ran down Tina's cheeks. 'I will, Alice, thank you.'

Alice struggled out of the chair and rummaged through a drawer in the old bureau. 'Here, this is Billy.' She pushed a dog-eared photograph across the table. Tina stared at the handsome young man in army uniform. 'If you do ever find his child, you give them this and tell them that their father was the kindest, bravest, most handsome man that ever lived.'

Tina slipped the photograph inside the envelope with Billy's letter. 'I promise you, Alice, I'll do everything I can to make sure Chrissie gets this letter. She, deserves to know that Billy wanted to do the right thing. Why he changed his mind and didn't post the letter we shall probably never know, but he did his best to get through to her and I am going to make sure she knows that.'

By the time Tina left Gillbent Road, it was 6.30 and already dark. As she waited at the bus stop, the heavens opened and she struggled to put up her umbrella. Mercifully, she could see the bus approaching in the distance and her spirits lifted a little. As it was Friday night, Rick would be going for a drink with his colleagues so would be late home. She thought about what Graham had said, but he was wrong. She could see no harm in Rick enjoying a pint or two once a week after work. He'd earned it, the hours he worked for her and the baby.

As she sat on the bus, the diesel fumes and the bouncing motion combined to make her feel nauseous. She reflected on Alice's words and was suddenly worried that she would not be able to love her baby enough. She told herself she was being stupid. Alice had loved Billy and he wasn't even her own natural-born son. Imagine how much she was going to love this baby that she had longed for and nurtured for nine months.

It was gone seven by the time she arrived home, and the house was in darkness. She unlocked the door and fumbled around for the light switch. The hallway was especially gloomy, with its dark brown Anaglypta wallpaper, and she made a mental note to ask Rick if it would be all right to paint it a lighter colour. She felt along the wall and found

161

the light switch with her palm. Before she could press it, a warm hand covered hers and she leapt out of her skin.

'Rick! Jesus, you scared me. I didn't know you were home.'

Three things seemed to happen all at once then. First she detected the distinct aroma of whisky; then she felt her head spin as Rick's fist connected with her cheek. And then slowly her mouth filled with blood and she swallowed and swallowed as she tried to make sense of it all before the blackness claimed her.

14

1939

Billy blinked and tried to open his eyes as wide as he could as he walked down the dark street. He was amazed at how seriously everyone was taking this blackout. Not a chink of light could be seen from any of the windows, the lamps were unlit and a car made its way cautiously down the street without the benefit of headlights. The inky blackness threatened to smother him. He was sure this practice was more dangerous than the threat of actual bombs falling, but he didn't make the rules. He became a little disorientated as he rounded the corner of the next street and struggled to recall where the nearest postbox was. It seemed the whole world had changed overnight. As he stood trying to get his bearings, he was aware of some-one standing close by. He stopped and listened carefully as he heard a match strike behind him. He spun round as the match flared into life and lit up the unmistakable features of Dr Skinner. Billy was immediately on the defensive.

'Are you following me?'

'I was coming to see you, yes.'

Skinner took a long drag on his cigarette and flicked ash on to the pavement. 'Where are you off to, then? Not to see my daughter, I hope. I told you she wants nothing more to do with you.'

'She told you that, did she?'

'Indeed. It seems she has finally come to her senses.'

'Can I ask you something, *Samuel?*' Billy knew that the use of his first name would rile the doc-tor no end. Dr Skinner, however, merely nodded. 'Why do you hate me so much? What have I ever done to you?'

'I'm sure you will make someone an adequate husband one day.' Skinner gestured with his hand along the gloomy street. 'This place is filled with little scrubbers for whom you would be quite a catch. But my daughter is special. She deserves someone better than an orphaned, illiterate baker's boy.'

Billy suppressed a little laugh. He knew he was holding an ace and he was just biding his time before he played it.

'At least I actually care about her happiness, about what she wants.'

'She doesn't know what she wants. I do, I'm her father.'

163

Billy noticed that the only source of light, the cigarette, was fading. He rummaged through his own pockets for his matches. He wanted to see every sinew, every muscle and every nerve in Dr Skinner's face when he spoke his next words. He struck the match and the doctor's features came into sharp focus again.

Billy could not suppress a smile as he stared Skinner in the eye. 'Would you prefer to be called Grandad or Grandpa?'

For a split second, before the match burnt itself to the end and Billy had to drop it, he watched Dr Skinner's face. His eyes narrowed, his lips pursed themselves into a thin line and the vein at his temple throbbed. 'You're a liar,' he hissed.

'Am I?' asked Billy. 'Are you sure about that?'

Darkness fell between them again, but Billy did not need his sight to know the depth of Dr Skinner's fury. He could feel it; could hear his breath coming in short gasps. Billy had known he would not take this news well but his rage was tangible.

He softened his tone. 'I love Chrissie, Dr Skinner. I know I'm not the husband you would have chosen for your daughter but she's having my baby and I'm going to honour that. I will not shirk my responsibilities. Chrissie and the baby will always be able to depend on me. I'll work hard and...'

Billy stopped abruptly as Dr Skinner cried out.

'Help me,' he gasped. He clutched his chest as he sank to his knees. Billy stood over him with his hands on his hips. Dr Skinner pointed to the pocket of his jacket. 'My pills.'

Billy fumbled around in Dr Skinner's pocket.

Although he was sure this was a ruse he reached inside and pulled out a little brown bottle. He struggled with the cap but eventually it gave way and he tipped the contents into his palm. 'I can't see too well. How many?'

'Here.' Dr Skinner groped around in his other pocket, pulled out a small torch and the yellow beam shone on the little pile of tablets.

'Torches aren't allowed, Dr Skinner.'

He glared at Billy. 'It's an emergency.' He picked up two of the tablets with his trembling thumb and forefinger and popped them under his tongue. Then he eased himself into a sitting position and leant against a lamppost.

'Thank you,' he said, and closed his eyes.

Billy didn't know what to do next. The doctor's breathing seemed shallow and laboured. The street was deserted, and there was no way he could carry a large man like Dr Skinner by himself.

'I'm sorry, Dr Skinner. Are the pills working?'

Skinner opened his eyes. 'Is it true? You have got my Chrissie pregnant?'

Billy lowered his gaze. 'Yes, sir, it is, but as I said, I want to do the right thing.' He fished in his pocket for the letter and held it up. 'I've written her this letter. I'm afraid I reacted rather badly yesterday when she told me the news, and I may have said some things I didn't mean. I called round to try and put things right but you wouldn't let me see her so I've written it all down. I was just on my way to post it.'

Dr Skinner's breathing had settled down. 'Help me up, lad, will you?'

Billy grabbed him under the arms from behind

and Skinner struggled to his feet. He dusted him-self down and drew himself up to his full height. 'There's no point in putting it in the post, is there?'

Billy frowned. 'Why not?'

'Think about it. War was declared yesterday; Everything's changed now. The postal system is sure to collapse and that letter will never see the light of day again.'

Billy doubted this was true but nobody could be sure of anything anymore. It seemed everything *had* changed overnight.

Dr Skinner continued. 'Give it to me, I'll pass it on to her.' He held out his hand.

'I'm not sure... I mean, how do I know you'll even give it to her? I'm sorry, and I don't wish to sound disrespectful, but I just don't trust you.'

'I don't blame you, but it's your best bet.'

Billy reluctantly handed over the letter. 'I'll be calling round tomorrow to make sure she has received it.'

'I don't doubt it.'

Dr Skinner took the letter and slipped it into his breast pocket.

Chrissie and her mother were seated at the kitchen table, talking in hushed tones, when Dr Skinner arrived home. They had been discussing the best way to break the news to him about the baby. They heard the front door slam and Mabel reached across the table and squeezed Chrissie's hand. Chrissie responded with an anxious smile. The sound of the doctor's footsteps as he thundered straight up the stairs without so much as a good evening puzzled and worried them both. Mabel

166

rushed along the hallway and gripped the banister as she called up to her husband. Chrissie stood in the kitchen doorway, biting the skin around her thumb.

'Samuel? Is that you? What's wrong?'

She could hear him banging around as she climbed the stairs. He was in Chrissie's room, and she entered with more than a little trepidation.

'Samuel?'

He had his back to her as he rummaged through Chrissie's wardrobe, flinging out clothes, on to the bed behind him. Then he reached up and pulled down the battered brown suitcase off the top of the wardrobe. The handle snapped off and the suitcase tumbled to the floor.

'Damn! Mabel, fetch me another case will you, and then arrange to send a telegram to your sister.'

'Kathleen? Why?'

Dr Skinner stopped and turned to face his wife. His face was crimson, his brow beaded with sweat and the corners of his mouth foamed with spittle.

'Because that daughter of yours is a little whore and there is no way she is remaining in this house to give birth to a bastard child. She'll have to go to Ireland and stay with Kathleen.'

Mabel slumped down on the bed. 'Samuel, please calm down. I know this is a shock for all of us, but–'

'You knew then? Don't even attempt to defend her. There is no excuse for this. You had no right keeping it from me. What about when the bastard is born? Were you going to keep it in a box at the bottom of the garden like some secret pet?'

Mabel had never seen her husband so livid.

His final words were spat out with venom. 'She leaves first thing in the morning.'

The next day, Chrissie stood alone in her bedroom and contemplated it for the last time. The wallpaper with its garish red roses, the lurid green paintwork, the dressing table with her hand mirror and hairbrush neatly arranged upon it, all so familiar and comforting. How had her life gone so suddenly and dramatically wrong? She had repacked her suitcase, which her father had so haphazardly filled the night before, and was struck by how insignificant it felt when she picked it up. Not much to show for her nineteen years on this planet. She stared at her pathetic reflection in the mirror. She was dressed in her best winter coat, despite the mild weather, her hair neatly curled and arranged under her hat. Her complexion was colourless and pallid and her baby-blue eyes were dimmed and filled with utter despair.

She sat down at the dressing table and tentatively picked up her newly acquired rouge. With trembling fingers she smeared a little over her cheeks, pinching them as she did so. The resulting glow made her feel slightly better, so she reached for her lipstick. *Sod it,* she thought. If *he thinks I'm a whore, I might as well look like one too.* She applied two coats of the pale colour and then applied dark kohl to her eyebrows and underneath her eyes. She shoved the make-up into her handbag as her mother's voice floated up the stairs.

'Chrissie, it's time to go.'

She took a deep breath, picked up her little

suitcase, took one last look around the room and headed down the stairs. Her mother and father were waiting at the bottom.

Mabel issued her instructions again. 'Write to me as soon as you get to Aunt Kathleen's, won't you. I'll be thinking of you, Chrissie. I'll visit whenever I can and I'll be there when the baby is born.'

Dr Skinner scoffed and Mabel cast him a vicious glance. 'I'm sorry it has to be like this, but you understand, don't you? Your father has a standing in this community and the shame of having a daughter who–'

'Mother, can we please not go through this again. I'm a terrible person who has done a wicked deed and for that I am paying the price.' She looked down at the floor. 'I honestly thought Billy loved me,' she whispered, 'but it just shows how wrong you can be.'

Just then Leo bounded in from the garden and circled round Chrissie's legs. She bent down and ruffled his ears. He shook himself vigorously.

'Goodbye, lad. I'll miss you. You be a good boy.' She buried her face in his fur and inhaled his delicious smell for the last time. Then she stood up and addressed her mother. 'Promise me you'll look after him.'

Mabel wiped a tear from her eye. 'Of course, Chrissie, I promise.'

She embraced her daughter and held her tightly. Chrissie suppressed a sob. She did not want to give her father the satisfaction of seeing her cry. Suddenly she was desperate to be on her way. The dark, narrow hallway felt claustrophobic, and

169

there didn't seem to be enough air for them all to breathe. She hugged her mother one last time and then stepped back to address her father. As she looked into his cold, dead eyes, she realised that words were futile, and with the slightest nod of her head she left the only home she had ever known and stepped outside to begin a new chapter of her life.

15

Later that evening, as the rain lashed the windows, Mabel was in the surgery updating patients' records. It was a task Chrissie would normally have done with much more efficiency than she could ever hope to match, and she realised she was going to miss her daughter in more ways than she could imagine. The doorbell rang, making her leap, and Leo scurried down the hall barking madly. Mabel dragged herself away from her paperwork and went to answer it. She was in no mood for visitors, and her glum expression, grey pallor and red-rimmed eyes would leave the caller in no doubt of this. She took hold of Leo's collar and pulled him back as she opened the door. Due to the inclement weather, the caller had pulled his cap down over his eyes and turned the collar of his jacket up round his ears, so that Mabel didn't recognise him at first.

'Mrs Skinner. Good evening. I'm sorry to disturb you, but I was wondering if I could have a word with Chrissie.'

Leo recognised Billy's voice and yelped excitedly as Mabel released her grip on his collar. Billy bent down and fussed over the dog.

'Er ... Mrs Skinner? Is she in?'

Without a word, Mabel opened the door wider and gestured for Billy to enter.

'Thank you,' he said, removing his cap and running his fingers through his hair.

'Follow me,' said Mabel evenly as she headed for the kitchen.

Once in the bright light, Billy registered Mabel's troubled appearance. 'Mrs Skinner, are you all right?' He looked around the kitchen. 'Where is everybody?'

'My husband is out on an emergency house call and Chrissie is on her way to Ireland.'

'Ireland! Whatever for?'

Mabel covered her face with her hands and began to weep.

'Mrs Skinner, please tell me what's happened. Did she read my letter?'

She wiped her eyes and looked up at Billy, her face creased into a frown. 'What letter?'

Billy spoke more urgently now, the words tumbling out. 'Last night, I gave a letter to Dr Skinner to give to Chrissie. I was on my way to post it, but I bumped into him and he persuaded me to give it to him. Said the postal system wouldn't work now that war had been declared. Tell me, did he give it to her?'

'I know nothing about a letter, Billy. All I know is that you broke my daughter's heart and now my family has been ripped apart.' Mabel banged her fists on the table. 'You couldn't keep your hands off her, could you? And then you cast her aside like yesterday's newspaper. It's a good job my husband isn't home, because I wouldn't rate your chances of getting out of here in one piece.'

Billy tried to placate her. 'Please, Mrs Skinner, listen to me.'

Mabel was sobbing openly now as she sat down and put her head in her folded arms on the table. Billy took deep breaths and paced the room.

'Look, I admit I didn't take the news of the baby very well. It was such a shock, you see. I mean, Chrissie and I had only, er, been intimate once, and that was–'

Mabel looked up, her blotchy face streaked with tears. 'Please, spare me the details.'

Billy continued in earnest. 'What I mean is, our relationship was always more about the way we felt. It was such a shock when she told me about the baby that I had to be alone to take it all in. To my eternal shame, I just left her and ran off when she told me. All I could think of was how we were going to bring a baby into a world where war had just been declared and I would have to go off and fight and leave her to bring the baby up on her own. I panicked, but it wasn't because I don't love her; it was because I do.'

'Why didn't you say all this to her, Billy?'

Billy's face was flushed with anxiety. 'I tried. I came round that night but Dr Skinner told me she didn't want to see me.'

Mabel shook her head. 'Samuel told us that you had got fed up of waiting and didn't think she was worth the bother anyway. I must admit, I thought that was particularly callous.'

Billy gritted his teeth. 'All lies. I can't believe he hates me that much.'

'He hated you before you got his daughter into trouble, so imagine how he feels now.'

'He didn't give her the letter, did he?' Billy snorted with derision. 'I knew I was right not to trust him. How could I have been so stupid?'

'You have been stupid, Billy, nobody could argue with that. What was in the letter anyway?' asked Mabel.

'An apology, a declaration and a proposal.'

Mabel's tone was serious. 'You want to marry her?'

'I've never been more sure of anything in my life. I love her, Mrs Skinner, really love her. I need to see her to put all this right.'

'It's too late, Billy. She's gone to Ireland to stay with my sister. She will have the baby over there, away from the prying eyes and the gossips here.'

'But she should be here with her family. Please, Mrs Skinner, this is my baby too. Aren't I entitled to have a say in where it's born?' He was practically pleading now. 'Please let me have her address so I can tell her how I feel before it's too late.'

'I told you, Billy, it's already too late.'

'No it's not. I mean, it needn't be.'

Mabel looked into Billy's dark eyes, and even with the pain reflected in them, she could see why Chrissie had fallen for him. He really was one of the most handsome men she had ever seen, and in other circumstances she would have been proud to have him as her son-in-law. She relented a little.

'Look, it's getting late and my husband could

return at any moment. If he finds you here... Well, do you really need me to tell you what will happen? I will write to Chrissie myself tomorrow, and if she wants to, she can contact you.'

Billy hung his head. 'I'd appreciate that, Mrs Skinner.'

'You will have to be patient, though. My sister lives out in the sticks, with no telephone, so the line of communication will be slow.'

Billy breathed a sigh of relief. 'I understand. Thank you, Mrs Skinner. I promise I won't let Chrissie down again.'

'You had better not. Good night, Billy.'

He retrieved his cap and bade her farewell. 'Good night, Mrs Skinner.'

When Dr Skinner returned home later that evening, he entered the kitchen shaking drops of rainwater from his overcoat.

Mabel looked up from her sewing. 'She'll be at the guest house in Dublin by now, I expect. Poor girl, having to make that journey on her own in her condition. It'll be another long day for her tomorrow, too. Heaven knows what time she'll eventually arrive at Kathleen's.'

Dr Skinner ignored his wife's remarks and reached for the newspaper.

Mabel placed her sewing on the table in front of her. 'Why didn't you tell me you saw Billy last night?'

'Must have slipped my mind.' He spoke without turning round, so Mabel was unable to read his expression. 'How do you know anyway?'

'He's been here asking for Chrissie. Says he gave

you a letter to give to her. Where is it, Samuel?'

Dr Skinner turned round now to give his wife the full brunt of his fury.

'He just doesn't know when to give up, does he? I've told him there is no way he will be part of Chrissie's life. She's a beautiful, intelligent girl; she could have any man she wanted.'

'She wants Billy.'

'She may think she does now, but that's only because of this blasted baby. Once that's been adopted, she'll come to her senses.'

'Adopted? What on earth are you talking about? She's going to keep the baby.'

'As long as I have breath in my body, I will see to it that those two have nothing more to do with each other and that that bastard child goes to a home that deserves it.'

'Chrissie will never agree to it. You can't force her to give up her baby.'

'We'll see.'

Mabel stood up sending the kitchen chair flying backwards. 'Over my dead body.'

The telephone in the hall rang out suddenly, the shrill tone making them both jump.

Mabel snatched up the receiver. 'Good evening. The Surgery. Oh, hello, Mr Henderson.'

After a short conversation, Mabel returned to the kitchen. 'That was Mr Henderson. His wife's gone into labour. Her waters have already broken, so I'm going round there now. When I get back, we are going to sort out this mess. I want to see that letter Billy gave you.' She pulled on her navy cape and looked around for her bag.

'You should take a torch with you, Mabel, it's so

175

dark out there. Would you like me to come with you? I don't like the idea of you going out alone.'

'I've done it hundreds of times before, Samuel. It's never worried you before. In any case, torches aren't permitted in the blackout.'

Samuel rummaged through the kitchen drawer and found an old brown envelope, which he tied over the torch. 'Here, take this; at least it's something.'

Mabel grabbed it. 'You are a stubborn old mule, Samuel Skinner, and I hate you sometimes.'

It was a foul night, and Mabel pulled the hood of her cape over her head and held it tightly at her throat. She battled against the wind and horizontal rain as she tried to avoid the swollen puddles. The torch was next to useless and she found it difficult navigating her way along the pavement. She tripped over a cracked paving slab, slipped off the kerb and fell headlong into the road, the contents of her medical bag clattering to the ground. She didn't see or hear the car that hit her. She only smelt the burning rubber as it tried to stop, and then felt the crushing blow that snapped her spine like a matchstick.

16

Kathleen McBride held the telegram to her chest and shook her head in disbelief.

'Holy Mary, Mother of God,' she whispered as she crossed herself.

From what she could gather, her pregnant niece was on her way and there was nothing she could do about it. In a fit of pique, she threw the telegram on the fire and pondered the news. It was so typical of her brother-in-law to shirk his responsibility like this. He was the most loathsome man Kathleen had ever met, and she had never forgiven him for taking her sister away to England. Mabel had been completely smitten with him and his Protestant ways, and now it seemed they had reared their daughter to be a promiscuous little madam.

Since the death of their parents, it had been left to Kathleen to keep the family farm going. Two of her siblings had died in infancy and both her selfish brothers had emigrated to America in search of a better life. She was the eldest of the six children, the only one who cared about the farm and the sacrifices Mammy and Daddy had made. Their parents had struggled all their lives to keep the farm viable and to provide a loving home for them all, and Kathleen was determined that it should remain in the family and that her parents' values should be upheld.

She lived a frugal life. The farm had no electricity or running water, and life was a struggle in this rugged, unforgiving landscape at the foot of the Galtee Mountains in the south of Ireland. The farmhouse was decrepit and the damp rose relentlessly from the boggy earth; seeping through the thick, crumbling walls and taking up residence in the bones. The fire in the kitchen was used for both heat and cooking and was never allowed to go out. At night, Kathleen covered the embers with the grey ash, and in the morning when this was raked off, the fire would still be glowing underneath and would come to life again. Water was drawn from the well each morning before breakfast and a pot set over the fire to heat it, a tedious, back-breaking process. The turf for the fire had to be cut from the bog and dried out before it was fit to burn.

Now Kathleen tugged at a fresh chunk of peat and threw it on the fire. Immediately the room was filled with smoke and she coughed violently. She stood up and eased herself slowly into an upright position, rubbing her back as she did so. She was only forty-five, but the years of hard work in the pitiless climate had taken their toll.

She had no idea what time her niece would be arriving, or how for that matter, but it was no concern of hers. There was no way that she could stay at the farm in her condition. The thought of it caused Kathleen's face to redden even though she was alone. It was only a tiny community, and the news of a pregnancy out of wedlock would spread like wildfire. She could picture the congregation nudging each other as she settled herself into her pew, her head hung low with the mortification of it all. In the name of God, what was her sister thinking sending her wayward daughter over like this?

She opened the door and called into the yard.

'Jackie, would you come here a minute.'

Jackie Creevy; nineteen years old and yet to be diminished by years of endless labour, looked up from the old carthorse he was attending to and jumped to his feet.

'Yes, Miss McBride, what can I do for yer?'

Kathleen smiled with something approaching fondness, but the worry was clearly etched on her face.

'Er, my niece will be arriving sometime today. I'm not sure when exactly, but would you mind keeping an eye out for her? As soon as she arrives, I want you to fetch me. Don't talk to her or ask her any questions. I expect she'll arrive on the donkey cart from town.'

'Of course, Miss McBride. Sure that will be nice for yer.'

Jackie doffed his cap and returned to where Sammy was still waiting patiently. He considered his employer's news as he tended to the horse's legs, gently rubbing away the mud with a soft brush. In the four years he had been at the farm, Miss McBride had never spoken of her family, and now all of a sudden a niece was coming to stay. She didn't have many visitors, so this should be an exciting event, but the look on her face had told him that this particular visitor was not welcome.

He finished the horse's legs with a rub-down of castor oil to keep out the damp, and led him into the barn for his hay. Then he whistled for the farm dogs that were asleep at the back of the barn, nestled amongst the straw. They immediately sprang into action and yelped excitedly around his legs. He called for the two other farm workers, Michael and Declan, who were also snatching a crafty forty winks, and they all set off up the lane to bring in the cattle for the evening milking. It

179

was only a small herd, but the milking would still take the four of them a good couple of hours to complete. As Jackie ambled along, he wondered if this niece would be staying long, and whether she would be pulling her weight around the farm. They could use all the help they could get.

Kathleen was hauling a dead sheep out of a ditch as the cattle came into the yard. She wiped her hands down her apron and went across to the milking shed. Michael led the cows in one by one and Kathleen tied a piece of twine around the more difficult animals' back legs. More than once she had had a farm labourer injured and out of action for days after a swift, vicious kick from a disgruntled cow.

The cowshed fell silent, save for the squirts of milk as they hit the metal pails, and Jackie turned to Kathleen, who was pulling on the cow's udders more savagely than usual.

'What's your niece's name, Miss McBride?' he ventured.

Kathleen squeezed harder, causing the cow to stamp her back legs in protest.

'Now, Jackie, you don't need to concern yourself with little details like that. She won't be here long.'

'That's a pity. She'll be company for you and she could help you with your chores.'

'She's a city girl, Jackie. I doubt she even knows where milk comes from. It just appears on her doorstep like magic, I imagine.'

'Ah well. You could educate her, Miss McBride, so you could.'

Kathleen straightened up and moved her stool to the next cow.

'You're quick tonight, Miss McBride,' said Jackie with admiration. Nobody could accuse her of not pulling her weight.

'There's a dead sheep outside, Jackie. Could you put it on one side for Pat.'

'That I will, Miss McBride.'

Pat was a local trader who visited all the farms in the valley and took away any eggs, cream, butter or vegetables they might have to sell. He took the produce into town and hawked it round the shops. The shopkeepers would pay the farmers directly, and Pat took a small commission. Kathleen also let him take away any sheep that had died of natural causes. You couldn't eat a sheep if you didn't know what it had died of, but Pat would be able to get a small amount for the wool. He would then boil up the carcass, skim off the resulting fat and sell it back to the farms as wagon wheel grease. He had even managed to sell some to the chemist in Tipperary Town, who made this foul, greasy substance into soap and face cream.

Dusk was falling as Jackie settled himself down in the barn. He slept on a bed of straw, cuddled up to the dogs, with a paraffin lamp his only source of light. Miss McBride provided him with thick blankets and always brought him a mug of hot cocoa before she turned in for the night. He had been happy here since being orphaned at fourteen, when she had taken him in. He didn't earn much, but he had food and shelter, and sometimes Michael and Declan took him down to the local pub for a game of dominoes or cards. It was a simple life that thrived on routine, with each day not varying greatly from the next. So when he heard the sound of the donkey's hooves as it trotted into the yard, Jackie's heart quickened.

He stood in the doorway of the barn and regarded the little cart. The driver alighted and offered his hand to Miss McBride's niece. She took it hesitantly and jumped down, taking in her surroundings as she did so. Jackie was captivated by the little scene and stood motionless before remembering his manners. He jogged over to greet the new arrival and removed his cap.

'Good evening. You must be Miss McBride's niece. Welcome to Briar Farm.'

'That's right. My name's Chrissie. How do you do?'

She looked absolutely exhausted. Her skin was pale and insipid, her lips were dry and cracked and her blonde hair was limp and had no style. In spite of all this, Jackie thought she was the most beautiful creature he had ever seen. She had an endearing sweetness about her, but she looked vulnerable and he instantly wanted to protect her. He took her little suitcase and guided her towards the farmhouse.

'My name's Jack Creevy, but everybody calls me Jackie.'

Chrissie smiled. 'It's nice to meet you, Jackie.'

'Follow me, I'll take you to your aunt.'

17

The farmhouse was tiny, with a low thatched roof and two little windows either side of the front door. It was absolutely ancient and looked as though it might fall down at any minute, but the glow from the fire within made it a welcoming sight and Chrissie was relieved to be here at last.

Jackie led her up to the house and knocked tentatively. He smiled at Chrissie and they both waited. Eventually the door opened and Chrissie caught her very first glimpse of her aunt. Kathleen's hair was completely grey, her face was weather-beaten and lined and she stooped like a woman twice her age. She was regarding Chrissie warily.

She turned to Jackie.

'Water, please, Jackie.'

'Of course, Miss McBride.'

It was then that Chrissie noticed the receptacle on the wall next to the front door. It was made of stone and the little basin was filled with water.

Jackie dipped his fingers in and sprinkled some over Chrissie. She shook her head as a few droplets ran into her eyes.

'Holy water,' whispered Jackie.

Kathleen held out her hand and Chrissie took it, embarrassed that her damp palms gave away her nervousness. Her aunt's hand was incredibly rough and calloused; it felt to Chrissie like she was wearing worn leather gloves.

'You must be Chrissie. Come in, won't you. That will be all, Jackie, thank you.'

'Sure. Good night, Miss McBride. Good night, Chrissie.'

Kathleen glared at him, but Chrissie turned and gave him a small wave as he retreated.

'Now then, Chrissie. Let's get you out of that coat, shall we?'

Chrissie pulled off the heavy coat and handed it to Kathleen, who slung it over her arm. She took a step back and looked her niece up and down.

'You can't tell, then?'

Chrissie smoothed down her dress and patted her stomach.

'I'm only two months gone. The baby's not due until April.'

Kathleen looked relieved.

'And you are fit and well?'

'Yes thank you.'

'And the baby's father?'

Chrissie was not in the mood for this barrage of questions from a complete stranger, no matter that they were related to each other. She merely shook her head.

'What were you thinking of, girl? Didn't your parents instil you with any morals at all? Have you no idea of the shame you have brought on this family?'

Chrissie exhaled deeply. 'I'm beginning to, yes.' Her chin started to wobble and Kathleen relented.

'We'll talk about this later. You look absolutely shattered. Come on, have a seat by the fire and I'll make a pot of tea.'

Chrissie sat down gratefully and took off her shoes.

'I wouldn't mind a bath if it's not too much trouble. I've been travelling for the best part of two days.'

'A bath? Jesus, Mary and Joseph! Where do you think you are, girl?'

Chrissie looked around the sparse room with its meagre furnishings and realised her mistake.

'Water is drawn from the well outside and heated up in this.' Kathleen indicated the large blackened pot that hung over the fire. 'It's quite adequate; you'll get used to it. The toilet is outside, behind the barn.'

Chrissie fought back her tears. 'And where will I sleep?'

'Over there. There's only one bedroom.'

She turned to see a small cot that had been made up in the corner.

'Now,' said Kathleen, adopting an official tone. 'It looks like we've been lumbered with each other for the time being. I'm not sure who's come off worse, but whilst you are here, we might as well try to get along. I take it you've no objection to hard work?'

Chrissie shook her head. 'Of course not. I help … that is, I *used* to help out in Father's surgery.'

Kathleen scoffed. 'I'm talking about proper work, girl. You ever milked a cow? Hauled a bale of straw? Cleaned out a stable or harvested crops in all weathers?'

Chrissie shook her head.

'Thought not. Well you haven't come here for a holiday. I'll expect you to earn your keep.'

185

She passed over a jam jar filled with tea.

'I got the best china out in your honour.' She winked as she sipped her own tea, and Chrissie managed a weak smile.

When it was time for bed, Chrissie was permitted to accompany Kathleen upstairs to her bedroom. In the corner was a table on which a pristine white cloth had been laid. There was a candle at either end, and in the middle were three statues of Our Lady, St Joseph and the Infant Jesus of Prague. Dried flowers were arranged neatly along the front.

'This is my altar,' said Kathleen proudly. 'You can pray here with me before you go to bed.'

'Thank you.'

'The family that prays together stays together.'

Kathleen knelt down and Chrissie followed suit. The hard wooden floor was unforgiving on the knees and she struggled to get comfortable. Kathleen clasped her hands and closed her eyes.

'Dear Father, we thank you for bringing Chrissie safely to our home. We pray for guidance regarding the unfortunate position she finds herself in. We pray that her soul is cleansed of its stain before she departs this world for the next. We give thanks for the harvest we have so far gathered from the fields and pray that our crops will continue to grow in abundance. We thank you for watching over our animals as they graze in your verdant pastures. We pray that you continue to watch over Jackie and the others and keep them free from disease and mishaps through the winter months. Father, we pray that you forgive us our sins. Amen.'

'Amen,' repeated Chrissie. She tried to struggle to her feet but Kathleen grabbed her arm and forced her back down.

'Mary, Mother of God...' said Kathleen.

Chrissie cast a furtive glance towards her aunt, unsure what she was supposed to do.

'Pray for us,' whispered Kathleen.

'Oh. I see. Pray for us,' repeated Chrissie.

'St Joseph...' Kathleen nudged her niece hard in the ribs.

'Pray for us,' said Chrissie.

'Amen,' said Kathleen, finally straightening up.

'Amen,' echoed Chrissie as she too got to her feet.

'Hmm. I gather you are not a regular worshipper.' Kathleen's tone was disapproving.

'No, not really. Father is a medical man, you see. He believes in the power of medicine over prayer so I've never really been to church. We would go to the midnight service on Christmas Eve, and of course to weddings, funerals and christenings, but other than that, no, I can't say I've regularly attended church.'

'Maybe if you had, we wouldn't be here now having this conversation.' Kathleen pursed her lips into a thin line and shook her head. 'You may retire to your bed now. We rise at five thirty for prayers. You can join me up here at the altar. Then there is just time to fetch the water in before the church bells ring for the Angelus at six. After that it's morning milking and then breakfast. You will help with the chores, but on no account must you discuss your situation with Jackie or the others. Do you understand?'

Chrissie nodded miserably. 'Yes, Aunt Kathleen.'

'You may take some of the hot water from the pot for washing, and there is a chamber pot at the end of your bed. That is only for night-time use, though; you must use the toilet outside during the day. Do you have any questions?'

'No.'

'Good, then I'll see you in the morning. Good night.'

Chrissie crept downstairs and pulled up a chair next to the fire. It was impossible to get warm in this place and her breath hung in the air, as she exhaled. Her aunt had settled the fire for the night, so the heat it gave off was minimal. The water in the pot was still warm enough for a wash, though, so she ladled some into a bowl, took up a flannel that her aunt had left on the bed and slowly began to clean off the grime left by two days of travelling. She shivered uncontrollably as she removed her clothes and washed her body. She would have given anything for a long soak in a bubble-filled bath right now.

She rummaged around in her little suitcase and found her nightdress. As she pulled it over her head, she caught the overwhelmingly familiar scent of home. Wood Gardens had a very distinctive smell, with its clinical aroma of medicine, the fragrance of the oily beeswax used to polish the cabinets in the surgery, and the welcoming scent of her mother's cooking. Chrissie suddenly felt very weepy. She longed for her own bed, the comfort of her mother's arms and the unquestioning devotion of Leo. She climbed in between the sheets and pulled the covers up to her chin. Even with the weight of three blankets pinning her down, she could not coax any warmth into her bones and all the shivering was making her back ache.

She wondered what Billy was doing now. Did he feel any remorse at the callous way he had abandoned her? She really had loved him and was sure she could have made him happy had she been given the chance. Her mother should have been stronger too, and not allowed her father to ship her out of the way like this. She was still a part of the family and was determined to return to it one day, her *and* the baby.

Samuel Skinner gripped his wife's hand in desperation, every fibre of his being willing her to live. The last twenty-four hours had changed the doctor's life irrevocably. He had already said goodbye to his only daughter as she made her way in shame to a new life in Ireland. He had only just got her out in time too, before that Billy had come grovelling for her forgiveness. It seemed he had managed to convince Mabel that he wanted to marry Chrissie. Dr Skinner laughed to himself at the absurdity of it. No, the baby would be adopted and out of their lives for ever. He let go of his wife's hand then, stood up and ran his fingers through his hair. He had just recalled Mabel's reaction when he told her his plans for the baby. *Over my dead body*, she had said defiantly.

He bent down close to her face and smoothed his thumbs over her cheeks.

'Mabel. Mabel, please wake up. I'm sorry,

Mabel.' He gently shook her shoulders, even though he knew this would make no difference. He laid his head on her chest so he could be comforted by her rhythmic breathing, but her ribcage was perfectly still. He gripped her hand in his; already he could feel her blood turning to ice. 'Mabel, no! Please don't leave me.' He let out a primal scream that brought a nurse running in.

'Dr Skinner, what is it?'

The doctor fell to his knees at the side of the bed. 'She's gone.' His voice cracked. 'She's gone.'

It was two o'clock in the morning before Dr Skinner arrived home. He should have been exhausted, but as it was, he felt as though he would never sleep again. He poured himself a large whisky and slumped into the armchair in the kitchen. Leo pawed at the back door and whined to be let out. Dr Skinner called to him. 'Come here, boy. You're all I've got left now.'

Leo ambled over and allowed the doctor to ruffle his head.

'It's just you and me now, Leo. What are we going to do?'

The dog sat at his master's feet and wagged his tail.

This whole situation was that damn Billy's fault. If he hadn't got Chrissie pregnant, she wouldn't be in Ireland now. Mabel would not have gone out last night in such an agitated state and maybe she would have seen the car that hit her. If only Chrissie had never set eyes on that … that... Dr Skinner hurled his glass of whisky across the room, and as it shattered, leaving the golden liquid running down the wall, Leo dived for cover under the table. Dr Skinner put his head back in the chair and closed his eyes. Of course there was no way he could tell Chrissie, about her mother's death. That would bring her running back from Ireland immediately and into Billy's arms. No, it was best left as it was. As far as he was concerned, Chrissie was as dead to him as his wife.

18

Chrissie had been at the farm for two months when her aunt was taken ill. She knew immediately that something was wrong, because she had seen a number of her father's patients with the same symptoms.

'Aunt Kathleen, I really think you should be in bed and not out here in the yard. It's freezing and you will only make matters worse.'

'How can I go to bed when there is so much work to be done? Stop fussing, girl, and let me get on with my chores. I've never had a day's illness in my life. I'll take an extra big spoonful of malt and cod liver oil tonight and I'll be right as rain.'

She coughed violently, snorted the resulting phlegm, which had accumulated in her throat, and spat the huge green globule on the ground. Chrissie turned away in disgust, but not before she had noticed the tell-tale streaks of blood. Kathleen was trembling as Chrissie put her arm round her shoulders and guided her to the wall so she could lean on it to get her breath back. Everywhere the ground was as hard as flint as another severe frost exerted its relentless grip. The cattle stood despondently in the fields and even the chickens, which normally ran freely round the yard, were huddled together, puffing up their feathers in a futile attempt to keep warm.

'Aunt Kathleen,' Chrissie tried again, 'I think you may be very ill. I think you might have tuberculosis. I've seen these symptoms before, many times.'

Kathleen wiped her eyes with a greying handkerchief. 'Nonsense. Tuberculosis, who ever heard anything like it? Where would I pick up a disease I have never even heard of?'

'You have heard of it, Aunt Kathleen, although you probably call it consumption.'

Kathleen looked doubtful for a second as she thought about this. 'Well, like I said, I've never had a day's illness in my life.'

'Then all the more reason for you to go to bed now. I can do more work around here; you know how quick I've become at the milking. Besides, if I'm right about this, tuberculosis is very, very contagious. You don't want to infect Jackie and the others, do you? And I'm sure I don't want to catch it. It wouldn't be good for the baby.'

Kathleen put her finger to her lips and looked around furtively at the mention of the baby. 'Maybe you're right. I feel dreadful, so I do.'

'That's settled then. You lean on me and I'll get you inside.'

Later that afternoon, as Chrissie stirred a pot of chicken broth over the fire, she heard her aunt coughing violently. She ladled some soup into a bowl, tore off a piece of soda bread she had baked earlier and crept up the stairs. The sight of her aunt startled her and sent her into a panic. Her face was as white as chalk and her eyes were red and swollen. Chrissie felt her brow, which was stinging hot in spite of the cold, damp air. She put the soup and bread down on the little bedside table, ran back downstairs, heaved open the front door and yelled into the yard.

'Jackie! Jackie!'

She heard the clanking sound of iron clattering to the stone floor as Jackie dropped his tools and appeared from the barn, two dogs in hot pursuit.

'What is it, Chrissie?'

'I need you to ride into town and fetch Dr Byrne – now.'

Jackie's face clouded with concern. 'Is it Miss McBride?'

'Yes, Jackie. Please hurry.'

Jackie turned on his heel, grabbed Sammy, the old carthorse, who had been tied up in the yard enjoying his hay, and without bothering with a saddle vaulted onto the startled animal's back. He kicked his flanks and the horse responded instantly. They cantered out of the yard, Jackie's arms flailing as he struggled to control his mount with just a head collar.

It was another two hours before he returned with the doctor. Chrissie explained the symptoms to him as they climbed the stairs together.

'I think she has tuberculosis,' she concluded.

Dr Byrne frowned at her. 'I'll be the one who does the diagnosing round here, thank you very much.'

'Sure, sorry. Will you have a cup of tea, Doctor? I've had the water on ready.'

Dr Byrne nodded. 'Two sugars.' He regarded Kathleen's dozing figure.

'Now then, Kathleen, what have we got here?'

Kathleen stirred and forced her swollen eyes open. 'Dr Byrne? What are you doing here? I've no money to pay you, so I haven't. It's my meddling niece, she shouldn't have called you.'

'I'll be the judge of that,' replied the doctor as he opened his medical bag and took out a thermometer. Anyway, you can pay me with a chicken and a tray of eggs.'

'I'm not well, Doctor,' gasped Kathleen. 'I've known for a while, to be honest.'

'I know, that's why I'm here.' He fumbled with his stethoscope.

'No, you don't understand.' Kathleen grabbed at his wrist. 'Now you're here, I need you to do something for me.'

'That's what I'm trying to do, if you'll just let me.' He pushed her hand away.

'Over there.' Kathleen pointed to a small chest of drawers. 'In the top drawer there is a note rolled around some money. I need you to give it to Father Drummond.'

'What am I? Some kind of postman as well as your doctor?'

Kathleen gave way to another violent coughing fit. 'Please, Dr Byrne. It's important.'

Later that evening, after Dr Byrne had left, reluctantly confirming her diagnosis, Chrissie stirred cocoa powder into two mugs of hot milk. Her aunt was sleeping soundly now, due to the medication the doctor had given her. Chrissie pulled on her coat and crept silently out of the house and over to the barn.

'Jackie?'

She could just make out his paraffin lamp at the back of the barn, and she heard the hay rustling as he stirred himself.

'Chrissie? Hang on, I'll be with yer in a minute.'

He looked as though he had been dozing, and bits of hay clung to his hair.

'I've made some cocoa. It's in the kitchen.'

'Oh, thank you. Do you want me to come and fetch it?'

'No, I want you to join me in the house so we can drink it together.'

Jackie hesitated. 'Well, I'm not sure Miss McBride will approve of that. She always brings my cocoa out to the barn.'

'Please, Jackie. I could do with the company, and besides, she's fast asleep. Dr Byrne gave her something.'

'I guess it will be all right, then. I'll just fetch my jacket.'

Chrissie had stoked the fire up in the kitchen and piled on some extra turf so that the room actually felt quite cosy. Once they were settled with the comforting cocoa in their hands, they both began to relax. Chrissie was at ease in Jackie's company; if it wasn't for him, she didn't think she could endure this place. Her aunt had mellowed slightly since her arrival, but was still adamant that no one should be told about the baby, so Chrissie was still somewhat isolated. She had written to her mother several times over the last couple of months and was disappointed not to have received a reply, but Aunt Kathleen had insisted that this was not unusual. The post was so unreliable it had always taken months to get through, and now with the war on in England it was bound to take even longer. Chrissie's heart ached as she thought about her mother, her home, Leo, and of course Billy. In spite of his behaviour, she had not been able to get him out of her mind and was secretly delighted that his child was now growing inside her. She just knew that one day they would be reunited, and it was this belief that kept her going. She patted her stomach gently and smiled to herself.

'Penny for them?' interrupted Jackie.

'Oh, I was just thinking about home. You know, how I miss everybody.'

'You never talk about your home, Chrissie. Tell me about it.'

Chrissie shrugged. 'Not much to tell really. I was born and raised in Manchester. I'm an only child, my father is a doctor and my mother is a midwife. That's about it.'

'You seem so sad, though. Why don't you just go home if you miss it so much?'

Chrissie sighed. 'I wish it were that simple.' Tears slowly began to make their way down her cheeks. Jackie put a tentative arm round her shoulders, casting a glance towards the stairs as he did so.

'Come on now, Chrissie. Why don't you tell me what's bothering you? I'm not pretending I'll have the answer, but I'm sure you'll feel better if you share it.'

'I can't,' whispered Chrissie.

'You can trust me. I know we've only known each other a short time, but we're friends, aren't we?'

This was true. Jackie reminded her of Clark in a way. Although much taller, he had the same red hair and kind face. Chrissie wondered where Clark was now. He would be off fighting somewhere, no doubt, and she shuddered at the thought of him, and probably Billy too, in some far-off place defending their country, with the threat of death never far away. Maybe she should count herself lucky. At least she was safe. Ireland had declared itself neutral and had no intention of becoming involved in the hostilities.

'Chrissie?' Jackie's concerned face brought her back to the present.

She pulled herself together. 'I'm fine, Jackie, honestly. It's Aunt Kathleen we need to worry about now.'

'You're right. What did the doctor say?'

'Well, with tuberculosis, surgery is a possibility, but Aunt Kathleen would never agree to that, and besides, it may not be necessary at this stage. My father used to perform a procedure known as the plombage technique, where the infected lung is collapsed so that it has time to rest and the lesions can heal, but I mentioned this to Dr Byrne and he didn't seem to know what I was talking about. Back in Manchester, my father would send

197

patients to a sanatorium, where a healthy climate and good nutrition help to combat the infection, but to be honest, even if such a place exists here, Kathleen would never leave the farm, would she? No, the two of us will look after her. I can make sure she eats well, gets plenty of rest and recovers her strength. You can take control of the farm so she doesn't fret too much.'

'I can make my mammy's Irish stew, that's sure to have her on her feet in no time.'

Chrissie looked at him fondly. 'That's kind. Thank you, Jackie. I'd appreciate that and I know my aunt will too.'

'I'd do anything for Miss McBride, so I would.'

'Do you miss your parents a lot?'

'Why, sure I do. I was an only child, you know, and that's a rare thing here in Ireland. My mammy never got caught with a child again after me.'

'What happened to them? Your parents, I mean.'

'They got the consumption. They died within a couple of days of each other. I held my mammy's hand as she took her last breath and slipped peacefully away.'

He reached into the neck of his jumper and pulled out a gold chain. On it were three rings, which jangled together and shone in the firelight. 'These are my mammy and daddy's wedding rings and my mammy's engagement ring. I never take them off.' He kissed them and tucked the chain safely back into his jumper, then closed his eyes and patted his chest gently.

His pain was obvious and Chrissie thought of her own mother. If anything happened to her, she knew she would not be able to endure it. 'I'm sorry, Jackie.'

His features clouded. 'This tube ... tuberclo...'

'Tuberculosis,' Chrissie corrected.

'Yeah, that. It's not as bad as the consumption, is it? I mean, I couldn't bear to lose Miss Mc-Bride too.'

Chrissie could not bring herself to tell him that they were one and the same.

'No, Jackie, don't worry. We'll make sure Miss McBride gets well. You just come in here again tomorrow and we'll make a batch of your mammy's Irish stew. It sounds as though that could revive the dead.' She gripped his hand and added defiantly, 'I promise you, Miss McBride is not going to die.'

The next day, Chrissie sat by the fire mending some sacks. She was used to darning socks, but this was much tougher. The needle was curved, flattened and very sharp and it was a struggle to push it through the heavy-duty fabric. Jackie was upstairs with her aunt, feeding her his mammy's Irish stew. There wasn't much meat in it, but he had chopped up an abundance of fresh vegetables to make up for the lack of protein, and the result was a delicious, nutritious broth that would be more beneficial than any fancy medicine. He had been up there for a while, and Chrissie wondered what could be taking so long. Her aunt would only be taking tiny sips, such was her weakened state, but surely Jackie should be back down by now?

She finished another sack, and noticing that the

water over the fire had come to the boil, she brewed a jam jar of tea for Jackie. She added the two sugars he preferred, even though this was an extravagance, and crept up the stairs.

She gently pushed open the bedroom door and peered round. Jackie was lying next to Kathleen, his head on her pillow and his arm thrown over her lifeless body.

'Jackie? What on earth are you doing?'

Jackie stirred briefly but did not answer.

With a sick feeling of dread in her stomach, Chrissie approached the bed, recoiling in horror at her aunt's waxy face. What little colour Kathleen had once had was now drained away, leaving her with the pallor of a weathered statue.

'Oh Jackie.' She placed her hand on his arm. 'Why didn't you come and fetch me?'

He shook his arm free and buried his face in the pillow.

'Jackie, I'm so sorry. I know what she meant to you.' She placed the jam jar of tea on the bedside table, then gently pulled the sheet over her aunt's face.

'Jackie, come on downstairs, will you? We need to fetch the doctor.'

Jackie sat up and stared at her. 'It's a bit late for that, don't you think? You promised me she wouldn't die.' His voice was no more than a strangled sob.

Chrissie gripped his hand in hers. 'I know. I'm so sorry. She was obviously sicker than we thought.'

'Why does this keep happening to me? Everybody I care about leaves me. Over four years I've been here. I thought I had a home for life, and now this.'

Chrissie glanced out of the window and noticed the greyness of the November day. 'We really need to think about riding into town for the doctor. It'll be dark soon and I have to try to call my mother too. Come on, Jackie, we'll go together.'

She stood up and held out her hand. He took it hesitantly and rose to his feet. At the door, he glanced back at the lifeless shape under the covers. 'Goodbye, Miss McBride,' he gulped. 'I'll never forget what you did for me.'

19

It was Christmas morning, and Chrissie and Jackie were seated by the fire in the kitchen. Kathleen had been dead for almost two months, but life at the farm carried on relentlessly. They had just come in from the morning's milking, a job that had taken twice as long because it was just the two of them. Michael and Declan had been given the day off to be with their families, a gesture they had readily accepted. Jackie owned the farm now. Kathleen had left it to him in her will, thus ensuring he would have a home for life just as she had always promised. They might not have been related by blood, but she had grown to think of him as part of her family. He had the same work ethic as her parents and she'd known the farm would be in good hands.

The funeral had been a quiet affair, just Chrissie,

Jackie, Michael, Declan and Father Drummond. After several attempts, Chrissie had finally managed to place a call home. She had spoken to her father in stilted tones, only to be told that her mother was out on an emergency call and anyway would not be able to make it to the funeral. Her father had not even asked after her well-being, and from that moment on Chrissie vowed she would never speak to him again. She could hear Leo barking in the background and she thought her heart would burst with grief.

Jackie had slaughtered a chicken for their Christmas lunch and it was now simmering in the pot. A jug of warm ale sat on the beam over the fireplace, a gift from Michael and Declan. Chrissie poured two glasses of the dark, frothy liquid and handed one to Jackie. 'Cheers,' she said. 'Happy Christmas.'

· Jackie raised his glass and clinked it against hers. She smiled and took a sip of the warm, malty drink. She pulled a face and Jackie laughed. 'It's an acquired taste, I think.'

She wiped the froth from her lips with the back of her hand. 'You look lovely when you laugh.'

He glanced at the floor in embarrassment and then poked at the chicken. 'Should be ready in another hour.'

'Jackie, sit down, please. I need to talk to you.'

His eyes widened in panic. 'You're not leaving, are you?'

'Why would you jump to such a conclusion? I need to tell you why I'm here and why I can't go home yet. My aunt was insistent that it should remain a secret, but I don't see how I can ignore the subject any longer.'

She unbuttoned her woolly cardigan and smoothed down her blouse so that the roundness of her stomach was clearly visible.

Jackie frowned and shifted uncomfortably. 'Are you...?'

'Yes, I am. Almost six months. I was sent here by my father, who could not live with the shame of having a daughter who was a slut,' she said bitterly.

'Don't say that!' Jackie was immediately on his knees by her side. 'What about the baby's father?'

Chrissie sighed. 'He is ... was ... the love of my life. I loved him with all my heart, but when he found out about the baby he didn't want to know.'

Jackie clenched his fists. 'The bastard...'

'Hush, it wasn't his fault. I think he panicked. War had just been declared, we were both very young, my father absolutely loathed him and we had only been seeing each other a short while.' Chrissie wiped a tear from the corner of her eye. 'I truly loved him, though, and I'm sure he loved me...' She cleared her throat and sat up straight. 'Anyway, it's all water under the bridge now. He has no idea where I am and I have no idea what happened to him either. He's probably away fighting.'

Jackie gazed up into her pale blue eyes. 'What are you going to do?'

'That's what I need to talk to you about. I was wondering if it would be all right for me to stay here, at least until the baby is born. Then I'll make my way back to Manchester with my head held high and my father will just have to accept it. As

203

soon as my mother sees her grandchild, everything will be fine.'

Jackie gave a weak smile. 'I like that plan. Apart from the bit about you going back to Manchester.' He stood up and kissed her lightly on the forehead. 'I'll take care of you and that babby. You'll have a home here for as long as you need it.'

Chrissie sighed with relief. 'Thank you, Jackie. I don't know what I would do without you. And by the way, it's about time you stopped sleeping in the barn. This is your home now. I think you should move into my aunt's old bedroom.'

'Oh I couldn't. It wouldn't feel right.'

'Well at least take my bed over in the corner. I'll move upstairs for now.'

He looked doubtful but had to admit it made sense. 'All right then, if you're sure.'

Chrissie smiled and picked up her beer again. 'Cheers!' The second sip was no more palatable, and she shuddered as the ale hit her taste buds.

Life on the farm continued throughout the winter months, and Chrissie and Jackie lived in contentment despite the bitter weather and the hard labour that defined their daily struggle. At the beginning of March, Jackie had Declan slaughter a pig to celebrate his and Chrissie's twentieth birthdays. It turned out they had been born within a week of each other. The carcass was now hanging upside down in the shed ready to be submerged in the boiling water that had been heated over the turf-fired burner.

Chrissie entered the shed and crept up behind Jackie.

'You're working hard, Jackie. When will it be ready?'

The steam from the water had flushed his face and his hair was stuck to his forehead. He wiped his brow with his sleeve. 'It'll be a while yet, I'm afraid.'

He placed his arm around her shoulders. 'You all right?'

Chrissie rubbed her aching back. 'I just want this baby born.'

'Only a few more weeks to go now.'

He picked up the four trotters that he had cut from the pig.

'Do you fancy these for tea?'

Chrissie wrinkled her nose in disgust. 'I certainly do not. I know what that pig has stepped in!'

Jackie laughed and tried not to think about how much he was going to miss her when she returned to Manchester after the baby was born.

A couple of weeks later, Jackie was alerted by an unfamiliar sound outside. The dogs were barking wildly and the chickens flew up in the air in a cloud of dust as a little donkey cart entered the yard and Father Drummond climbed down from his seat. He tied the donkey to a post and called out a greeting to Jackie.

'Father Drummond, this is an unexpected pleasure. Won't you come in for a cup of tea?'

'I wouldn't say no, Jackie, thank you.'

The two men heaved open the stiff front door of the cottage. Chrissie was knitting by the fireside. She looked up in surprise.

'Father Drummond! How nice to see you. I'll

put the water on. Jackie, find the best cups, would you?' She couldn't have a man of the cloth drinking out of a jam jar.

When they were all settled with their drinks, Father Drummond cleared his throat and began to speak. 'The thing is, people are, well, you know ... talking.'

'About what?' asked Chrissie, immediately bristling.

Father Drummond looked distinctly uncomfortable. 'Er, your aunt always used to put a nip of whiskey in my tea.' He held out his cup. 'Would you mind?'

Jackie reached for the bottle from the top shelf, blew off the dust and poured a measure into their visitor's cup. The priest took a sip. 'Ah, much better. Now where was I?'

'People are talking.' Chrissie folded her arms defiantly.

'Ah yes, well. This situation you find yourselves in. I mean, living as man and wife when you are not even married and–'

Chrissie interrupted. 'We are not living as man and wife. I sleep upstairs in my aunt's old room and Jackie sleeps over there.' She indicated the cot in the corner.

'I see, but the baby...'

Jackie spoke quietly. 'The baby is nothing to do with me, Father. I mean, I am not the father. Chrissie is here as my guest and I will take care of her and the baby until she decides it is time for them to leave. It is my fervent hope that that day will never come, but Chrissie is free to return to her old life any time she wants. It is nobody's busi-

206

ness but ours, Father, and I will not have gossips making it into a sordid little affair. Chrissie means the world to me. I could not have got through the last few months without her, and I have no idea what I am going to do if she decides to leave.'

He stood behind her and placed his hands firmly on her shoulders. She reached up and grasped one of his hands. They both stared resolutely at Father Drummond, who at least had the grace to look uncomfortable.

'Well I can see you have inherited your aunt's stubbornness, Chrissie. However, arrangements were made long ago for the birth of your baby.'

'Arrangements? What kind of arrangements?'

Father Drummond spoke quietly but with determination. 'Your aunt told me about your condition.'

'Pregnancy,' interrupted Chrissie.

'Yes, quite. She asked me to find a place for you to give birth, a place that would be away from prying eyes and gossips, a place where you could have the baby safely and peacefully.'

'You mean a hospital?'

'Er, no. But the next best thing. I have arranged for you to go to the convent.'

'A convent? But I'm not a Catholic. Would that even be allowed?'

'As I said, your aunt begged me to help and I promised I would. Trust me, this is the best thing for you.'

Jackie spoke up. 'Maybe he's right, Chrissie. Imagine giving birth here in this damp cottage with no heating or running water, and what if something was to go wrong?'

Chrissie had to admit he had a point. With all her experience of watching her mother's patients go through labour, she was well aware of the risks involved.

'What would it cost?'

'Why, nothing,' explained Father Drummond. 'That's the beauty of it. You enter the convent and they look after you and the baby, and in return you work for the nuns for a while.'

Chrissie was wary. 'What sort of work?'

'Well, let's see. They take in laundry from local hotels, restaurants, priests' houses, that kind of thing, and they also have a small farm where they grow vegetables to sell. You're used to that.'

'What do you think, Chrissie?' asked Jackie. 'It sounds like the perfect solution. We could never afford to pay for a hospital, and Miss McBride obviously thought it would be for the best.'

'Listen to Jackie,' insisted Father Drummond. 'He talks sense, so he does.'

'How long would I have to stay there?'

Father Drummond hesitated before giving his answer. 'That's up to you, Chrissie. You could stay as long as you liked.'

'You make it sound like a holiday.'

He gave a nervous laugh. 'Well you would be well looked after.'

'I think you should go,' urged Jackie.

Chrissie smiled weakly. 'All right then, Father. Please finalise the arrangements, would you?'

Father Drummond stood. The two men shook hands and Jackie showed him to the door.

'Thank you very much, Father. We appreciate your help.'

He stared at the floor. 'It was all down to Miss McBride. You remember that, son.'

Jackie frowned. 'Of course, Father. Mind how you go.'

As Father Drummond climbed back onto the donkey cart he patted Kathleen McBride's note in his breast pocket. How was he supposed to ignore the wishes of a dying woman, no matter that they spelled heartache for her young niece?

20

1973

Tina lay on the couch in the lounge with no recollection of how she had come to be there. Her head throbbed with each beat of her heart as the blood was forced through her veins. Her cracked lips felt enormous and one eye was fixed tightly shut as though someone had poured glue between the lids and sandwiched them together. Through her one good eye she could just make out the shadowy form of Rick as he hovered over her. She tried to speak but her tongue would not co-operate and remained stubbornly fixed to the roof of her mouth. She could taste congealed blood, which reminded her of a childhood visit to the dentist when she had had two teeth removed. The memory was suddenly so vivid she could smell the gas that had been used to send her to sleep. Sleep. That was what she needed, what she craved. If only she could sleep she would wake up and find this was all a terrible nightmare. She felt herself falling deeper and deeper into oblivion and she welcomed the comforting blackness of it.

Some time later she was aware of a warm sensation on her lips. She forced open her eye and saw Rick's face only inches from hers. He was gently pressing a damp flannel to her swollen mouth.

'Morning, love. How are you feeling?'

It took her a while to register this question and even longer to formulate an answer.

'What happened?' was all she could manage.

Rick turned away as he wrung out the flannel in a bowl of warm water and reapplied it to Tina's cheek.

'You had an accident. Last night, you came in late, it was dark. I came to meet you in the hall to find out where you'd been, if you were all right, and you must have tripped. I tried to catch you, but you fell and hit your head on the banister. I've been worried sick. I sat up here all night with you.'

Tina's thoughts were muddled. She had a vague memory of meeting Rick in the hall, but after that all she could remember was the searing pain. She was sure there was something, though...

'The baby!' She tried to sit up, but the effort made her head swim.

'Shh, the baby's fine,' Rick placated.

'How can you be sure? I need to see a doctor.'

'No,' Rick almost shouted. 'No doctors.'

Tina lay back on the couch. 'My head hurts, Rick.' She began to weep softly.

Rick gently smoothed his hand over her brow. 'I'll fetch you a couple of paracetamol.'

He returned a few minutes later with the tablets, a cup of tea and a slice of toast.

'Here, I've made you some breakfast. You can't take those tablets on an empty stomach.'

He placed his arm around Tina's back and eased her into a sitting position, plumping the cushions up to make her more comfortable. She winced as the hot tea touched her lips.

'I'm sorry to cause you all this trouble, Rick.'

'Tina, you're my wife. In sickness and in health and all that.'

'But what about work?'

He glanced at the clock on the mantelpiece. He had forgotten to wind it up again. 'I start my shift in an hour. Will you be all right?'

'Yes, of course. You go, I'll be fine. What day is it?'

'It's Saturday. Don't go worrying about the shop, I've sorted it.'

She was too tired to protest. 'OK, I just need to sleep.'

'Good girl.' He planted a firm kiss on her lips, making her wince once more.

Rick had been gone for a few hours when Tina began to feel hungry. She gingerly swung her legs off the sofa and sat upright. Dizziness overcame her for a few seconds, but then she steadied herself and stood up carefully. She was still wearing yesterday's clothes, and she felt grubby and sticky with blood and sweat. She teetered into the kitchen and surveyed the carnage. Rick had obviously made himself a meal the night before, and

211

the remnants of this were in evidence on every surface. Dried baked beans were welded to the bottom of a saucepan. Empty eggshells lay on the worktop, and two pieces of blackened toast had been abandoned on a greasy plate.

She sighed and began to clear away the dishes. She picked up a glass and noticed that the bottom of it was covered with a thin brown stain. Hating herself for what felt like snooping, she raised it to her nose and inhaled deeply. As she sniffed the stale aroma of the whisky, the events of the previous evening were brought into sharp focus. She hadn't tripped at all; the blow to her face had not been caused by the banister but by something far more dangerous – her husband's fist. She stumbled into the hall and stood at the foot of the stairs. Her husband was a violent drunk who would never change. The realisation hurt far more than any bruise he had ever given her.

As she lay soaking in the bath, she pondered what to do. She was seven months pregnant and trapped in this violent marriage. Graham and Linda had been right all along. She was ashamed and embarrassed that she had got herself into this situation. She would have to leave for good now, for her own sake and that of the baby, but the thought of returning to the grubby little bedsit filled her with dread. Besides, there was no way she could be seen in public now. She looked as though she had gone ten rounds with Henry Cooper.

By the time Rick returned home from work, Tina was feeling a little better, physically at least. She had managed to prepare a meal, and they sat at the kitchen table attempting to make normal conversation.

'How was work?' she asked casually.

'Not bad. Had a couple of yobs do a runner without paying. Conductor chased after them, but he didn't have a hope in hell of catching the little blighters. Then a snotty kid wet himself, so the seat smelt of piss all day.'

He pushed another forkful of food into his mouth.

'Thanks for the tea, love. I would have made it, you know. You need to rest.'

'I'm all right.' Tina pushed away her plate of uneaten food.

'Don't you want that?' asked Rick, reaching across and helping himself to a forkful of her mashed potato.

'I'm not hungry.'

'You need to keep your strength up, if not for you then for the baby.'

Tina took a deep breath and covered her face with her hands.

'I know it was you, Rick.'

Silence descended as Rick put down his knife and fork. He peeled her fingers away from her face and stared straight into her eyes.

'You know *what* was me?'

'Last night. I didn't trip at all. You punched me in the face. I remember the smell of the whisky and–'

He was on his feet in an instant.

'What? How can you think such a thing? Punch you in the face? I would never do that.' He noticed Tina's disbelieving expression. 'I mean, I know

I've hit you in the past, and I regret that more than anything, but I've changed, you must realise that. We're going to be a family now. I wouldn't jeopardise that.'

He sank to his knees at Tina's side and laid his head in her lap. 'I can't believe you would think that of me. I wouldn't dream of hitting a pregnant woman.'

Tina was in turmoil now. He sounded so contrite and seemed genuinely horrified that she could think, he was capable of such violence. Maybe she hadn't remembered the events of yesterday correctly after all. She placed her hand on his head and ran her fingers through his thick dark hair. 'I'm sorry, Rick. My memory must be playing tricks on me.'

He looked up at her imploringly.

'Please, Tina. You have got to start trusting me again if this is going to work.' He gripped her wrists firmly.

'I know. It's just that–'

He reached up and put his finger to her lips to silence her.

'No more talking. Let's just forget about it.'

He took both her hands in his, and she smiled even as she tried to ignore the purple bruising that was visible across his knuckles.

21

The weather became ever more cold and damp, and the whole country sank into a depression as the oil crisis grew and power cuts were introduced. Rick and Tina listened to Prime Minister Heath's broadcast in which he warned that the nation was facing the hardest Christmas since the war. The next day, all six hundred and fifty bulbs were turned out on the Christmas tree in Trafalgar Square.

It was in this gloomy atmosphere that they went shopping for a pram in Manchester. Tina had been badgering Rick to come with her for weeks. She felt it was something they should do together and he had finally agreed. He gripped her hand firmly as they battled through the crowded streets. A young man walking towards them accidentally knocked into Tina, causing her to stumble. Rick grabbed her elbow to steady her as he turned on the young man.

'Oi, mate. Watch where you're going.'

The stranger noticed Tina's heavily pregnant state and immediately apologised profusely.

'I'm so sorry.' He touched Tina's forearm gently. 'Are you OK?'

Rick immediately let go of Tina and grabbed the man by his lapels. 'Don't you touch my wife. Can't you see she's pregnant? She's not interested in you. I'm the only one allowed to touch her. Do you understand?'

The stranger held his palms aloft submissively.

'Take it easy, squire. I didn't mean anything by it. I'm sorry I bumped into your wife, all right?'

Rick grunted and shoved him against the wall.

Tina stood cowering, trying to blend in with the small crowd that had gathered. Rick sought her out and grabbed her by the hand. 'Come on, love.' He turned to the curious bystanders. 'Show's over, folks, now bugger off.' He strode off, dragging Tina behind him.

'Jesus, Rick. What was that all about?'

'Don't tell me you didn't notice. That clown was all over you. The way he looked at you, and you nearly nine months pregnant. It was sick.'

Tina sighed. She knew Rick was convinced that every man she came into contact with was trying to get her into bed. Part of her was pleased that he was so protective of her. It showed how much he loved her. He was breathing heavily now, a combination of his anger and the quick pace at which they were travelling. Tina had to run to keep up with him.

'It's no good.' He stopped and took a deep breath. 'I can't go shopping now, I'm too wound up.'

'Rick, please. Don't spoil things. I've been looking forward to this for ages.'

He pointed to a pub over the road. 'Why don't we nip in there for a quick drink and a bite to eat?'

She hesitated. She knew it was a bad idea, but she desperately wanted to buy the pram today. After lunch and some quiet time together, maybe he would have calmed down.

'All right then, but not for too long.'

He perked up and took hold of her hand again. 'Lovely. Come on then.'

He skipped across the road, expertly dodging the traffic as he pulled Tina along in his wake.

That evening, Rick lay on the sofa in a foul mood. The electricity had been cut again and they sat in silence surrounded by candles. Needless to say, the pub lunch had turned out not to be such a good idea. After several pints, Tina had managed to coax him back on to the street, but he was in a belligerent and argumentative mood and had no interest in shopping for prams. She suggested they should get the bus home and Rick had readily agreed, but not before making an extravagant purchase of his own. That purchase was now sitting in its box in the middle of their lounge, completely redundant.

'Bloody government! Who do they think they are, cutting off our power like this?'

'I'm sure if they had known you were going to buy a colour television today they would have made an exception.'

Tina was silently fuming. A colour TV for God's sake! What was wrong with their old rented black-and-white one? That was the pram money gone. She knew there was still money left from the National win, but Rick had put it where she couldn't get her hands on it. She sighed and struggled to her feet.

'Do you want a brew?'

217

Rick looked at her in disbelief. 'Are you trying to be funny?'

Tina realised her mistake and sat back down. 'I forgot.'

'We're sat here in near-darkness and you *forgot* the power was off?'

'Just leave it, Rick, please. I'm not in the mood for an argument.'

He sidled over to her on the couch and whispered in her ear. 'You know what *I'm* in the mood for?'

Tina's heart missed a beat. 'Rick, please. Look at the state of me. I'm huge.'

He slipped his hand inside her blouse and fondled her breast clumsily.

'So are these.'

He nuzzled into her neck and bit her ear painfully. She turned to ask him to stop, but he closed his mouth round hers and parted her lips with his tongue. Tina forced herself to relax so as not to incur his wrath, and managed not to recoil as he shifted his weight on top of her.

The next day, the power was back on and Rick unpacked the television from its box. When he switched it on, the images bloomed into a kaleidoscope of colour. Everybody seemed to have an orange glow and Tina thought the old black-and-white screen was much more natural. Rick was pleased, however, and he fiddled with the knobs, adjusting the contrast and brightness until he was satisfied he had the perfect picture.

He stood back and admired his new toy. 'Look at that,' he proclaimed. 'It's so sharp. Hey, it's so good I'll get dust in my eyes when I watch a Western!'

He laughed at his own joke and continued to flick through the three channels.

'Pass us that *Radio Times*, would you, love.'

Tina picked up the double issue with its promise of fabulous festive viewing: *Morecambe and Wise, Look. Mike Yarwood, The Black and White Minstrel Show.* The irony of watching this last programme on the new colour television was not lost on Tina. She flung the magazine across the floor and Rick scooped it up. He was oblivious to her bad mood.

'When do you think we can go for the pram?' she ventured.

'You're not still going on about that, are you? Let's just sit back and enjoy our new telly. We can go next week.'

Tina rubbed her belly. 'The baby might be here by then.'

Rick stopped-scouring the *Radio Times* and digested this. 'Bloody hell! You're right. We had better enjoy ourselves while we can. Fetch us a drink, will you?'

A couple of days later, Tina was in the charity shop when Graham came in.

'When are you going to give this lot up? You must be about ready to drop.'

'Morning, Graham. End of the month,' replied Tina. 'Can't come soon enough.'

She eyed the battered pram in the corner. It had been donated to the shop some weeks ago, and Tina had pitied the poor mother who would have no choice but to buy it because she couldn't afford a new one. Now, however, she was resigned to the fact that this rather ancient, battle-scarred contraption would be the one into which she herself would lovingly place her longed-for baby. She began to lift out the books that had been stored there. Graham rushed over.

'Here, let me help you with those.'

He took a pile of books from her and laid them on the counter.

'Why are you emptying it anyway? Does somebody want it?' He ran his fingers over the dusty hood and grimaced at the ripped and shoddy interior. Tina looked away in embarrassment and moved some more books to the counter.

'No,' said Graham. 'Please tell me you're not having it.'

'Oh it's not that bad really. A bit of Ajax on the inside and it will be like new.'

'I thought you were going shopping for a new one.'

Tina scoffed. 'We did. It's a long story, but we came back with a colour telly instead.'

Graham shook his head and gripped the counter. He gritted his teeth and inhaled deeply.

Tina gently placed her hand on his shoulder.

'Graham, it's not your problem. I'm fine, honestly. The baby won't need a pram for long anyway, and that telly will last us for years.'

'You are a saint, Tina. I don't know how you put up with him.'

She shrugged. 'I love him, Graham. I know I have every reason to hate him, but I can't. He hasn't been too bad since...' She instinctively raised her hand to her cheek.

'Since what? Has he hit you again, Tina?'

She leapt to Rick's defence. 'No, of course not. Everything's fine. We're both really excited about the baby.'

Graham looked doubtful.

'Look, I know you mean well, but I have to make this work. I don't want you to think I'm weak. I know what I'm doing. I can't bring a baby up on my own, you know, and I'm sure Rick will be a great father. If I thought for one second that he would harm the baby, then believe me I would go. I don't know where, but I wouldn't risk my own child's safety. You have to trust me, Graham.'

Tina closed the shop early and prepared for the long walk home with the pram. She thrust the shop keys into her pocket and cursed herself again for coming out without her handbag.

The pram wasn't that bad really. It still had plenty of suspension, and the bumps and cracks in the pavement were absorbed by the large wheels. She wondered about all the babies who had been pushed in this pram in its previous life. She suddenly felt alive as she proudly wheeled it through the streets. In a couple of weeks she would be pushing her very own baby, and strangers would smile fondly and ask if they could have a peep. She would peel back the covers to reveal the most beautiful baby anybody had ever seen. Rick would wheel the pram proudly round the depot, and all the other drivers and conductors would gather round and admire their adorable child. They would all agree that they had never seen such a delightful baby.

With these thoughts and scenarios going round in her head, Tina was surprised to find herself back in her own street. It didn't seem as far when you were pushing a pram. She left it on the doorstep as she entered the hall and called out to Rick.

'Come and see what I've got!'

She pulled off her coat and hung it up on the peg.

'Rick? Where are you?'

She went into the kitchen. Rick was staring out of the window.

'There you are. Didn't you hear me come in? I've got a pram. It's only second-hand, but it's nice to push, and once it's cleaned up it will be—' She stopped abruptly as Rick turned towards her. His face was thunderous and he was seething with every sinew. He had something in his hands, a piece of paper, one that Tina recognised.

'I had a headache,' he began slowly, struggling to keep the anger from his voice. 'I couldn't find any tablets in the cupboard, and then I noticed you had left your handbag on the kitchen table. There weren't any tablets in there either, but I found this.' He held Billy's letter aloft, and a feeling of dread settled into the pit of Tina's stomach.

'Well, *Christina*.' He emphasised her full name. 'When were you going to tell me about this Billy?'

Tina was frantic. 'God, Rick, you've got this all wrong. That letter is not to me. Look at the date, for God's sake.'

But Rick wasn't listening. He lunged forward and caught hold of her long dark hair. She screamed in fright, but he slapped her savagely across the face, and then clenched his fist tight and thrust it into her swollen stomach. Tina gasped and doubled over in pain as she fell to the ground. The last thing she remembered seeing was the faded photo of Billy Stirling, which had fluttered to the floor.

'You've got this all wrong,' she said over and over again. There was no one there to hear her. She heard the front door slam as she tried to struggle to her feet. Then she felt a warm sensation between her legs.

'The baby,' she whispered. And then she passed out.

22

Rick thundered down the street in a blind fury, Billy's letter clutched in his right hand. He spotted a bus approaching and held out his hand even though he was nowhere near the bus stop. It slowed down a little but did not stop altogether. It made no difference to Rick. He simply caught hold of the silver pole and expertly swung himself aboard. The conductor was taken by surprise.

'Oi, you can't just hop on and–' He stopped as he recognised Rick. 'Oh, it's you. Where are you going in such a hurry?'

'Gillbent Road, Frank.' He pushed past and slumped down in the nearest seat. 'Now leave me alone.'

By the time the bus had dropped him at Gill-bent Road and Rick had found number 180, he had worked himself into a state of complete apoplexy. He badly needed a drink. He rapped on the door with his fist and waited impatiently. Two seconds later he rapped again, and this time he shouted as well.

'I know all about you, Billy. Come out here now and face me like a man.'

He rapped on the door once more and this time he could hear movement inside. Slowly the door was inched open.

'What a racket. At least give me a chance to get to the door.'

Rick was more than a little surprised to see an elderly lady, but he pushed past her roughly and entered the small sitting room. 'Where is he?'

'Who?' asked the old lady. 'My husband?'

Rick looked her up and down and scoffed. 'I don't think so. Billy. Is he your son?'

She stiffened. 'Who wants to know?'

Rick caught hold of her elbow. 'Don't play games with me. I know he lives here and I know he's been shagging my wife.'

The old lady bristled. 'He'd have a job. Billy's been dead for over thirty years.'

This stopped Rick in his tracks. 'What did you say?'

The woman stared him in the eye. 'Look, I don't know who you are, but I'm not scared of you. You can't just come barging in here accusing my Billy of all kinds. Like I said, he's dead. He died during the war in 1940.'

Without invitation, Rick slumped into one of

224

the armchairs by the fireside.

'Be my guest,' said the old lady, sarcastically.

He slowly unfolded the letter he had been clutching since he left home and began to read it properly for the first time. When he had finished, he held his head in his hands.

'Oh my God. What have I done? What have I done?'

23

Graham knew that if Sheila ever found out, she would kill him. He peeled off a wad of banknotes from the roll in his pocket and handed them to the shop assistant.

'Thank you, sir. I'm sure your wife will be very happy with it.'

He hesitated. 'It's not for my wife.'

The shop assistant gave him a knowing look. 'Oh, I see. My mistake.' She punched some buttons on the till. With a loud ring the drawer shot open and she counted the notes into it.

Graham was flustered for a second. 'No, it's nothing like that. It's for a friend.'

The assistant gave a low whistle. 'Must be a good friend.'

'She is, yes. A very good friend.' He wasn't sure why he was even having this conversation with a complete stranger. He was too honest for his own good.

He bade the shop assistant a good evening and

pushed the brand-new, top-of-the-range Silver Cross pram out on to the pavement. He heard the door click behind him as the shop girl turned the sign round to read 'Closed'.

He wheeled the pram over to his van, cursing the wet streets as the virgin tyres collected their first traces of grit and grime. He knew it was an extravagant gesture, but the sight of Tina pushing that battered old second-hand thing had really stirred him. He knew he was a soft touch where Tina was concerned, but he couldn't help himself. He only hoped that Rick would not be there when he delivered the pram.

When he pulled up outside the Craigs' house, he was confused to see it in darkness. He glanced at the street lights; they were all lit, so there couldn't be another power cut. He left the pram in the van and rang the doorbell. He noticed that the old charity shop pram was standing outside the front door.

After the third ring, he gave up and returned to the van. He started the ignition and the engine coughed into life. Then it occurred to him that he could leave the pram in the shed at the back. He could put a note through the front door explaining what he had done. It would be a nice surprise for Tina when she returned home.

He manoeuvred the big Silver Cross down the narrow ginnel at the side of the house. When he reached the shed, he had to squeeze past the pram in order to open it. There was a lot of junk in there, as well as a lawnmower and some under-used garden tools, but with a little rearranging Graham managed to squeeze the pram in. He hesitated for a second, and then on a hunch, he cupped his hands to his face and peered in through the kitchen window. In the blackness, it took his eyes a while to adjust and then his brain a few seconds longer to register what he had seen. With a swift jab of his elbow, he broke the glass in the back door, reached for the key and burst into the kitchen.

'Tina. Tina...' A sob emerged from his throat. 'Jesus, what happened to you?'

He ran down the hall to the telephone and dialled 999. His fingers were trembling and clumsy, and it took him three attempts before he managed to get through.

He returned to where Tina lay and knelt beside her. His hands shook and he hardly dared to touch her. Her face appeared ethereal, while her lips had a bluish tinge and her dress had ridden up to expose an expanse of bone-white thigh. He gingerly pulled it down to preserve her modesty, and that was when he noticed it. A dark red stain had spilled out from between her legs and congealed on the lino, and Graham knew instinctively that she would not need either of those two prams.

24

The first thing she noticed was the smell. Disinfectant at first, but then another less familiar scent, one that caused her pulse to quicken. The pungent, metallic aroma of blood. She opened her eyes and tried to lift her head off the pillow, but it felt as heavy as a medicine ball. Her arm was stiff and pinched slightly on the inside of her elbow. She craned her neck and saw that she was attached to a drip. Her mouth felt parched and furred up and her lips were cracked. And something else, something a lot more sinister. She felt empty.

The door to her room was eased open and Graham walked in carrying a plastic cup of coffee. She saw him register the fact that she was conscious and he rushed over to the bed.

'You're awake!' He smoothed his hand over her brow and stroked her hair, still matted with sweat.

'Graham! What are you doing here? Where am I?'

Graham took hold of her hand and kissed the back of it. 'You're in the hospital, love.' His eyes shone with tears and he looked away as he tried to compose himself.

'Graham?'

He took a deep breath. 'I'm really sorry.'

Tina held up her hand to spare him. 'I know. I lost the baby.'

'Oh Tina.' He leant forward and kissed her on the forehead.

'Where's Rick?'

Graham clenched his hands into fists and fought to control himself. 'A long way from here if he knows what's good for him. You're going to press charges, I assume.'

Tina was weary. 'I can't think about that now. I just need to see him.'

Graham shook his head with incredulity. 'After what he's done, Tina? You're not thinking straight.'

Tears began to burn their way down her cheeks. She tried to wipe them away with her hand, but this caused the bag of fluids to sway on its stand. 'My baby,' she whispered. 'My baby's gone.'

She gave way to huge racking sobs as Graham enveloped her in his arms. He rocked her back and forth. 'That's right, let it all out.'

She could hardly form the words. 'Was it a boy or a girl?'

'A beautiful baby girl, Tina. A perfect bundle of loveliness.'

Tina pulled back to look at him more closely. 'You've seen her?'

'Yes, I was here with you the whole time. Well, not for the actual birth, I waited in the corridor then, but they let me see her afterwards.'

Tina propped herself up on her elbows. 'I want to see her.' Her voice was surprisingly calm.

Graham hesitated only for a second. 'Of course, I'll fetch a nurse.'

As Tina gazed down on her newly delivered daughter, she marvelled at how perfect she was. Her eyes were closed, and her long dark eyelashes swept across her cheeks. She looked as though she was asleep, like she would open her eyes any second and gaze adoringly at her mother.

'Are you sure she's...'

Graham removed his head from his hands. 'She didn't stand a chance, Tina. That bastard hit you with so much force, you suffered something called a placental abruption. You've lost a lot of blood. It's a wonder you didn't die as well.'

Tina squeezed her eyes closed. 'I wish I had.' She hugged her daughter closer to her chest. 'This is all my fault... I shouldn't have gone back to him. You and Linda told me I was mad, but I wouldn't listen. Now my baby has paid the ultimate price. I'll never forgive myself for this.'

Graham squeezed a clump of bedclothes in his fist. 'There is only one person to blame here, Tina, and it's not you.'

'Katy,' whispered Tina.

'Sorry?'

'I'm going to call her Katy.' She managed a weak smile.

'That's a lovely name.' Graham took out his handkerchief and blew his nose noisily.

Tina cradled her baby and sang to her softly, gently rocking her in time to the words:

Sleep my child and peace attend thee
All through the night
Guardian and God will send thee
All through the night

She smiled and traced her hand round the infant's face, then turned to Graham, who was watching from a chair nearby. 'Can you get the nurse to take her now?'

He jumped up. 'If you're sure.'

He rang the bell, and a few moments later a nurse appeared. Tina adjusted Katy's pink blanket so that it fitted snugly round her little face. 'I don't want her to get cold,' she said firmly. She gazed down at her perfect baby and kissed her on the forehead. 'Goodbye, my little angel. I'll never forget you. Sleep tight.' Then she handed her baby over for the last time.

It was past midnight when Tina woke from a fitful sleep. Graham was slumped in the chair beside her, snoring gently. Tina looked at him fondly and smiled. There were some decent men out there. Her thoughts turned to Rick and she felt the bile rising. Her heart began to quicken and she wished she had more energy to give way to her feelings of anger, but the trauma of her daughter's still-birth had sapped her of all her strength. Graham had tried to telephone Rick at her insistence, but had received no answer. Tina thought about ringing her mother-in-law, but could not face the woman and the excuses she would no doubt try to make for her son's abominable actions. He was probably unconscious somewhere, his pickled brain unable to cope with reality. All she could remember, apart from the searing pain, was him storming out of the house clutching Billy's letter, his evil mind full of foolish thoughts, incapable of seeing the truth.

It was the early hours of the morning by the time Rick returned home. After leaving Gillbent Road, he had gone to the nearest pub to try and gather his thoughts. He had made a complete fool of himself, and when he read Billy's letter again, this time calmly and thoroughly, he realised what an irrational idiot he had been. The problem was, he loved Tina so much and was terrified of losing her to another man. His jealousy had now turned to

231

paranoia of epic proportions. Not only was Tina incredibly beautiful, but she was also kind and caring, and her quiet intelligence stunned him at times. He knew he was not the best husband in the world. His behaviour could be erratic and his lack of judgement sometimes bordered on lunacy, but he loved her intensely.

He sank another pint and staggered to his feet. He had made his mind up. He would make Tina proud to call him her husband. He knew he had let her down too often, but he was determined to make amends. They would be wonderful, doting parents to their child, who would want for nothing, and their little family unit would be unbreakable.

As he put the key into the lock of his own front door, he noticed the old pram on the doorstep and stopped. He couldn't remember seeing it when he had stormed out earlier. He tiptoed down the hall quietly so as not to wake Tina. He badly needed a drink of water. The long walk home might have sobered him up somewhat, but now he was parched. He switched the light on in the kitchen and ran the tap for a few seconds to allow the cold water to come through. He gulped down two glasses and then stopped as he felt something crunch under his feet. He bent down and examined the shards of glass. Frowning, he stood up and registered the broken window in the back door.

'What the...?' His heart was pounding, and despite the water, his mouth was dry again. He backed away from the door, fear rising like mercury through his body. Slowly he turned round and surveyed the kitchen. Something did not feel right. An icy river of sweat trickled down his spine and his heart thumped wildly against his ribcage.

And then he saw it. He backed away in a panic and leant against the sink. He covered his face with his hands and rubbed his eyes fiercely, then forced himself to look again. It was still there, as he'd known it would be. The dark red stain on the floor that couldn't be anything other than his wife's blood. He turned and retched into the sink.

After confirming that their bed was empty, Rick returned to the kitchen and pulled out a chair. He rested his head on the table and closed his eyes. His breathing became shallower, then suddenly his body jerked and he was alert again. He stood up and searched around for a pen. He found one by the phone in the hall, then felt in his trouser pocket and pulled out Billy's crumpled letter. With shaking hands he smoothed it out, turned it over and wrote one word: *Sorry.*

He cut a forlorn figure as he made his way out of his marital home for the last time. He knew with absolute certainty that Tina would never forgive him. He neither expected nor wanted her forgiveness. As he shuffled his way down the street, he was finally giving her what she deserved. He was setting her free.

25

Tina sat on the edge of the hospital bed and swung her legs absently. She had been in the hospital for almost a week now and there had still been no word on Rick. Graham had been back to their house on a couple of occasions, primarily to clear up the kitchen and get rid of the two prams, but Rick was nowhere to be seen. In the end Tina had telephoned Molly, but she had not heard from him either. She was devastated to hear of the loss of her grandchild and frantic with worry that Rick seemed to have disappeared.

'My Ricky would have made a wonderful father,' she sobbed.

There was a hesitant knock at the door and Graham bobbed his head round.

'Are you ready, love?'

Tina slid off the bed and picked up her little bag. She swayed slightly and Graham caught her at the elbow. 'Easy now. Look, I've brought your coat. It's freezing out.'

Tina took the heavy winter coat and pulled it on. She realised there was something different but could not work out what it was. Then it dawned on her. She could fasten all the buttons. The last time she had worn it she had been nearly nine months pregnant. Her bottom lip trembled and she bit down on it firmly.

'Are you OK?' Graham asked.

'What do you think?' she responded wearily.

'I'm sorry, stupid question.'

'No, *I'm* sorry, Graham, but please don't keep asking how I am.'

'Sure,' said Graham. 'Look, why don't you come back and stay with me and Sheila? I don't like to think of you in that house on your own. And what if *he* comes back?'

'So what if he does. I need to see him. There are things we need to sort out.'

'I can do that for you. You don't ever have to set eyes on him again. After what he's done.'

Tina held up her hand. 'There's something I have to say to him, Graham. Something I should have said a long time ago.'

Her tone told him there was no point in arguing further.

When they arrived home, Tina was taken aback at how cosy the place looked. Graham had cleaned the house from top to bottom and had even erected a small Christmas tree in the lounge. She slumped down on the settee and struggled to take off her boots.

'Here, let me,' said Graham. He tugged them off and set them on the floor at Tina's feet. 'Cup of tea?'

'Lovely, thanks.'

A few minutes later, Graham returned with the tea tray and something else. 'I found this.' He handed her Billy's letter.

Tina took it and observed its crumpled state. As she smoothed it out, she noticed it. One word. One word in his childish scrawl was all he thought she deserved.

She stared at the word and it was a long time before she spoke. 'He's been back,' she said simply.

Graham and Tina sat together on the settee, the silence between them comforting rather than awkward. He chewed the end of his pen whilst he pondered over a crossword clue, and she flicked absently through *Woman's Weekly*. There were recipes for star-shaped Christmas biscuits, instructions on how to make your own crackers from the inside of a toilet roll and suggestions for last-minute stocking-fillers. She let the magazine slide to the floor. As far as she was concerned, Christmas was cancelled and a magazine full of festive cheer was not going to change that. It was good of Graham to put up the tree, and she knew he had meant well, but she just wanted to tear it down and crush the cheap little baubles beneath her feet. She suddenly wanted to be alone.

She turned to face Graham. 'Don't you think you should be getting back to Sheila?' The Christmas tree lights twinkled and the electric fire was glowing with heat. 'I'm fine here now, honestly. You have been a wonderful friend to me, Graham, you really have, but you have your own life to be getting on with. You have to go back sometime.'

'You've been through a lot, Tina. I just want to make sure you're all right. I know I'm an old fusspot, but I'm worried that Rick will come back.'

'He won't. He's lying low for a while, I'm sure. Too ashamed to come crawling back.'

They both froze as the doorbell rang out loudly. They stared at each other, neither one daring to move. Tina was the first to react. 'I'll get it.' She began to struggle to her feet.

'Oh no you don't,' said Graham, gently pushing her back down again.

At the front door, he peered through the window, but the frosted glass made it impossible to see who was there. He put the chain on and eased the door open a little.

A rather striking red-haired girl was standing there holding a casserole dish wrapped in a checked tea towel.

'Oh, hi. I'm here to see Tina.'

She looked friendly enough, so Graham took off the chain and beckoned her in. 'And you are?'

'Linda. Linda from work. Is she in?'

She peeped round the lounge door as Tina looked up. 'Linda! Oh my God, come in. Thanks for coming.'

The two women embraced affectionately, then Linda took hold of both Tina's hands and scrutinised her. 'How are you feeling? I know it's a daft question, but I don't know what else to say. I'm hopeless in situations like this.'

Tina smiled. 'You don't need to say anything. Just being here is enough.'

Graham cleared his throat. 'What do you want me to do with this?' He was standing there awkwardly holding the casserole dish.

'Oh, just put it in the kitchen for now, please,' instructed Linda. She turned to Tina. 'I've made a luxury fish pie for our tea.' She fished around in her handbag and pulled out a bottle of Blue Nun. 'And stick this in the fridge, would you?'

Tina was impressed. 'You've made a fish pie?'

'*Luxury* fish pie,' Linda corrected.

'What's luxurious about it?'

'It's got prawns in.'

Tina laughed for the first time in what seemed an eternity.

Graham came back into the room. 'Look, you two must have loads to catch up on. I'll get going now.' He turned to leave.

'Wait,' Tina said. She wrapped her arms around him and laid her head against his chest. 'You know I couldn't have got through this without you.'

Graham bent and kissed the top of her head.

'I'm always here for you, Tina. Call me if you need anything, anything at all.'

She looked at him gratefully. 'Thanks, I will.'

After the luxury fish pie and half a bottle of wine, Tina felt more relaxed than she had for a good while. She tucked her legs underneath her and hugged a furry cushion to her chest. Linda was always such a good tonic and was guaranteed to lift her spirits. They had just had time to heat up the pie before the power was cut again, so now they sat in the lounge by candlelight.

'Where do you think he is?' ventured Linda.

Tina swirled the wine around her glass. 'I honestly have no idea. He doesn't really have any close friends and his mother hasn't heard from him. Probably lurching from pub to pub in a drunken haze.' She hesitated for a second before adding, 'Thanks.'

'For what?' asked Linda.

'For not saying "I told you so".'

'Well I won't deny I haven't *thought* it, but it's

238

the last thing you need to hear right now.'

For the second time that evening, Tina jumped as the doorbell broke the silence.

'Who's that now?' asked Linda. She noticed Tina getting to her feet. 'No, I'll go.'

A few seconds later, she reappeared accompanied by two uniformed police officers. Tina felt her scalp prickle as she stood to greet them.

'Mrs Craig?' one of them asked nervously.

'Yes, that's me. What can I do for you?' She fought to keep her voice steady.

The other policeman took over. 'It's bad news, I'm afraid. Your husband, Richard Craig, has been found... Well, he's been found dead.'

Even in her shock, Tina felt sorry for the young officer having to impart this news. 'Dead?'

'Yes. I'm really sorry, Mrs Craig.'

'Dead?' Tina repeated. 'I mean, how? Where?' Linda put her arm around her.

The policeman cleared his throat and looked down at his notebook. 'He was found by a man walking his dog along the towpath at the side of the Ship Canal.'

Tina clung to Linda for support as she felt her knees weaken.

'I don't understand. How can he be dead?'

The two policemen looked at each other, and then the first officer spoke again. 'There will have to be a post-mortem, of course, but early indications are that he choked on his own vomit.'

Tina gave a half-laugh. 'Drunk, you mean? He was found dead beside the canal because he was drunk?'

The policeman exchanged an awkward glance

with his colleague. 'Well, nobody's saying that at this stage.'

Once the police officers had left, Linda took charge. 'Let's get you a glass of whisky. You've had a nasty shock.'

The irony was not lost on Tina. In a daze, she took the glass and brought it to her lips. The smell, of the liquor brought back so many painful memories.

'I feel cheated, Linda. I desperately wanted to see him again. I *needed* to see him, and now he's had the last word and I never got the chance to tell him how much–'

She threw the glass of whisky into the sink, where it shattered, causing Linda to jump back in alarm. Tina was sobbing now, her whole body heaving as she slid down the wall and on to the floor. She gritted her teeth as she spat out the words. 'And I never got the chance to tell him how much I *hate* him!'

PART TWO

PART TWO

26

William Lane straightened up and placed his hands in the small of his back. After a couple of deep breaths, he wiped his beaded brow with his forearm and took a long swig from his water bottle. In spite of the hard work, it was his favourite time of year. The harvesting of the sap from his sugar maples began in late February and ended roughly six weeks later as he collected the last of the buckets that had been strapped to the trees. The sticky amber liquid would now be boiled away until all that remained was the thick, rich syrup that his fellow Americans loved to pour over their breakfast pancakes.

He could hear his father splitting logs over in the garage and he felt a sudden rush of affection for the old man, accompanied by a good dollop of guilt for what he was about to do to his parents. They both worked so hard to provide a comfortable living for them all, and while their lifestyle was homely and relaxed, for all the hours they put in they deserved a greater reward. They would disagree, of course. His mother loved running the guest house; she thrived on meeting people and treated their paying guests more like members of her own family.

William heaved the last bucket into the sugar

shack. The fire-heated boiler was searingly hot now and the sugar sap was boiling away, reducing nicely. Once it had all been bottled and labelled with their own brand, Lane's Maple Syrup, he knew that the time would be right. At least that was what his head told him. His heart was another matter.

A month later, with the late April sunshine warming up the soil and the maple syrup bottled and distributed, William sat on his suitcase and bounced up and down as he grappled with the buckles. Once the case had surrendered and was securely fastened, he swung it from his bed and placed it by the door. He patted his jacket pocket and felt the reassuring bulk of his passport and plane ticket. His mother's warm voice floated up the stairs.

'Will, honey. You must have some breakfast before you go. I've made blueberry pancakes. Come and eat them while they're still hot.'

As he dragged his suitcase down the stairs, his heart was heavy with anguish. He had waited for this day for a lifetime, and now it felt like a betrayal of his mother's love. His parents had nurtured him for the past thirty-one years, and now he was kicking them in the teeth. They deserved better.

The smell of the fluffy pancakes flooded his nostrils as he entered the kitchen. His mother smiled, wiping her hands on her apron.

'There you are. Come on and sit down, I'm just about to dish up.'

William pulled out a chair and slumped down. He rested his head in his hands and hunched his shoulders like an old man. His mother laid her arm across his back and then ruffled his hair as though he were a nine-year-old.

'Come on, Will. You've waited a long time for this day.' She managed to keep her voice steady.

William looked up and met her eyes, his own moist with tears that threatened to spill over at the slightest kind word from her. He cleared his throat.

'I feel like I'm betraying you. You and Dad.'

His mother sat down beside him. 'We've been through all this. Your father and I support you fully. We will always be your parents and will always love you. You are our precious son and it pains me to see you struggling for inner peace.' She patted the back of his hand. 'I just pray you find it.'

A sudden gust of wind nearly took the back door off its hinges as Donald Lane stomped into the kitchen, a rifle slung over his shoulder, a couple of dead rabbits in his free hand.

'Morning, son. How you doin' today?' Even with his New York drawl, his father struggled to make the question sound casual.

'OK, I guess.'

'What time's your flight from Idlewild?'

William shook his head and managed a smile. 'It's JFK, Dad. It's been JFK for the past eleven years.'

Donald grunted and laid his rifle on the table. 'Same thing.'

'The flight's not until this evening, but I'm setting off shortly. Dirk's giving me a lift. We've got a few hours on the road and I want to arrive in plenty of time.'

Donald turned to his wife. 'Coffee on, Martha?'

William had known from an early age that he was adopted. During his idyllic childhood in New England, however, the fact had never been relevant. His adoptive mother and father were the kindest, most honest, God-fearing people you could wish to meet, and the fact that they had never been blessed with children of their own made William question the very existence of the God they worshipped so dutifully. If anyone had been born to be a mother it was Martha Lane.

The first three years of his life had been spent with his natural mother in a convent in southern Ireland, where he had been born. He had always been aware of this fact – his adoptive parents had made no secret of it – but he could not remember much about his 'real' mother or the place he had lived as a toddler. When he was around ten years old and they had moved into the farmhouse in Vermont, his mother was down on her hands and knees scrubbing the wooden floor with Sunlight soap when William walked in. From behind, the hunched figure clad in a grubby apron and with a scarf wrapped around her head could have been anyone, and for a minute William was confused. Then the smell of the soap wafted over, filling his nostrils and stunning him into inertia. He was rooted to the spot. The lemony smell had transported him back to his beginnings with a jolt. He could suddenly visualise a long corridor filled with young girls scrubbing the floor until it shone like a mirror. He had quietly backed out of the room without a word.

On another occasion, some years later, his then-girlfriend, Jenna, a girl not known for her culinary skills, had cooked him a romantic meal. He'd forked through the mound of greying mashed potato, complete with hard lumps where she had missed with the masher, then put his cutlery down and stared out of the window.

'Is everything all right, Will?' Jenna had asked.

'Pandy,' replied William. 'This is pandy.'

Jenna looked affronted. 'That doesn't sound like a compliment.'

'No, it's not an insult, sorry. I mean, that's what we used to call this. I remember my mother feeding it to me.' He squeezed his eyes shut and rubbed his temples as he tried to conjure up a more detailed image. It was no good. However hard he tried, his mother's face was always featureless, but what memory he had of her was one of tenderness and devotion.

Now he stood with his parents on the porch of the farmhouse and prepared to say goodbye.

Martha Lane clutched a pretty floral handkerchief in her hand and dabbed at her eyes. Donald Lane embraced his son in a bear hug that William returned with deep affection. Then he pulled away and looked his father in the eye.

'Thanks for letting me do this, Dad. I know how hard it must be for you and Mom. I just want you to know that I love you both so much. You will always be my mom and dad and I'm grateful for everything you have given me. I'm not looking for a new mom; I just need to know where I came from and what led to me being born in those circumstances.'

He took hold of his mother's hand and kissed her on the cheek.

'You come back real soon, son. We'll miss you.' Martha turned quickly on her heel and went back into the house.

'Dad?'

'Don't worry, son. She'll be fine. You just make sure you come back safely, that's all. And if you do find your other mom, you tell her thanks.'

William raised his eyebrows. 'For what?'

Donald sniffed loudly. 'For giving us the most precious gift of all. A boy to be proud of. A boy who has made our lives complete.'

'I will, Dad, thanks. And look after Mom.'

Some hours later, as William settled himself into his seat for the long transatlantic flight, he took out the piece of paper his mother had given him. He already knew all the details by heart, but he read them again anyway, running his fingers over the words. His birth mother's name was Bronagh Skinner and he had been born in St Bridget's Sacred Heart Convent, near Tipperary Town, on 10 April 1940. She had been twenty years old when she had given birth to him, which would make her fifty-four now. He folded the paper in half and slipped it into his jacket pocket. As he stared out of the window at the disappearing New York skyline, he felt a flutter of excitement mixed with apprehension. For better or worse, he was about to uncover his roots.

27

It took William a few moments to register where he was. His body clock was all over the place and he had slept in for longer than he meant to. He threw off the thick eiderdown and padded into the bathroom. His appearance shocked him momentarily: heavily lidded eyes, dark circles beneath, and his hair looking as though it had never been acquainted with a comb. He splashed his face with cold water and wandered over to the window. Below him lay Tipperary Town, with its brightly coloured facades and where, according to his guidebook, a warm welcome was assured. He had certainly been given a warm welcome by his landlady. His mother would have been impressed.

He looked around the bedroom and nodded his approval. It was newly decorated, and the smell of paint still lingered in spite of the huge jar of fresh flowers Mrs Flanagan had positioned on the dressing table. He was startled by a knock on the bedroom door. He grabbed a towel to cover his modesty and inched the door open.

'Ah, sorry to disturb you, Mr Lane, but I was wondering if you'll be wanting any breakfast. I usually stop serving at ten, but I understand you must be tired after all the travelling.' Her soft Irish accent brimmed with kindness.

'Oh, Mrs Flanagan. Yes please. I'm so sorry. What time is it?'

'Well, let's see now.' She pushed up the sleeve of her blouse and squinted at her watch. 'Well, it's quarter to now.'

'Ten?'

'Er, no, a quarter to eleven.'

'Oh my gosh, it's later than I thought. I wouldn't want to put you to any trouble, but I am suddenly ravenous.'

Mrs Flanagan's ruddy face broke into a wide smile. 'That's settled then. It'll be on the table in fifteen minutes.'

The dining room was small but homely. The carpet sported a busy pattern and all the furniture was dark mahogany and seemed to crowd the room. William thought it was a shame to have net curtains on the windows, which blocked out the view of the pretty town. He sipped at the cup of coffee Mrs Flanagan had set before him, then pulled out a map and laid it on the table. Mrs Flanagan bustled in with his breakfast.

'This will set you up for the rest of day.'

William immediately started to salivate. There were thick, juicy sausages, grilled tomatoes, black pudding, two fried eggs and a couple of home-made potato cakes.

'This is a feast, Mrs Flanagan, thank you.'

'Ah, go on with yer. You're very welcome.' She beamed as she backed out of the room, leaving William to devour his breakfast.

Ten minutes later she was back, enquiring whether he would like any more. William sat back and rubbed his belly.

'Mrs Flanagan, that was truly wonderful,

ma'am. I could not eat another thing.'

'Well if you're sure. I don't want any of my guests going hungry, especially when they have travelled so far to see us.'

'I don't think I'll need to eat for the rest of the day.'

Mrs Flanagan laughed as she cleared the plate away. 'Tell me, is this your first time in Ireland?'

William hesitated before answering. He didn't feel ready to start talking about his past, especially with a complete stranger. Mrs Flanagan was hovering, waiting for an answer to a question she had not thought was particularly difficult.

'Er, well no, since you ask. I've lived in America with my adoptive parents most of my life but I was born here.'

'Well now, would you believe it? Born here in Tipperary Town?'

'Not far away, I believe. In a convent.'

Mrs Flanagan's face clouded and she hurriedly stacked the rest of the dishes without meeting his eye. 'Well, you would never know it from your accent.'

William decided to press on. 'St Bridget's Sacred Heart. Do you know it?'

Mrs Flanagan met his gaze and narrowed her eyes. 'Why, to be sure I do. My friend who runs the Cross Keys Hotel in town sends all her laundry there – bedding, tablecloths, that sort of thing.'

William frowned. 'Your friend sends laundry to a convent?'

Mrs Flanagan set down the dishes and lowered herself into the chair opposite William.

'How much do you know about your birth

251

mother?' He shrugged. 'Not a lot. Just her name.'

'And you plan to visit the convent?'

'Yes, of course. That's the whole purpose of my trip.'

Mrs Flanagan shuffled uncomfortably. 'Don't expect too much, will you? I mean, there will be a very good reason why your mother was sent to the convent in the first place.'

'What makes you think she was *sent* there?'

Mrs Flanagan scoffed. 'Believe me, Mr Lane, no girl in their right mind would enter that establishment voluntarily.'

William's brow furrowed as she continued.

'Look, how can I put this? That place is full of girls who have brought shame on their families, moral degenerates if you like. To get yourself pregnant out of wedlock is a sin indeed, but the nuns make sure that the girls' souls are cleansed and that the stain is washed away through hard work. They give them a home when their own families want nothing more to do with them, and in return the girls earn their keep by doing the laundry, growing vegetables and making rosary beads.'

'But they are free to leave when they choose, are they not?'

Mrs Flanagan shrugged. 'Well, I suppose so. Look, that's all I know. I'm just saying it's a blessing that the sisters are there for these girls when even their own families disown them.'

William rubbed his chin. 'So let me get this right. Are you saying my mother must have been rejected by her family?'

Mrs Flanagan stood up. 'I'm not saying anything. I've just given you a view of things. Each

252

girl's case is different. Try not to get your hopes up. The sisters will not be forthcoming with information. It's very much a closed shop, that place.'

William stood up too and gathered his map. 'Well, would you be so kind as to give me directions so that I can at least see for myself?'

'Of course, no trouble at all.' She pulled a pen out of the pocket of her apron. 'Will I write on the back of this map?'

The bus journey had taken over thirty minutes, and by the time William alighted, he was the only passenger left. The driver pointed up the road. 'This is as far as I go. You need to walk up that way for about a mile and a half and it'll be there on your left. You can't miss it.'

William nodded his thanks and jumped off on to the grass verge. The doors closed with a loud hiss, and he was suddenly all alone in the peaceful countryside. The day had warmed up and the sun shafted through the trees. The fields were full of sheep, and it was so quiet he could hear them munching on the grass, the sound only broken by the lambs bleating as they gambolled around with each other.

He heaved his rucksack over his shoulder. Mrs Flanagan had insisted on giving him a flask of coffee and a huge slab of her famous porter cake, crammed with dried fruit and moistened with Guinness. After a short while, he stopped to take off his jumper and roll up the sleeves of his thick checked shirt. He removed his baseball cap and ran his fingers through his sweat-drenched hair.

He was sure his guidebook had promised cool temperatures accompanied by varying amounts of rain. He shivered involuntarily as his rucksack pressed against the clammy wetness of his shirt, but his pace quickened at the thought of his destination, now only a few hundred yards away.

As he rounded the next bend, he caught a glimpse of the convent that had been his home for the first three years of his life. He stopped in his tracks and breathed deeply, placing his hands on a nearby tree for support. He had expected to remember the building, but he had no recollection of it whatsoever. He inched forward until eventually he was standing right outside the front gates. There was a long driveway leading up to the main door, but the gates were locked and he could not see a way in. He walked round the perimeter and eventually found himself at the rear of the property. The back yard was completely surrounded by thick walls, at least twenty feet high and topped with shards of broken glass. *They take security very seriously here*, thought William. *Anybody would have a job breaking in.*

Or indeed, breaking out, he mused grimly.

He walked back round to the main gates and peered through the railings. From what he could make out, the convent was imposing indeed. A huge grey double-fronted property with stone steps climbing up to the black-painted front door. Dark green ivy snaked its way up the masonry, and there was a beautifully kept white marble statue just to the left of the door.

William sat down on the grass verge in frustration. He had travelled three thousand miles, and now that he was here, there seemed to be no way in. He pulled out Mrs Flanagan's fruit cake and unwrapped it from its greaseproof paper. His mouth watered as he took his first bite. The fruit was plump and juicy and his taste buds revelled in the richness of the Guinness. He poured himself a cup of coffee and pulled out his map. There was a tiny village, more of a hamlet really, around the bend, and he was just contemplating walking there when he became aware of the faint rumbling of a car engine and a van approached along the road. He waved his arms in order to attract the driver's attention, and he duly slowed down and leaned out of his window.

'What can I do for yer?'

William hurriedly folded his map and approached the man.

'Are you going to the convent?'

'I certainly am, yes.'

'Oh, that's grand. I'm trying to get in but can't seem to open the gates.'

The van driver laughed. 'This place doesn't accept casual visitors, son. Do you have business here?'

'Yes, you could say that.'

'The nuns are expecting you then?'

'Not exactly, no.' William scuffed the ground with his boot. 'Look, I've come a long way and I just need to get inside and have a chat with whoever's in charge.'

'The mother superior? You'll be lucky.' The driver nodded his head towards the driveway. 'Here comes one of them now. She's going to let me in. They need to be expecting you, see.'

William stared at the elderly nun as she made her way down the driveway. Her black habit brushed the gravel and she glided along as though on casters.

The van driver groaned. 'It's Sister Mary. You'll get nowhere with her. Look, jump in the back with the laundry and I'll take you to the front door. Keep me out of it, though.'

William smiled gratefully. He wrenched open the back doors of the van and climbed in amongst the piles of dirty bed linen. As he waited for the van to move forward, he lay back on the sheets and laughed to himself. He felt like a fugitive, but at least he was one step closer to finding his mother.

28

William waited until the van had come to a complete stop. He could feel it rocking as the driver climbed out, could hear muffled voices in conversation, then suddenly the back doors were flung open and bright sunshine flooded the van. He came out squinting.

'Coast is clear now. Quick, jump out and go round to the front door. When they ask how you got in, just say you happened to arrive at the same time as the laundry van. Tell them you walked up the front drive bold as brass. They'll never believe you, of course, but at least you're in.'

William grabbed his rucksack and jumped out. He held out his hand to the driver. 'Thanks a lot, buddy, I owe you one.'

The driver gripped his hand and winked. 'I hope you find what you're looking for.'

William climbed the stone steps to the heavy front door and, noting the absence of a bell, rapped firmly with his knuckles. The wood was hard and unforgiving and he winced as he massaged his hand. He pulled himself up to his full height as the door opened.

'Good afternoon,' he began. 'I was wondering if I might come in and have a word with the person in charge.'

The nun who had answered the door raised her eyebrows.

'Do you have an appointment?'

'Well, no, but I've come–'

He was unable to finish his sentence as the door was abruptly slammed in his face. He stood there open-mouthed for a second before the blood began to course through his veins and he felt a sudden rush of anger. He clenched his fists and breathed deeply through his nose. Ignoring his sore hand, he rapped on the door again, and continued to rap until it was once again opened by the same nun. Her forehead wrinkled as she glared at him.

'How rude! As I was just saying, I would like to speak to the person in charge. I've come a long way and will not be leaving until I have seen somebody who can help me with my enquiry. So if you don't mind, could you please fetch someone in authority before I camp out on your doorstep. And don't think I won't. I've got a flask, cake and all the time in the world.'

Without a word, the nun began to close the door again, but William was too quick for her and he jammed his heavily booted foot in the doorway.

'Take your foot out of the way!' spat the nun.

'Not a chance,' replied William as he pushed past her and found himself standing in the hallway. He was immediately hit by the familiar lemony smell. He glanced around, taking in his surroundings, and noticed a group of girls at the end of the corridor. They were all dressed in the same shapeless brown pinafore dresses and on their feet they wore what looked like old rags. William frowned, then realised that they were using them to polish the floor. One girl, with a shaven head, turned to face him. He noticed the huge swell of her belly and glanced away in embarrassment, but not before he saw her smiling coyly.

'Bernadette, turn your eyes away, you disgusting little temptress,' berated the nun who was overseeing the group. 'Have you not learnt anything? Look at the state of you. I fear for your soul, girl, I really do.'

William cleared his throat uncomfortably and turned to the nun who was still standing beside him. She had now closed the door, and he became aware of the stifling atmosphere of the convent.

'We don't take kindly to intruders. Wait here while I go and see Sister Benedicta.'

William bowed his head respectfully. 'Thank you, ma'am, but I prefer to think of myself as a visitor rather than an intruder if it's all the same.'

As he waited patiently, the group of girls shuffled off and the hall fell eerily quiet. William jumped at the sound of a voice.

'I'm Sister Benedicta. How may I help you?'

She was a tall woman, with a ruddy complexion and piercing blue eyes. Her mouth was already set into a grim line of determination.

'Good afternoon. My name is William Lane, and you might say I have come home. I was born here.'

If the nun was surprised by this statement, she did not show it.

'I repeat. How may I help you?'

William was taken aback. 'Are you in charge here?'

She nodded her head slowly. 'Indeed I am.'

William pressed on. 'Look, Sister Benedicta, I don't want to cause any trouble. I've just come to see if you can help me trace my mother. I know she was an inmate here–'

'Resident,' interrupted Sister Benedicta. 'Not inmate.'

William bowed his head. 'Of course, I'm sorry. I know she was a resident here. I was born in April 1940. I assume you keep records, so any information you can give me would be greatly appreciated.'

Sister Benedicta's lips eased into a sly smile. 'Your naivety is breathtaking, Mr Lane. Come this way, would you?'

William followed in her wake as she led him to her office. In the centre of the room was a large mahogany desk covered in stacks of paper of varying heights. A plaque on the wall read: *When lust hath conceived, it bringeth forth sin. James 1:15.*

Sister Benedicta gestured towards a chair opposite the desk and they both sat down. She propped her elbows on the desk and leaned in towards William.

'Tell me, Mr Lane. Do you love your parents?'

William was indignant. 'Why, of course, more than anything!'

'And they have given you a good home, have they not? Nurtured you?'

He shuffled in his seat. 'That is not in question, nor is it the point. I have their full blessing in my search for my real mother.'

'Your real mother is the woman who brought you up, the one who picked you up when you fell over, the one who comforted you in the night when you had had a bad dream, the one who–'

William held his hand up. 'Point taken, Sister. What I mean is, I have their full blessing in my search for my *birth* mother. Is that better?'

'I don't care for your tone, Mr Lane. I don't think you appreciate the work we do here. All the girls who pass through this convent are fallen women, moral degenerates who have been shunned by society and rejected by their own families, to whom they have brought nothing but shame. We give them a home, look after them throughout their pregnancies and then ensure that their babies are given to loving homes. We make certain that through hard work, their souls are cleansed. These girls know they will be damned to hell if they tell anyone they have had a baby, so I can assure you, Mr Lane, that no good can come of this search of yours. I suggest you leave right now, and then get down on your bended knees and thank the good Lord that this convent had your best interests at heart when it placed you in such a kind and loving home.'

William felt like a naughty schoolboy sitting in the headmaster's office, a feeling that intensified when he spotted the thin cane hanging on the wall behind Sister Benedicta. He wondered if this had ever been used on his own mother, and he struggled to keep his rage under control.

'Sister Benedicta, your work here is not in question, and of course I am grateful for the upbringing I have had, but I spent the first three years of my life here. I even have flashbacks to my time here and to my mother, but I can never see her face. I feel as though a piece of my life is missing, and because of that I can't find peace. What difference does it make to you? Please just give me any information you have about my mother and I'll be on my way. I won't bother you again.'

Sister Benedicta sighed and shook her head. 'It's like you haven't heard a word I've said.' She stood up and walked over to a large filing cabinet. Using a key that she wore on a chain round her neck, she unlocked it and pulled out a huge leather binder. She slammed the file down on the desk, causing a sheaf of papers to flutter to the floor.

'What was your mother's name?'

William's heart gave a little leap of hope and his mouth was suddenly dry. 'Bronagh Skinner.'

'And you were born in 1940, you say?'

He nodded and rubbed his sweating palms down his trouser legs.

Sister Benedicta flicked through the ledger for what seemed like an eternity. There were literally hundreds of names listed, and it gave William some comfort that he was not the only one in this position. Presently she picked up her fountain pen and wrote down a number on a piece of paper. She stood up and heaved the ledger back into the filing cabinet. Then with an exaggerated movement, she locked it again and stared William in the eye as she hung the key round her neck.

'Wait here,' she commanded as she left the room.

Fifteen minutes passed, and still there was no sign of Sister Benedicta. William stood up, and paced the room. He went over to the window and stared out at the garden below. Several girls, all heavily pregnant, were digging over a vegetable patch as a nun watched on carefully. One girl stumbled and fell to her knees. She seemed to have trouble standing again and another girl offered her hand to help her up. The presiding nun immediately interjected and pushed the two girls apart. William could not hear the conversation through the glass, but he saw the girl who had stumbled cowering from the nun as she raised her hand. He was left in no doubt that this girl was used to being beaten.

The door to the office opened again. A middle-aged woman in a nurse's uniform looked at him and raised her eyebrows.

'Oh, I was looking for Sister Benedicta.'

'She's just stepped out for a while. She's gone to find some information for me.'

'Oh, I see.'

'What is it, Nurse?' Sister Benedicta had returned, a thin brown file tucked under her arm.

'I need a word, Sister.' She nodded towards

William. 'In private.'

Sister Benedicta did not hide her impatience. 'Can't it wait?'

'Not really. It won't take a minute.'

Sister Benedicta ushered the nurse into the corridor and closed the door. Intrigued, William crossed the room and pressed his ear to the wood. The two women were talking in hushed, urgent tones, but he could just make out the conversation.

'It's Colette, Sister. I've just delivered her, but she's torn really badly. She desperately needs stitching.'

'You know the rules, Nurse. No stitching. If she's torn, then it is God's will. She will atone for her sins. She should have thought about that before she got herself into this situation.'

'Sister! You know she was raped.'

'We only have her word for that. She's a temptress, Nurse. She has brought this on herself. Now stop wasting my time. I have business to attend to.'

William took two huge strides back into the middle of the room as he heard the door opening again and adopted a casual air. Sister Benedicta frowned at him and pointed to the chair. 'Sit.'

She took her place opposite him and opened the file. Perching a pair of reading glasses on the end of her nose, she began to leaf through the papers. William craned to see, but the desk was so wide it was impossible to make out anything other than a number: 40/65. Eventually Sister Benedicta found what she was looking for and pulled out a piece of yellowing notepaper.

'See the signature at the bottom?'

William leaned across and caught a glimpse of a name written in a rather childlike hand: Bronagh Skinner. He reached out to take the letter, but Sister Benedicta whipped it away before he could touch it. 'Your mother signed away all rights to you the day you left this convent. You are never to have contact with her and she has vowed in this letter never to contact you, interfere with you or make any claim over you in the future. We will never divulge her whereabouts, Mr Lane, so I am afraid you have had a wasted journey. Now if you don't mind, I have work to do.'

Her dismissive tone left William in no doubt that this meeting was over. He stood up and heaved his rucksack on to his shoulder. He already detested this woman and found it difficult to speak.

'I will be back, Sister. You can count on it.'

'Like I said, you're wasting your time.'

But William had got the bit between his teeth now, and nothing, especially not this vile woman, was going to keep him from finding his mother.

29

William found himself out on the narrow road again. The afternoon sun was growing weaker and the nip in the air reminded him that it was still only early April. He pulled his jumper back on and set off at a brisk, determined pace towards the bus stop. He covered the mile and a half in well under twenty minutes, such was his desperation to put distance between himself and that loathsome place. He was sweating again now, so he took off his jumper again as he studied the bus timetable, which was nailed to a post. The next bus wasn't due for another fifty minutes. He groaned and slumped down on the grass verge. He suddenly felt incredibly drained, a combination of his alter-cation with the unbending Sister Benedicta and his lingering jet lag.

Using his rucksack as a pillow, he lay back on the grass, welcoming its coolness against his per-spiring skin. It seemed like he had been asleep for hours when he was suddenly aware of a ringing sound. The sun disappeared, and behind his eyelids William felt the world become darker. He propped himself on his elbows and rubbed his eyes. It wasn't a cloud that had blocked out the sun but a human being standing astride a bicycle. He couldn't make out her features, silhouetted as she was, but he knew it was a female from the ball of curly hair that surrounded her face

'I hope I didn't startle you. I rang my bell because you seemed out for the count.'

William struggled to his feet. It was only when he was level with her face that he recognised the nurse from the convent.

'Not at all. I just thought I would grab forty winks while I waited for the bus. I hope I haven't missed it.' He rolled up his sleeve and studied his watch. He had only been asleep ten minutes.

'The bus comes at ten past the hour, so you can wait here for the ten past five or you can come back with me to my house and then catch the ten past six. That's the last one.'

William frowned. 'Come back to your house? Why would I want to do that?'

'Because you need to tell me everything you know if I am to help you find your mammy.'

Grace Quinn had been a midwife at the convent for as long as she could remember – thirty-six years to be exact – and had delivered countless babies. As William sat beside her on her lumpy floral sofa, he was mesmerised by her soft voice and her deep-set grey eyes, which she frequently cast towards the ceiling as she told her tale.

'I suppose you must be wondering how it is that I can work in such a miserable place?'

William gave a huff of agreement and blew out his cheeks. 'It didn't look like a barrel of laughs, I must admit. And that nun. She really was something else.'

Grace clasped her hands and rested them on her lap. 'I know some of their methods may seem a little unorthodox. To an outsider they may seem downright cruel, but these girls would have nowhere to go otherwise. The shame they have brought on their families is mortifying. What kind of a life would you have had if your mother had been allowed to keep you?'

William shrugged. 'I have no idea, but you've just hit the nail on the head – if she'd been allowed. She didn't have a choice, did she? I stayed with her for the first three years of my life and then I was torn away and sent to America. Don't get me wrong, I love my mom and dad, but that just seems wicked to me.'

Grace bowed her head. 'I know. That is why I am going to help you.' She stood up and shuffled over to the bureau, returning with a pen and paper. 'Now, tell me everything you know.'

William cleared his throat. 'My mother's name was Bronagh Skinner and I was born on the tenth of April 1940.'

Grace looked up from her pad, her pen poised for more. 'Is that it?'

'Oh, and she was twenty years old.'

Grace frowned. 'Not much to go on.'

William suddenly remembered the slim brown file that Sister Benedicta had brought into the room.

'Her file number is 40/65.'

Grace looked startled at this information. 'Quite the detective, aren't you? That means you were the sixty-fifth baby born in 1940.' She made a note and drew some heavy black lines underneath, as if this made the information all the more important. 'All right, is there anything you can remember about your time at the convent? Anything at all that might jog my memory?'

William stood up and paced the room. 'I can remember the smell of the soap, and the lumpy mash we were served, pandy I believe it was called.'

'Anything about your mother? I had only been at the convent for two years when you were born, and since nuns were not allowed to train as midwives prior to 1950, I would almost certainly have delivered you.'

William closed his eyes and pinched the bridge of his nose. 'There is something else.'

Grace sat forward expectantly. 'Go on.'

'Well, she used to sing to me.' He began to hum a tune. 'I can't remember the words, it's so frustrating. I can almost hear her now, but there was something different about her...'

'Different?'

'The way she spoke. She didn't sound like anybody else.'

He slumped back on the sofa and held his head in his hands. After a while he began to rock gently back and forth. *'Sleep my child and peace attend thee...'* he sang.

Grace looked up from her notes. *'All through the night.'*

William raised his head and smiled. *'Guardian angels God will send thee...'*

The two of them finished in unison: *'All through the night.'*

Grace covered William's hand with her own. 'I am kind to the girls, you know. I mean, I try to make it as comfortable as I can for them. I have dedicated my whole life to that place. Never had a husband or children of my own.'

'I just can't understand why Sister Benedicta is so obstructive. What difference does it make to her whether I trace my mother or not?'

'Penance, William. Your mother had a baby out of wedlock, and in the eyes of the Lord that's a sin, but through the hard work she endured at the laundry, the stain on her soul has been cleansed and her passage to heaven assured. I know it seems harsh but your mother signed away all claims to you. Sister Benedicta is not in a position now to divulge her whereabouts.'

'Do you really believe that my mother will be forgiven?'

Grace nodded. 'Yes I do. I believe God has the capacity to forgive any sin. She is assured of her place in heaven now.' She rubbed the back of his hand. 'You were saying your mother sounded different to the others. What do you mean by that?'

'Some words ... I don't know... She said them differently. Her vowels were flatter and–'

Grace covered her mouth with her hand. 'Sweet Jesus! I remember her now. She was English!'

William's eyes widened. 'You remember her? You mean I'm half-English?'

'If it's the girl I'm thinking of, then you're all English, William. And her name wasn't Bronagh. It was Christina.'

30

'You're a lucky boy, so you are,' began Grace, her eyes shining with excitement. 'I have to be honest with you, the chances of me remembering your mother were pretty slim, but Bronagh was difficult to forget.'

'You said her name was Christina,' William interjected.

'When girls enter the convent they are given a new name, chosen by the nuns, a more holy name if you like. St Bronagh was a sixth-century abbess, and I wouldn't mind betting that the day your mother arrived at the convent was her saint's day.

That was often how the names were decided at St Bridget's.'

Grace put her notebook down and wandered over to the bookcase. After leafing through the pages of a heavy antiquated volume, she finally found what she was looking for.

'Ah-ha!' she declared. 'St Bronagh – the second of April. That would fit in nicely. Your mother entered the convent on the second, and you were born eight days later.'

'Another piece of the jigsaw, then.' William felt excited as he pressed Grace for more information. 'You said she was difficult to forget.'

Grace sat back down next to William on the sofa and took his hand. 'That poor girl. All the girls that enter the convent have sad stories to tell, but hers really tugged at my heartstrings. She was from Manchester, I think. She had been sent to Ireland to stay with her mother's sister on her farm. We hadn't had an English girl before, or since for that matter. She wasn't Catholic either.' She attempted a smile, but it was more like a grimace. 'I kept that bit to myself, though. Anyway, her own mother was a midwife too, so she knew more than most about childbirth. She even helped me in the years following your birth. She was always so kind to the other girls, and they could relate to her.'

William shook his head. 'How did she end up at the convent if she was from England?'

'Ah,' Grace began. 'That's the sad part. A combination of a draconian father and a capitulating mother. She had a very sheltered upbringing, from what I could gather. She was forbidden from seeing unsuitable boys, or any boys for that matter, until one night she met Billy. Oh, she never stopped talking about him. It was Billy this and Billy that. She wept all the way through your birth, calling out his name and glancing at the door as if expecting him to walk through it any minute begging for her forgiveness.'

William sat with a rapt look on his face. At last his mother was emerging as a person to him and not just a name.

'What did she have to forgive him for?'

'That was the strange thing. After what he had done to her, I couldn't believe she still held a candle for him, but she said true love could endure anything. Apparently, when he found out she was pregnant, well, he panicked and disappeared. They hadn't been courting for that long, and of course her father was not at all supportive. He was a doctor, you know, a well-respected man, and his reputation was everything to him. But incredibly, she never stopped loving Billy. It's why you were given his name.'

'So she loved Billy then, but it sounds as though he didn't feel the same way. Did they ever get in contact again?'

Grace shrugged. 'I couldn't say. Bronagh left St Bridget's after three years. That's the rule, you see. You look after your babby for three years and then you're free to go. But alone, of course. No girl is ever allowed to take her little one with her. If you want to leave before that, you have to be claimed by a relative and pay a vast sum for your freedom. That sort of money is completely out of reach of the majority of girls, and of course their families

271

have disowned them anyway. Her dearest wish was to raise you herself, but she was a victim of her circumstances. All her rights had been taken away from her and she was powerless. It's not a perfect system but those were the rules at St Bridget's.'

William shuddered at the thought of this callous regime and wondered what kind of religion allowed this sort of thing to happen. His parents were both God-fearing people and he had been brought up to respect the Bible, but surely such treatment was unacceptable. He was sure his mother had had no idea of the extent of this cruelty.

'Where did she go after she left?' asked William.

'That's the part I don't know, I'm afraid. I know her aunt's farm was not far from the convent.' Grace sighed. 'All this information will be in that file, but getting my hands on it will be difficult, if not impossible.'

'Please,' implored William. 'I've come all this way and I feel so close to her now. I can't give up.' He struggled to keep the impatience out of his voice. After all, Grace did not have to help him.

Grace chewed on her bottom lip and a silence descended between them as she tried to remember the past. 'It was thirty-four years ago, William,' she said helplessly. She closed her eyes in concentration and tilted her face towards the ceiling. Suddenly the old grandfather clock struck six and they both jumped.

'The bus!' cried William, leaping to his feet. 'I'm going to miss my bus!'

'Oh my,' cried Grace. 'Where has the time gone? Look, take my bike to the bus stop. Just leave it in the hedge and I'll collect it tomorrow.'

William picked up his rucksack and threw it over his shoulder.

'I can't thank you enough, Grace.'

'Oh, be off with you now,' she laughed. 'Thank me when you've found your mother. It's my day off tomorrow, but why don't you come for tea and I'll tell you what I've managed to find out. But don't get your hopes up too much, William. You've seen how stubborn Sister Benedicta can be.'

When William arrived back at Mrs Flanagan's, he was greeted by the salty aroma of a boiled ham and his stomach suddenly complained of a hunger he had long forgotten.

'Oh, you're back then. Any good?' greeted Mrs Flanagan.

'You were right about the nuns,' he sighed. 'No help at all.' He slumped down on the sofa in the kitchen and closed his eyes.

'You look worn out. Will you have a wee nap before supper? I can keep it warm for you.'

'You are very kind, Mrs Flanagan, but I feel if I go to sleep now I shall be eating that meal for breakfast.'

'Very well, you go and wash up now and I'll put it out. It'll be ready in five minutes.'

After his meal of the boiled ham, accompanied by mashed potato with cabbage, William felt sated, but the emotions of the day had left him utterly drained. He thanked Mrs Flanagan and made his way upstairs to bed. He knew it was a mistake to lie down before he had even undressed or cleaned his teeth. He had only meant to close his eyes for five minutes, but the jet lag exerted its grip and by the time he opened his eyes again the sun was filtering through the red velvet curtains and dust particles were dancing in its rays. He rubbed his eyes and tried to open his furred-up mouth as he staggered to the bathroom in a desperate search for his toothbrush.

Arriving at Grace's house the following day, he was filled with hope and expectation. But Grace had been right to warn him not to get his hopes up. It had been impossible for her to retrieve the file without the key, the one that was guarded so closely by Sister Benedicta's bosom. They sat at the little wooden table in Grace's kitchen. Her washing hung on a line by the stove and the aroma of the apple pie that was baking in the oven suddenly reminded him of home and his mother's wonderful cooking. He felt the guilt rising again and struggled to fight against it.

'What's the matter, William?' enquired Grace.

'I was just thinking about Mom; you know, Mom in the US.'

Grace patted his hand. 'You know you have her blessing, don't you? Just because you want to know where you came from doesn't mean you love her any less. She sounds like a dear, selfless woman to me, and in that regard Sister Benedicta was right. You do have the most wonderful parents, don't you?'

William nodded his head in agreement, not trusting his voice.

'Well then,' continued Grace. 'Will you have another cup of tea while we wait for that pie?'

William smiled. 'That would be grand, Grace, thank you.'

She busied herself with filling the kettle and dropped two tea bags into the old stained pot. 'It's so frustrating. I mean to actually find the safe that contains the file but not be able to open it. I feel so helpless.'

'Please don't worry, Grace. It was good of you to try. I'm grateful I really am.'

She filled the teapot and returned it to the table. She popped on the knitted tea cosy with its blue and pink stripes and a bobble on the top, and William smiled to himself at the thought of the teapot wearing a hat. His parents would never believe it!

'Anyway, think about it. You haven't had a wasted journey, have you?'

'How do you mean?'

'Well, when you came here, all you knew was that your mother's name was Bronagh Skinner and that she was twenty years old, right?'

William narrowed his eyes. 'Go on.'

'Now you know her real name was Christina Skinner and that she was born in Manchester in 1919 or 1920.' Grace paused for William to catch up, but seeing his blank expression she pressed on. 'Don't you see? You could travel to Manchester and try and locate her birth certificate. She was already twenty years old when she entered the convent, which we know was at the beginning of April. So her date of birth must be sometime in the year before April 1920.'

Grace began to pour two cups of tea while William digested this information.

'How would that help, do you think?' His brain was still befuddled from the exertions of his travels.

'The birth certificate would tell you not only the exact date and place of birth, but the names of her parents. I'm pretty sure her mother's maiden name will be on that certificate too. I just wish *I* could remember the name of her aunt. It's so frustrating. I know she was a spinster and that she died shortly before Christina entered the convent. I also know she'd inherited the farm from her parents, so if we could get hold of the maiden name of Christina's mother, there's a chance someone might know the farm.'

William clasped his hands behind his head and leant back in his chair. 'You're a marvel, Grace.'

She flushed slightly. 'Go on with yer. You'd have worked out the same thing eventually.'

'You think there's a chance she could be back in Manchester?'

Grace shrugged. 'I don't know, William. It's possible, I suppose. I mean, she was sent here in disgrace to have the baby, but after that she was free to return. I can't imagine there was much to keep her here in Ireland, so yes, I would say it's possible that she returned to her home town.' She paused. 'Manchester is a big city; though; the chances of finding her there are slim.'

'I know. You're right, I need to find out the whereabouts of the farm first. If I can find that, then maybe somebody there will know where she went.'

Grace opened the oven door, and the aroma of cooked apples spiced with cinnamon filled the room. She placed the golden pie on the table.

'Allow me,' offered William, taking the knife and slicing into it. A plume of steam rose between them and Grace wafted it away with her hand.

'You know, Grace, I think I will take a trip to Manchester. I've come all this way across the Atlantic; another short hop over the Irish Sea wouldn't do any harm. I may just find the key to unlock this mystery.'

31

William had been informed by a fellow passenger on the ferry that it always rained in Manchester. He couldn't say if this was the case or not, but as the month of April ended, this new May day had dawned with skies as clear and blue as a swimming pool. He had found himself a cheap bed and breakfast on the outskirts of the city, only a short bus ride from the centre. The landlady had provided him with a map and had drawn a bright red ring around his destination. He sat on the top deck of the red double-decker bus, a novelty that had him grinning from ear to ear as the huge, hissing vehicle trundled along Oxford Road. He got off outside the Palace Theatre and spread out his map. He glanced in the direction of St Peter's Square, and there it was, just as his landlady had promised, the huge dome of Manchester's Central Library.

He quickened his pace as he strode towards the

impressive neoclassical circular building. The Corinthian porticoed entrance was two storeys high, with six imposing stone columns. As he climbed the steps, he felt as though he was entering a Roman palace rather than a municipal library. Inside, the splendour and majesty of the building was still in evidence, with polished woodwork of oak and English walnut. He ascended the huge staircase and entered the Great Hall. It had originally been known as the Reading Room, and William could not imagine a more peaceful place to indulge in the study of literature, or take a leisurely browse through the morning papers. With some trepidation he approached the young librarian behind the desk.

'Good morning, ma'am, I was wondering if you could help me.'

'That's what I'm here for,' she smiled. 'What can I do for you?'

'I need to obtain a copy of a birth certificate.'

The librarian, whose badge told William she went by the name of Miss Sutton, took out a form from under the desk.

'I'll need to take some details. First, do you want the certificate posted out to you or would you like to collect it?'

William was taken aback at how easy the process appeared to be. 'I'll collect it, please. I don't have a permanent address here in the United Kingdom.'

Miss Sutton smiled sweetly. 'I could tell you're not from round these parts. You Canadian?'

'I'll try not to be offended,' laughed William. 'I'm from the US, Vermont. I was born in

Ireland, though, but my parents are English.'

Miss Sutton frowned.

'It's a long story,' explained William.

She gave a sideways smile. 'You'll have to tell it to me sometime.'

Gosh, thought William, *are all English girls this forward?* 'Maybe…'

'I was only joking! Now, what's your name?'

William composed himself. 'William Lane.'

'And the name on the birth certificate?'

'Christina Skinner.'

Miss Sutton's pen moved swiftly across the paper, and without looking up she said, 'Date of birth?'

William was confused. '*My* date of birth?'

She gave him a withering look. 'Christina Skinner's date of birth.'

'Well I don't know that exactly. I only know it was sometime between April 1919 and March 1920.'

'Do you have any other details? Address? Place of birth, father's name?'

William suddenly felt foolish. 'No, is that a problem?'

'Not for me it's not, but you're going to have to search through the General Register indexes and see if you can locate the correct Christina Skinner. I can't order a copy of a birth certificate with so little information.'

William sighed. 'And how do I do that?'

Miss Sutton pointed over to a table in the corner of the room. 'You park yourself over there and I will bring you the first of the ledgers.'

After two hours, William felt as though his eyes

would never be able to focus on the horizon again. The close-up work had caused his distance vision to become blurry and he felt the beginnings of a headache. He badly needed some fresh air. He approached the desk and spoke to Miss Sutton, who he was now addressing by her first name.

'Karen, sorry to disturb you,' he whispered. 'I need to go out and get some fresh air. Can you keep that table for me?'

'Of course. How are you getting along?'

'I've found two possible Christina Skinners, but have another ledger to check. I'll be back in about half an hour.'

As William wandered the streets of Manchester, he wondered if his mother had ever trodden these pavements. Was it possible she was actually here in Manchester now? And what of his father, Billy? Why had he so cruelly deserted his mother just when she needed him most? He didn't seem to be a father to be proud of, that was for sure. He thought of Donald then, back home in Vermont, tirelessly working on the farm to provide for his family, his calloused hands and bent back testament to his labours. The usual feeling of guilt at what he was trying to do engulfed him again and he felt suddenly homesick. He yearned for the tranquillity, peace and love of his family home, the warm homely smells of his mother's cooking and the temple-achingly sweet aroma and solitude of his sugar shack. Manchester was a world away from all that, and he began to question the wisdom of his endeavours. Nevertheless, deep inside was an insatiable desire to uncover the circumstances surrounding his birth. Already he had found out that it was his mother's dearest wish to raise him herself. That she had been forced to give him up against her will made him both desperately sad and incandescent with rage. He needed to know the whole story of his mother's courtship with his father and why she had been so heartlessly abandoned. With this renewed determination he climbed the library steps once more to continue his search.

It was almost time for the library to close when William approached Karen Sutton again with a list of three possible Christina Skinners. He pushed it over the counter with a grim expression. Karen scanned it quickly.

'You want to order all three certificates at once?'

William pondered this for a moment. 'How long does it take?'

'A few days, maybe more.'

'If I try them one at a time I might get lucky and order the correct one first, I suppose, but then again it could be the last one and by then a couple of weeks will have passed. I don't have enough money to stay in the UK that long, and anyway my parents will be needing me back home.'

'We could post the certificates back to you in the US,' suggested Karen.

William rubbed his forehead as she stared at him, waiting for a decision.

'I don't want to rush you,' she urged. 'But the library closes in ten minutes.'

'I'm sorry,' said William. 'I guess I'll have to order all three at once.'

As Karen began to write down the details, she was joined behind the desk by a colleague, an officious-looking grey-haired lady in a brown tweed skirt and jacket, with a row of dull pearls at her throat. She peered over Karen's shoulder and then moved her glasses to the end of her nose for a closer look.

'Christina Skinner? We already have that birth certificate. It was ordered last week and is awaiting collection.'

Both William and Karen stared open-mouthed at this startling news.

Karen turned to face her colleague. 'I'm sorry, Mrs Grainger, you mean we have a birth certificate here already for a Christina Skinner?'

Mrs Grainger did not hide her impatience. 'That's what I just said, wasn't it? Now come on and get this desk cleared. I need to lock up.'

Karen gathered together a sheaf of papers and piled stray pens into a pot. 'Would it be possible to look at it, to see if it's the one William needs?'

'Certainly not. That certificate has been paid for and is the property of the person who ordered it. Only they may open that envelope.'

Karen raised her eyes to the ceiling. She looked as though she had been expecting that response. Mrs Grainger was clearly a stickler for rules and officialdom.

'When is this person coming to collect the certificate?' asked William.

Mrs Grainger shrugged her shoulders. 'I don't know. It only came in yesterday, so maybe tomorrow or the day after. It depends how urgently it's required.'

Could that birth certificate really be his mother's? William couldn't imagine who else would require a copy of it. Did he have siblings who were also trying to trace their mother? Or perhaps it was Christina herself. Had she ordered it to replace the original? Was it for a completely different person altogether? He desperately needed answers.

Mrs Grainger had now left the desk area and was busy returning some books to their shelves. William leant across to Karen. 'I need to know who ordered that copy,' he whispered.

Karen turned round and checked that Mrs Grainger was still occupied. She had now climbed a stepladder and was reaching up to the top shelf with a particularly hefty volume in her hand.

'Give me a minute,' she replied.

She dug deep into a drawer under her desk and rummaged round, withdrawing a key. Then, without taking her eyes off Mrs Grainger, she crossed to a filing cabinet and silently pulled open the top drawer. Her fingers were swift and nimble as she flicked through the files. She found what she was looking for and just had time to glance at the name on the envelope before Mrs Grainger called over. 'Have you finished yet, Karen?'

'Just tidying up the last few things, Mrs Grainger,' she replied. She winked at William. 'Meet me outside in five minutes.'

It was rush hour in Manchester city centre, and William watched as people made their way home. The square was filled with the noise and fumes of traffic as people ran for buses and cars impatiently sounded their horns. He heard high heels clacking on the stone steps behind him and turned to greet Karen. She took him by the arm and propelled him on to the street, glancing furtively over her shoulder.

'She's right behind me,' she whispered. She bundled him into a shop doorway as Mrs Grainger strode past, her eyes fixed on the pavement ahead. Both William and Karen breathed a sigh of relief and Karen started to giggle. 'I feel like an international arms smuggler.'

William smiled.

'Did you get it? The name of the person who ordered the certificate?'

'I did. It was ordered by a Mrs Tina Craig. Does that mean anything to you?'

William shook his head. 'Never heard of her. But then I don't know anyone here in Manchester. Maybe it's a different Christina Skinner.'

'Maybe, and maybe not. There is a way to find out.'

'How?' asked William.

'Come in again tomorrow and wait for her to show up.'

'What if she doesn't come, though? She may not decide to pick it up for days, weeks even.'

Karen shrugged. 'Depends on how desperate you are to see that certificate.'

32

Tina shook out her umbrella before turning to climb the steps to the library. The street glistened as the rain bounced off the pavement, soaking right through the thin soles of her sandals. She cursed herself for being so stupid. Boots would have been a more sensible option today, but it was May after all and she stubbornly refused to revisit her winter wardrobe at this time of year. She took her compact out of her bag and flipped open the mirror. Her long hair clung to her cheeks and her so-called waterproof mascara ran in long streaks down her face. She wiped underneath her eyes with the back of her hand as she climbed the stairs to the Great Hall. She approached the desk and propped her umbrella up against it. Immediately a little pool of rainwater collected on the polished floor. She ran her fingers through her hair and addressed the young woman behind the counter.

'Hello, I'm here to collect a copy of a birth certificate I ordered.'

'Your name?'

'It's Tina Craig. C-R-A-I-G.'

'Of course. Please take a seat for a minute.' The girl gestured to a row of upholstered chairs nearby and then turned to a filing cabinet and thumbed through the various folders. She smiled at Tina apologetically.

'I'm sorry. I just need a word with my colleague.'

Tina waved her hand. 'No problem. I'm not in any rush.'

William was ensconced at a table in the corner, hidden behind a newspaper. Karen slapped her hand down on the table and he looked up, startled.

'Hey! What do you think–'

Karen cut him off. 'She's here.'

No further explanation was needed. He stood up, carefully tucked the newspaper under his arm and followed Karen to the desk, where she pulled an envelope from a drawer.

'Mrs Craig,' she called. 'Here's your certificate.'

The woman who had been waiting on a nearby chair took the envelope and dropped it into her handbag. 'Thank you very much. Goodbye now.'

William stood open-mouthed and mute as he watched her leave without a backward glance. He gave Karen a stricken look and then made a decision. 'I have to follow her.'

He caught up with the woman as she stood in the portico wrestling with her umbrella.

'Excuse me, ma'am. I wonder if I might have a word.'

She looked around, surprised. 'A word with *me?*'

'If you don't mind. I won't keep you long.'

He was mesmerised by her striking blue eyes, now accentuated by a smudge of dark mascara underneath. He was conscious of the rainwater trickling under his collar, making him shudder involuntarily. The woman took a step towards him, offering him refuge under her umbrella. They faced each other in total silence for what seemed an eternity but was in fact only a split second. Two total strangers sharing a space on the planet no bigger than a paving slab. William spoke first.

'My name is William Lane and I've been waiting for you for some time.'

'All your life, I suppose.'

William froze momentarily, and then blushed as he realised that his remark had been misconstrued.

'Oh no, I didn't mean that. I just meant that I've been waiting for you to come and collect that birth certificate. I wasn't hitting on you or anything.'

The woman looked confused. 'I'm sorry, I thought you were trying to pick me up.'

'Pick you up?' William frowned. Considering they both spoke the same language, communication was proving difficult.

'You know ... ask me out.' She shrugged her shoulders and smiled faintly.

William searched her face. Though she was undoubtedly beautiful, there was a certain sadness in her eyes.

'Look,' he said finally. 'Shall we start again? Is there somewhere we could go to talk?'

'Oh, I'm not sure. I don't even know you.'

'Please,' urged William. 'It's important. I won't keep you long.'

'Well, there's a cafe on the corner. We could go there, I suppose.'

'Perfect,' said William. 'Shall we?'

Once they were seated with their coffees, and pleasantries were out of the way, William began to tell his story.

'I came here from America in the hope of tracing my birth mother. I was born in a convent in Ireland in 1940 and was told my mother's name was Bronagh Skinner.'

Tina shuffled in her seat at the mention of the name Skinner, but did not interrupt. William continued.

'I went to the convent to see if they would help me, but it was no use. The sisters there would not give me any information at all. Anyway, a midwife who works there took pity on me and offered to help. It turns out she remembers my mother because she was English, from right here in Manchester. And her real name was not Bronagh, but Christina. I came to the library to order a copy of her birth certificate and found out that you had already beaten me to it. I don't know if it's the same Christina Skinner I'm looking for, but I wondered if you'd mind if I took a look at it.'

Tina already knew that the birth certificate was surely that of William's mother. Both Alice Stirling and Maud Cutler had told her that Chrissie had been sent to Ireland in disgrace. She bent down to retrieve her handbag. William watched expectantly as she reached inside and pulled out not the envelope she had been given by Karen Sutton, but an older, yellowing one. She solemnly slid it across the table. 'I think you should read this.'

William's hands were shaking as he picked it up. 'It's addressed to Miss C. Skinner.'

'Your mother,' confirmed Tina.

'I don't understand.'

'Just read it. Afterwards, I'll explain everything.'

He carefully eased the letter out of the envelope

288

and unfolded it. He glanced at Tina before beginning to read. She held her breath as he first scanned the letter and then read it again more carefully. When he had read it twice, he set it down on the table between them and smoothed out the paper. 'Where did you get this?'

'I work in a charity shop and someone left a bag of old clothes on the doorstep. Inside there was a suit, and tucked into the jacket pocket was that letter.' Tina tapped it with her forefinger. 'As you can see from the envelope, it was never posted. When I opened it, I was so moved by the words and mystified as to why Billy never sent it that I vowed to try and find Chrissie and hand the letter to her myself.' She blushed slightly. 'You might think it was none of my business, but it stirred something in me.'

William stared at the letter again. 'This baby he mentions, that's me.' His eyes began to mist with tears. 'I thought he had abandoned my mother. She thought he wanted nothing more to do with her. Grace told me she never stopped longing for him, even though he had treated her so badly, and now I find this.' He held the letter up to his face and breathed in the scent of it. 'Why, didn't he post it, Tina? What happened to him?'

Tina knew there was no easy way to break the news. 'After I found the letter, I called round to 180 Gillbent Road, and believe it or not, Billy's parents still live there.'

William's eyes widened in astonishment 'My grandparents are here in Manchester?'

'Yes, William, they are.' Tina smiled briefly at his enthusiasm, but then continued solemnly. 'Your grandmother, Alice Stirling, told me all about her son. She and her husband adopted him when he was ten months old. I showed Alice the letter and she remembered him writing it; in fact it was her idea. He called round at Chrissie's house the next day and spoke with her mother, but she knew nothing about the letter. He was heartbroken to learn that Chrissie had been shipped off to Ireland and begged Mrs Skinner to let him have her address. She promised to contact Chrissie on his behalf.'

'What happened then?' asked William eagerly. 'Did they get in touch?'

Tina shook her head. 'Mabel Skinner was killed in the blackout that night, and as far as I know, she never made contact with her daughter.' She delved into her bag again and took out the photograph of Billy that Alice Stirling had given to her. 'This is your father.'

William took the photo and studied it carefully. 'He was a handsome man,' he declared. 'Do you know what happened to him?'

Tina steeled herself. 'I'm afraid he was killed in action in 1940. I'm so sorry.'

The tears spilled over now and William wiped them away with the back of his hand. Tina handed him a paper napkin from the little pot on the table. 'He was a good man, William. He didn't desert your mother. He loved her and wanted to be a family. Alice said he would have made a wonderful father.'

'But my mother never knew this. If only she had received this letter, things would have been different.'

'I know. That's why I felt I had to try and find her and give her the letter.'

'So this is why you ordered her birth certificate?'

Tina nodded. She told William about going to Wood Gardens and meeting Maud Cutler. 'Maud knew the Skinners well. She told me about Dr Skinner's fearful temper and that Chrissie had been sent to Ireland.'

'This is unbelievable, Tina. Thank you so much for caring. You could have just tossed that letter into the trash, but the fact that you took time out to try and trace my mother is just so...' He searched for the right word. 'Well, it's just remarkable.'

'It was over a year ago now that I found the letter, and it intrigued me from the start.' Tina took another sip of her coffee and stared at the raindrops running down the window. The glass on the inside had steamed up and she absently drew a line along the window pane with her finger. 'Anyway, I had a lot going on in my life at the time, so it just got pushed to one side. When I rediscovered it, it occurred to me that maybe Chrissie wouldn't want to be found. I mean, what if she's in a happy marriage now and doesn't want to be reminded of the past?'

'That had crossed my mind,' admitted William.

'In the end I decided to make a start with the birth certificate. I thought I could always change my mind at a later date.'

Just then a waitress appeared at the table, her once-white apron now stained with tea and coffee. 'Excuse me,' she began. 'I'm not being funny or owt, but will you be ordering anything else? We have a queue for tables, you see.' She gestured towards the door, where a line of irritable-looking people were glancing in their direction.

William stood up. 'So sorry. We got a little carried away.' He helped Tina on with her raincoat and beckoned her to lead the way to the exit. Once out on the street, they stood facing each other, not sure what to say next. The rain had stopped and the thick clouds had parted to allow the sun to tentatively shine through.

'Shall we go for a walk?' suggested William. 'I'm not holding you up, am I? Is there anybody waiting for you? A husband? Boyfriend?'

Tina shook her head. 'There's no one. Come on, we'll head towards Piccadilly Gardens and find a seat there.'

They found a relatively quiet bench and watched for a moment or two as office workers hurried past clutching brown paper bags containing sandwiches and fruit to be snatched as an early lunch.

'Tell me, how did you manage to locate my mother's birth certificate when all you knew was her name?'

Tina smiled. 'Well, like I said, my first port of call was Wood Gardens, where I met Maud Cutler. It was Maud who told me the names of Chrissie's parents. She also told me where Mabel was buried. She still lays flowers on the grave every year. Mabel saved Maud's baby's life, you know. He was so tiny when he was born.' She closed her eyes for a second as she remembered her own little girl.

'Are you all right?' asked William.

'I'm fine. I was just... Nothing. Anyway, once I

knew her parents' names, tracing her birth certificate wasn't too difficult. Shall we have a look at it?'

William had completely forgotten about the certificate. 'Yes please.'

Tina spread the certificate out on her knee and William leaned over to get a closer look.

'That's the name I need,' he said excitedly. 'May I?' He took the certificate and studied it more closely. 'McBride. That's Chrissie's mother's maiden name, so it must be the name of her aunt. This will help enormously when I go back to Ireland. The McBride family.' William's eyes shone with excitement. 'Someone's bound to remember something.' His hands trembled as he handed the certificate back to Tina. 'I'm going to find my mother!'

Tina pushed the certificate back to him. 'You keep it.' She rummaged in her bag. 'And you might as well have these.' She handed over Billy's letter and photograph. 'Good luck, William.' She stood up and held out her hand. 'It's been a pleasure meeting you.'

William was on his feet in a second. 'Come with me,' he blurted.

Tina took a startled step back.

'I mean, please come with me. To Ireland. I couldn't have got this far without you and I would really love you to be by my side to see how it all ends.'

Tina knew it was preposterous to even think about going all that way with a man she didn't even know. She had done her bit. More than most people would have done, in fact. She didn't owe him anything, and yet as she stared into his dark brown eyes, she suddenly realised how much like his father he was. The similarities were startling. Billy was dead, but here was his son standing right in front of her, asking her to accompany him on a journey he must have been planning for most of his life. And she had made it happen. She had given him the information he needed to trace his mother. She felt a flutter of excitement she had not experienced for many months. It was a mad, impulsive and downright ridiculous idea.

She threw her head back and laughed. 'William, it would be an honour.'

33

Tina heaved open the cumbersome green door of the telephone box and was immediately grateful for the quiet sanctuary it provided. There was something about the inside of a telephone box that immediately calmed her. A feeling of being cut off from the outside world, a place to gather your thoughts and reflect on the chaos going on else-where. Of course, most of the telephone boxes in Manchester smelled of stale urine, but this one here in Tipperary Town was simply delightful, with no obnoxious odours to cloud the senses. She picked up the chunky black receiver and began to dial. After a few rings, she cursed under her breath as she heard Sheila's voice on the other end. She had no choice but to push in the first coin.

'Sheila? It's Tina. Can you fetch Graham for me?'

Fortunately Sheila was her usual uncommunicative self and she merely grunted before putting down the receiver and shouting for her husband. Tina bounced on the balls of her feet as she waited for Graham to come to the phone. After what seemed like an eternity, she heard his voice.

'Tina?'

Before she could speak, the pips started. She pushed another coin into the slot.

'Hello, Graham. Look, I haven't got much money so I'll have to be quick. You got my note?'

'This morning. What on earth are you doing in Ireland?'

'It's a long story. You remember that letter I found last year?'

'No, what letter?'

Tina inwardly groaned. 'I found an old letter in the pocket of a suit that had been donated to the shop. I'm sure I told you about it.'

'I don't remember, but what's that got to do with you flitting off to Ireland?'

Pip ... pip ... pip...

Tina was beginning to lose patience. She thrust some more coins into the slot.

'I'll have to be quick now, Graham. When the pips go again, that's it. I've no more money left. Just listen and don't say anything, OK? To cut a long story short, I've come to Ireland to try and trace the woman the letter was written to. I'm with her son, who's also looking for her. I just wanted to let you know that I'm all right and not to worry about me.'

Graham sounded utterly confused. 'You're with who? When will you be back?'

The pips went for the final time. Tina ignored his questions and hurriedly said goodbye.

As she replaced the receiver, she could just hear him shouting into the phone, 'I'll never stop worrying about you!'

Back at Mrs Flanagan's guest house, William was waiting for her in the lounge.

'Everything OK? You want some tea?' His mouth was full as he spoke and his words came out muffled.

Mrs Flanagan had set out a tray with a vast pot of tea and warm potato cakes with smoked salmon, and William was tucking in eagerly. He swallowed, wiped his mouth with the back of his hand and tried again.

'Sorry about that. These potato cakes are delicious. Did you manage to speak to your friend?'

Tina sat beside him on the couch and began, to pour herself a cup. 'Yes, I did, thanks. I left him a note to say where I had gone, but he worries about me.'

William took another bite. 'This Graham? Is he an old boyfriend?' Crumbs spilled from his mouth as he spoke, and Tina frowned.

'Do you Americans always speak with your mouth full?'

William took a swig of his tea and grinned. 'I'm sorry. It's a terrible habit, I know. I'm not very refined, I'm afraid. Just a country boy really.'

She glanced at her watch. 'It's only four o'clock in the afternoon. What meal is it you're having

296

anyway? Late lunch, early tea?'

'It's Mrs Flanagan. She thinks I need fattening up!' He shrugged his shoulders and Tina smiled.

'To answer your earlier question, Graham is just a very good friend. He's been a huge support to me during the last twelve months or so and I owe him a lot. It wouldn't be fair of me to just take off and not let him know I'm all right.'

'More like a father figure then?' asked William.

Tina considered this. 'More like a brother, I suppose.'

Mrs Flanagan popped her head round the door. 'Do you need anything else?'

'You're too kind, Mrs Flanagan, but I think we have enough here.'

'Very well. You just give me a shout if you want some more.'

She backed out of the room, leaving William and Tina alone again.

'So what's the plan then?' asked Tina.

'Well, tomorrow morning I'm going to take you to meet Grace Quinn. After all, if it hadn't been for her, I would never have gone to Manchester and we would never have met. We'll see if she can remember the McBride family and where they might have lived.'

Tina smiled. 'Sounds like a plan.'

Tina thought Grace Quinn's cottage was just charming and would not have looked out of place on a chocolate box or a jigsaw. The white stone walls positively dazzled in the sparkling sunlight and she had to shield her eyes as they walked up the crazy-paving pathway to the bright red door, which, was perfectly framed by a smoky-blue wisteria. Once inside, they were greeted with warmth by Grace, who was delighted that William had brought Tina to meet her. They sat round the kitchen table and William took out his notebook.

'Christina Skinner's mother was called Mabel McBride before she married. Does that name mean anything to you, Grace?'

Grace clasped her hands in front of her on the table and thought hard. She desperately did not want to disappoint this young man and the sweet girl he had brought with him, but she had to admit that she was not familiar with anyone called McBride.

'I'm sorry, William. I really am, but that name doesn't mean anything to me.'

William tried to hide his disappointment. 'Don't worry. I've come this far and I'm not giving up now. I learnt so much in Manchester, you wouldn't believe it.'

He leafed through his notebook and pulled out Billy's letter.

'Here, read this.'

Grace placed her glasses on the end of her nose and read the letter. 'This is incredible. Where did you get it?'

Tina explained how she had come by the letter, and that it was she who had traced Chrissie's birth certificate.

'You were right, Grace,' interjected William. 'Chrissie's father was a doctor and her mother was a midwife.'

'That poor girl, she had no idea that Billy wanted to marry her. When I think of the anguish

298

she went through during the birth, and the sadness in her eyes that never left her. When she held you for the first time, William, I knew she was overjoyed, and her smile lit up the room, but her eyes ... if you looked into her eyes, you knew. There was a pain in there that would never subside.' Grace blew her nose quietly. 'What I can't understand is why Billy didn't post his letter. I mean, it's written with such love and feeling, I just can't believe he didn't send it.'

Tina explained how Alice Stirling remembered Billy going out to the postbox but was as mystified as anyone else as to why he changed his mind.

'I've never heard such a heart-rending story in my life,' sniffed Grace. 'Do you know what happened to Billy?'

Tina and William looked at each other. William spoke first.

'He was killed in action in 1940.' He opened his notebook again. 'This is his picture.'

Grace looked at the handsome young man in army uniform.

'You look just like him, William.' It was all she could manage. She folded the letter in half and went to pass it back to William but then stopped herself. 'Oh look, there's something written on the other side.' She peered carefully at the back of the letter. 'It just says "Sorry".'

William took the letter and studied it again. 'I'd not noticed that before, had you, Tina?'

Tina stiffened at the memory. She felt the familiar feeling of repugnance well up inside her. It started in the pit of her stomach and crept upwards until it burnt the back of her throat and made her want to retch. She clamped her hand over her mouth.

'Tina? Are you all right?'

She could feel perspiration breaking out on her top lip, and her whole body bristled with hatred.

'I'm f-fine...' she stammered. She stood up. 'Grace, would you mind if I used your bathroom?'

Grace glanced at William, an anxious look on her face. 'Of course, dear, it's this way.'

Tina took refuge in the bathroom and splashed cold water on her face. Her chest and neck were flushed and her face was blotchy and crimson. She clung to the edge of the sink as she breathed deeply, trying to lower her pulse rates, Rick had been dead for five months now, but he still had the power to stir these violent emotions in her. She managed to keep her hatred for him buried most of the time. She didn't want it to eat away at her and define who she was. He had sabotaged the last five years of her life and she was determined he was not going to do the same to the next five.

When she had composed herself, she returned to the small living room to find William and Grace huddled over the table, a plate of warm, fluffy buttermilk scones between them. It seemed that Irish hospitality centred on food. William turned as he heard her come in.

'We're just looking at a map, Tina. We've marked the convent, here, look.' He showed her where he had drawn a red cross. 'Now we know that Chrissie's aunt lived fairly locally, but in rural terms that could mean a number of miles away.' He checked the scale of the map and then drew a circle around the spot where the convent was. 'That's everything within a two-mile radius.' He drew another, wider circle. 'And that's everything within a five-mile radius.' He sat back to look at his handiwork. 'It's a bit rough, but in the absence of a pair of compasses, it's the best I can do.'

'My brother is coming round tonight,' announced Grace. 'I'll ask him to mark all the pubs within your two circles and that can be your starting point. Rural communities thrive on their pubs and they really are a cauldron of information.'

William smiled at Tina. 'Are you ready for this?'

She smiled back. 'Of course.' His enthusiasm was infectious and it was too late to back out now. She had no idea whether they would be able to trace William's mother, but she wanted to be at his side whatever the outcome.

34

William and Tina sat in the Malt Shovels, the third pub they had visited. Grace's brother had dutifully marked the pubs on the map, four in the inner circle and three in the outer. That meant there were seven pubs within a five-mile radius of the convent.

William picked up his half-pint of Guinness and took a sip. 'This pub must have an entrepreneurial landlord, it actually serves food. Shall we order some? I'm starving.'

Tina laughed. 'Do you ever think about anything else? I've never known anybody eat so much. I think you must have a tapeworm!'

'All this cycling from pub to pub has given me an appetite.' He pointed at the blackboard. 'Look, they have a nice Irish stew, so they do.'

Tina nudged him playfully in the ribs. 'You're beginning to sound Irish.'

He took another sip of his drink. 'I am Irish, aren't I? Born, if not bred.' He raised his glass to the barman, who nodded and began to fill another for him.

'Are you sure you want that? We have one more pub after this to investigate tonight and you don't want to be caught drunk in charge of a bicycle.'

'I suppose you're right. Look, we'll order some food and then start asking around. It looks a bit more promising than the last two places.'

Tina agreed. 'All right then. I'll just have the cheese salad. I want to save room for *that*.'

She pointed at the menu on the table and William leaned over to get a closer look.

'Bread and butter pudding. What on earth is that?' He wrinkled his nose in apparent disgust.

'You wait and see. I'll ask for two spoons. I guarantee you'll want some!' Tina gazed wistfully into the distance. 'It was my mother's speciality. She made it to perfection, with thick slices of white bread spread with creamy butter. The fruit was plump and juicy and the custard was set just right. The top was always slightly crispy and caramelised and if there was any left it was even better cold the next day.'

William smiled. 'You've never spoken about your

family before. Tell me about them.'

Tina picked at a loose thread on the sleeve of her sweater, avoiding eye contact. 'Both my parents are dead.'

William was shocked. 'Oh my God, I'm so sorry, Tina. I didn't mean to upset you.'

'You weren't to know. My father died when I was sixteen and my mother died seven years after that. She never got over his death, you know. It sounds clichéd, but they really were soulmates. Anyway, I'm an only child and I found myself orphaned at the age of twenty-three.' She managed a weak smile. 'I had a good job, though, in an office, and I worked in the charity shop at weekends, so I was never short of company. I work in the charity shop full-time now.'

'What happened to your office job?'

Tina hesitated. 'It's a long story. I left there when I got pregnant.'

William's eyes widened. 'You have a baby?'

'No. She was stillborn.'

William instinctively took her hand and pressed it to his cheek. 'I don't know what to say. You poor thing. What about the father? Were you married?'

Tina was rapidly losing her appetite. 'Yes, I was, but he's dead too.'

William was aghast. 'How much pain is one person supposed to endure?'

Tina stared ahead levelly. 'I don't shed any tears over *him*.' She picked up the menu. 'Now, shall we order?'

The sun was beginning to set as William and Tina left the pub. The smell of the pungent hawthorn hedgerows hung in the air and the May evening now had the faintest hint of a chill.

'Well that was another waste of time,' declared William, as he tucked his trousers into his socks. He looked across at Tina as she fiddled with the basket on the front of Grace's bike. She had been quiet all through dinner and William cursed himself for opening up old wounds.

'Are you up to another one?'

Tina looked up. 'Another one?'

'The last pub in the inner circle. We'll only have the three further out to do if we get no joy in the next one.'

'If you're sure your bike is up to it!' Tina giggled as she regarded the antiquated rusty bike William had borrowed from Grace's next-door neighbour.

William grimaced. 'I know. It's the one Noah refused on the grounds it was too old-fashioned.'

Tina laughed out loud. 'You are funny, William.'

'You look lovely when you laugh. Look, I'm sorry about in there.' He nodded towards the pub. 'I hope you don't think I was prying.'

'It was perfectly reasonable of you to ask about my family. You didn't know it was going to take on Shakespearean proportions. Come on, let's press on. Where to next?'

The final pub of the evening was no more than a tiny thatched cottage. The windows were small, so inside it was dark and gloomy, with scuffed wooden floorboards that even the sawdust could not disguise. There were half a dozen tables, around which were seated groups of old men, some playing cards or dominoes, some just staring into their pints. All of them looked up as William and Tina walked in. William nodded as he took Tina by the arm and approached the bar.

'Evening,' said the barmaid, who looked as though she would be more at home giving orders in the army. 'What can I get yer?'

William turned to Tina.

'Oh, just an orange juice for me.'

'Make that two, please.'

There was nowhere to sit, so they leant against the bar and surveyed the little room. The initial curiosity had worn off and now the regulars were immersed in their previous activities. William turned to the barmaid.

'I wonder if I might ask you something?' It was a well-worn routine now, albeit one that had turned out to be fruitless in the previous three pubs. 'Do you know of a family round here named McBride, a farming family?'

The barmaid stopped polishing the glass she was holding and frowned. 'You'll have to be more specific, I'm afraid. McBride's not that uncommon a name round here.'

William sighed. It had been the same story in every pub. It seemed they had just not got enough information.

'I'm afraid that's all we know. The family name is McBride and they used to live on a small farm in a remote location, although that was over thirty years ago.'

The barmaid continued to vigorously polish the glass as she mulled this information over. 'Why do you want to know, anyway?'

William cleared his throat. 'I'm trying to trace my mother. I was born here thirty-four years ago at St Bridget's convent and was given up for adoption. I went to live in America, but I've come back to try and find my mother.'

The barmaid pursed her lips. 'I see. You tried the convent, I suppose, and they were most unhelpful.'

William cast a knowing glance at Tina. 'You could say that.'

'Well let's see if we can do any better. This was all thirty-odd years ago, you say?'

William and Tina nodded in unison.

The barmaid put down her glass and called out to one of the men playing cards. He put down his hand and approached the bar. 'What is it, Morag?'

She nodded towards William and Tina. 'These two are looking for a family by the name of McBride, Father. Do you think you can help them?'

'McBride, you say? Can you be more specific?'

Morag smiled. 'That's what I said.' She turned to William and Tina. 'This is Father McIntyre, priest of this parish. If anybody can help you, he can.'

Half an hour later, William and Tina found themselves outside the pub clutching a piece of paper. Father McIntyre could not recall a McBride family matching the vague description William gave him, but he knew a man who might. William read the name the priest had written down for him.

'Well that's tomorrow's task sorted.' He tucked the paper into his shirt pocket and mounted his decrepit bicycle. 'Let's hope this Father Drummond can help us find another piece of the jigsaw.'

35

When William and Tina arrived back at Mrs Flanagan's, the landlady was already tucked up in bed. William groped around underneath the doormat and found the chunky key. It groaned and clinked as he forced it into the lock and he winced as they both tiptoed across the threshold, careful not to disturb Mrs Flanagan.

'Would you care for a nightcap?' he whispered.

Tina hesitated for a second, but then nodded her head in agreement. Once they were seated in the front room, each cradling a tumbler of whiskey, they relaxed a little and their hushed tones were replaced by a more normal level of conversation. Tina laid her head back on the sofa and closed her eyes. The whiskey burned its way to her stomach and the smell of it brought back memories of Rick. The lump in her throat made it difficult to swallow and she felt the tears start to well up. She silently prayed that William would not notice, but he was far too astute.

'Tina? Are you OK?' He rushed to her side on the sofa. 'Oh my God, you're crying.'

She flicked away a tear with her little finger and forced a smile.

'I'm fine, William, really, don't worry.'

He took hold of her tumbler and placed it on the coffee table, then grasped both her hands in his. 'From the second we met, I've sensed a sadness in you. It's in your eyes, Tina. You are so beautiful and have a gorgeous smile, but you never smile with your eyes.' He gripped her hands more firmly. 'You've been so kind to me, coming all this way, I want to help you. Tell me what's wrong.'

Poor William. He looked as though his own heart was breaking and there was no doubt his concern was genuine.

Tina indicated her tumbler on the table. 'Would you mind?'

William passed it to her.

'See this liquid here?' She swirled the glass so violently that whiskey sloshed over the rim and landed in her lap. She didn't seem to notice. 'This liquid,' she continued in a more venomous tone, 'has literally ruined my life and cost the life of my daughter.'

William put his own glass down now, his appetite for the strong stuff suddenly vanishing.

'Do you want to tell me about it?' he asked cautiously. 'I'd like to help if I can.'

Her tone softened as she turned to face him. 'It's too late, William. It's too late. I've been a total idiot, blind to the obvious. I can see that now.'

William squeezed her hands again. 'Go on.'

She took a deep breath, wrestled her hands free from William's grip and wiped them down the length of her thighs.

'I was a battered wife, William,' she began. He went to say something, but she shushed him with a finger to his lips. 'Everybody could see it but me. Graham, my friend Linda, my boss at work, they could all see what was happening, but not me. Oh no, I was convinced he would change and that's why I went back to him, gave him chance after chance. After he had beaten me, he was always so apologetic, so humble and incredibly loving. Sometimes he even cried at the way he had treated me and I felt sorry for him.' She shook her head and paused before continuing. 'Of course each time he promised he would never raise his fists to me again, and like a fool I believed him. But then something would rile him, usually something small and insignificant. He would convince me it was my fault, and I believed him then as well. Drink was at the root of it all, of course, but it's too simplistic to blame it all on the booze. He was a controlling bully who manipulated me in any way he could. I thought about leaving him for years but never had the courage. He always said he would track me down and I was scared of him. Besides, I felt I would be deserting him when he obviously needed help.'

William stared at her, his breathing becoming deeper and harder the more he heard of her story.

'Anyway, one day I did pluck up the courage to leave. But the truth of it was I was lonely. I missed him.' She turned to William. 'Can you believe that? I actually missed him!'

William shook his head but said nothing.

'He stopped drinking then and seemed to turn his life around. He coped without me and for some reason that hurt. He found a job and never harassed me to go back to him. He just sorted himself out and became the man I'd always wanted him to be. It was like he didn't need me anymore, but he was playing the long game, of course. Then I found out I was pregnant so I had no choice but to go back to him. At least that's what I told myself. It was wonderful for a while and I was so happy. He was too and we were both excited about the new baby. I knew I'd made the right decision, even though Graham and Linda told me I was mad. *What do they know?* I thought.' She forced out a sarcastic laugh. 'Quite a lot, as it turned out.'

'What happened then?' William's voice was thick with emotion.

Tina pointed to the glass. 'That's what happened. He started drinking again. Just a little bit at first, but it was a downward spiral into disaster. I should have seen it, but I had such an idealistic view of my marriage that I made excuses for him. I see now I was deluding myself, of course, but that's the clarity of hindsight. It has twenty-twenty vision all right.'

William steeled himself to ask the next question.

'What happened to your baby? A little girl, you said? How did she ... you know...'

Tina rubbed her face with her hands, then looked up at William. Taking a deep breath, she told him the story of what had happened on that terrible day.

William was aghast. 'I feel sick,' he whispered. 'If Rick hadn't seen Billy's letter, then you would still have your daughter.' He got up and heaved open the sash window, gulping in the fresh air. Tina crossed the room and placed her hands on his broad shoulders.

'I don't think of it like that. I've learned not to. Rick was an evil, spiteful bully and any one thing

310

could have caused him to lash out. He's to blame, and nobody else. It's taken me a while to accept that, but now I know it's true. It's that belief that helps me move forward little by little. I was the victim, me and my baby girl, and none of it was my fault.'

William turned round and embraced her firmly. He buried his head in her long dark hair. It smelled of freshly cut grass mingled with the tang of an evening bonfire.

'I'm so sorry,' was all he managed to say.

Father Drummond was not used to rising early. At the age of ninety six, he felt he had earned the right to stay in bed as long as he wished, all day if he pleased. This morning, however, his house-keeper-cum-nurse-cum-dictator had informed him that he had visitors arriving at ten. This meant being wrestled from his bed at eight so that he could be bathed, shaved and dressed in good time. He lay back and reluctantly let Gina lather his face with shaving foam. She took hold of the cut-throat razor and pulled his skin tight as she ran the blade over it. The wispy grey hairs came away easily and she wiped the blade with a flannel. On the second stroke she nicked his skin slightly and a minute speck of blood mingled with the foam.

Father Drummond was not amused. 'For the love of God, Gina. Can't you for once shave me without me needing a blood transfusion?'

Gina tutted and carried on with the task in hand.

'Stop exaggerating, Father. I don't know what you've got against those electric razors anyway. It would be much easier for me to use one of those.'

'I've been using a cut-throat all my life and I don't intend to change my ways now.'

Gina cast her eyes to the ceiling, and with a few more swift strokes the job was complete.

'There you are, Father Drummond, all done.'

'Hmm. Are my ears still attached?'

Gina ignored him and began to take off his pyjama top. 'You need a clean pair. I don't know how you manage to spill so much down your front. Now let's see. Do you want to put a suit on?'

Father Drummond looked confused for a second. 'Who did you say was coming again?'

Gina was exasperated. 'I told you. His name is William Lane and he is looking to trace his mother. Her name was Christina Skinner and she was sent here from England to have her baby. She lived with her sister, whose surname was McBride, and gave birth in the convent. Father McIntyre thought you might remember the McBride family, although I doubt it very much considering I've told you all this once not ten minutes since and you've forgotten it already.'

He scowled at Gina as she scrubbed mercilessly under his arms with the rough facecloth. The woman didn't know what she was talking about. There was nothing wrong with his memory.

Gina greeted William and Tina warmly and showed them into the front parlour. The old priest's house was enormous and the interior smelled musty. Tina wrinkled her nose.

'Half the rooms are closed up,' said Gina apologetically. 'There's only me and Father Drummond rattling round in here now.'

'Oh, it's beautiful, though,' said Tina, taking in the oak panelling. 'I mean, it really is a majestic building.'

Father Drummond was waiting for them by the fireside. In spite of the warm May weather, there was a roaring log fire in the grate and the old priest had a tartan rug wrapped around his legs.

William extended a hand. 'I'm William Lane, Father Drummond. Thank you for agreeing to see us. This is my friend Tina Craig.'

Tina held out her hand too, and Father Drummond clasped it briefly. 'Excuse me if I don't get up.'

'Not at all,' said William. 'We'll try not to keep you too long. I believe you may know the Mc-Bride family from around these parts.'

William explained about his journey so far. He told Father Drummond about Billy's letter. How Tina had vowed to deliver it to Chrissie and how they had met each other in Manchester. Father Drummond cast his eyes downwards as William told him how unhelpful the nuns at the convent had been.

'So you see, Father,' he said, 'you are really our last chance. I know it's all a long time ago, but perhaps you could think back thirty-odd years and tell us if you remember anything at all about a Mc-Bride family. If we could find the farm to which my mother was sent, there may be someone living there now who remembers what happened to her and where she went. Is there anything in my story that sounds familiar to you?'

Father Drummond stared at him for a long time,

then rubbed his temples and closed his eyes. William thought he had fallen asleep. Eventually the old priest opened his eyes and looked directly at him. 'I'm sorry, no. I don't recall a McBride family fitting that description.'

William and Tina strolled along the lane towards the bus stop.

'Well that was another waste of time. What do we do now?'

Tina squeezed his arm. 'Keep looking, that's what. We'll just have to broaden our search. We've still got those three pubs to check. We're bound to get lucky sooner or later.'

William smiled at her optimism. 'Thanks, Tina. You really know how to keep my spirits up.'

Father Drummond continued to sit by the fire. He went over things in his head several times and managed to convince himself that he had done the right thing. He had made a promise to Kathleen McBride and had carried out her wishes to the letter. No sense in raking up the past now. She would not have wanted that. He nodded his head firmly. No, there was no doubt about it: he had done the right thing.

Gina popped her head round the door. 'Are you ready for lunch, Father Drummond?'

'Yes, Gina. I think I am.'

'What a pity you couldn't help that young couple. I told you your memory's not what it used to be, but you wouldn't have it.'

Father Drummond smiled to himself. 'You were right, Gina. No memory at all.'

36

By the end of the month, William had reluctantly come to the conclusion that his search was over. Nobody in the vicinity could recollect the McBride family he was looking for, and he had exhausted all avenues. It was time to go home. They would leave first thing in the morning.

Tina was in her bedroom, carefully folding her clothes into her little suitcase, when William knocked on the door. She smoothed down the shirt she was holding and laid it on the top. 'Come in.'

He popped his head round the door. 'Are you nearly finished?'

'Yes, more or less, come in.'

He sidled into the room and slumped down on the bed.

'Are you all right, William?' She placed her hand on his shoulder and gave it a squeeze. He reached up and found her fingers, which he entwined with his own.

'I can't believe we didn't find her. We came so close. To be this near and still not locate her is so frustrating.'

Tina sat down on the bed beside him and laid her head on his shoulder. 'Don't ever give up, William, you hear me?'

He patted her knee and pulled himself together. 'I won't. Now come on, let's enjoy our last evening together.'

'I'm really going to miss this place,' said William as they strolled home a couple of hours later. 'I mean, everything about Ireland is just so warm and inviting. And the food...' He rubbed his stomach appreciatively. 'If I stay here much longer, I'll be the size of a barn door.'

Tina laughed and slipped her arm through his. 'I've loved every second of it. It was just the tonic I needed and I know we will always be friends.' She stopped and looked up into his face. 'We will stay in touch, won't we? I mean, I know we have an ocean between us, but we can write, and maybe on the odd occasion we could speak on the telephone. I know it's expensive, but–'

William put his finger to her lips. 'Let's just enjoy tonight and not think about going home. Care for a little walk before we head back to Mrs Flanagan's?'

An early summer shower had made the pavements glisten, but there was an almost tropical humidity to the evening. They walked through the park and sat down on a bench under a weeping willow, which had done a good job of keeping the seat relatively dry.

'I can't believe that this time tomorrow I'll be at home,' said William.

'You must be looking forward to seeing your parents again.'

He pondered this for a second. 'Of course, but I feel as though I've let them down.'

Tina frowned. 'In what way?'

'Well, they were so supportive in my quest to

find my birth mother, but I know it caused them a lot of anguish, and now that has all been for nothing. I should have just left well alone.'

Tina paused for a second. 'Then we would never have met.'

He considered this for a moment. 'Meeting you has been the highlight of this trip. I can't imagine how I would have felt if I'd had to make this journey alone. The disappointment at not finding my mother would have been so much harder to bear without you by my side.'

She reached up and caressed his cheek tenderly.

'Oh William,' she whispered. 'We've only known each other a short time, but already I feel as though you are part of my life. After Rick, I thought I would never trust a man again.' She turned away as she blushed slightly. 'I know that sounds ridiculous, and I'm sure that once you're back in America with your family you will forget all about me.'

William gave a short laugh. 'You're wrong, Tina. I'll never forget about you. In any case, I'm not giving up the search for my mother just yet. I'm sure I'll return to Ireland some day, and of course I have my grandparents in Manchester.'

'You think you'll visit them?' Tina asked hopefully.

'One day.'

'Then be sure to look me up.' She nudged him in the ribs.

He stood up and offered her his hand. 'Come on, it's getting late. We'd better get back to Mrs Flanagan's.'

Tina rose from the bench. As she straightened up, she went to pull her hand away again, but William strengthened his grip and she saw no further need to resist.

It was almost dark as they turned into Mrs Flanagan's street, and they were both so absorbed in their own thoughts that it took them a while before they realised that the landlady was calling to them from her front door.

William, still clutching Tina's hand, quickened his pace.

'What is it, Mrs Flanagan?' he asked breathlessly.

'There you are,' she cried. 'I've been waiting up for you.'

Even though she was a good foot shorter than William, she placed her hands on his shoulders and looked up into his eyes. 'There is a gentleman in my front parlour. No I don't want you to think I make a habit of letting strangers into my house at this hour, but for him I made an exception.'

William frowned. 'Go on,' he urged.

'I made an exception because he wanted to wait for you. I told him you were leaving first thing in the morning, see.' She paused, took a deep breath and then her face cracked into a broad smile. William, the gentleman sitting in my front room says he knows your mother.'

PART THREE

37

Not a lot had changed at Briar Farm in thirty-five years. After all, it was a simple existence and one that both inhabitants were accustomed to. Of course, farmhands had come and gone, animals too, but the essence of the farm was the same. It was back-breaking work for long hours with little reward. When Chrissie had first arrived here all those years ago, she had viewed it as a temporary measure, and if someone had told her then that she would still be here thirty-five years later, she would have shrugged it off as the ramblings of a madman.

While life had not been exactly good to her, she had found some contentment in the familiarity of her surroundings and the kind-hearted man with whom she lived. Jackie Creevy had been her rock, unstinting in his loyalty and devotion, and it was a constant source of sadness to Chrissie that she had never been able to give more of herself to him. She had offered to leave many times over the years so that he might find a wife, have children and make Briar Farm his own family home, but he would never hear of it. It wasn't that she didn't care for him. On the contrary, he was the one person on whom she could depend. So many people had betrayed her in the past. Her father in sending her to Ireland in the first place, her mother for completely abandoning her in spite of her promises to keep in touch, and Aunt Kathleen for arranging to have her sent to the convent to endure three years of hell she would not have wished on her worst enemy. Then of course there was Billy. Even after all this time, she could not comprehend why he had so cruelly rejected her. She had been so completely in love with him and knew he felt the same, so why had the baby changed everything?

The baby. There wasn't a single day when Chrissie did not think about him. These days she tried to picture him as a grown man, perhaps with a family of his own, instead of the small, terrified child she remembered. The day he was taken away from her and driven to Shannon airport to begin his life without her was the day Chrissie truly died inside. For three years she had nurtured him, and then she had been forced to sign him over to a childless American couple. The humiliation and degradation of the regime at the convent was nothing compared to the desolate anguish she felt when her beloved little boy was taken from her. She fought like someone demented as she was made to say her final goodbye. She managed to compose herself long enough to give him one last cuddle before he was placed in the car. He held his arms out to her through the open door.

'Mammy, me not want to go. Please.'

Chrissie reached out for him, but it was too late. The car door was slammed shut and she felt herself being pulled backwards as she watched the vehicle slowly crunch away on the gravel. Little William stood up on the back seat and looked through the window, his face contorted with grief as he cried out for his mother. Chrissie could not hear his words but his little blotchy red face was indelibly etched on her memory. She knew he would be well cared for. But she also knew that no mother could love him as much as she did. In the three years they had been together, she had lavished all her attention on him and made him the centre of her world. Billy might not have wanted his child, but she had more than enough love to give for the both of them.

Of course, over the years Chrissie had attempted to trace her little boy, but the nuns were immovable. She had been forced to sign a letter saying she had no rights to him and wouldn't attempt to contact him at any stage in the future. This piece of paper had been waved in her face several times over the years.

Now she stood in the kitchen waiting for the kettle to boil. This was one of the few changes that had been made, and it was more than welcome. Gone was the huge pot in the middle of the room that was used for heating water, and tucked neatly into the former fireplace was a cast-iron range cooker. Admittedly, it still required turf cut from the bog for fuel, but at least it was all done inside the oven and Chrissie could close the little door to keep out the worst of the smoke. She poured water into the little stained teapot and waited for it to brew. She could see Jackie through the window as he led the carthorse through the yard. Old Sammy had passed away years ago, and Jackie had bought this new one as an unbroken three-year-old at the horse fair. At nearly eighteen hands high, he was a tremendous beast, dark in colour, with a white stripe down his face. Jackie had said he chose him because he reminded him of George Orwell's horse, Boxer, from *Animal Farm*. He remembered that that fictitious horse was stoic in the face of adversity, incredibly loyal and worked until he literally dropped. He told Chrissie that if he named his new horse after him, maybe some of this work ethic would rub off.

It hadn't. In all his years of farming, Jackie complained, he had never encountered a more stubborn, bad-tempered, work-shy beast. Boxer could not have been more different from his namesake.

Chrissie crossed the yard carrying two mugs of tea and handed one to Jackie. Boxer snorted at her arrival and looked sideways at her, showing the whites of his eyes.

Chrissie laughed. 'He looks demonic sometimes.'

Jackie patted the horse's flank and took the drink.

'He's all right really, aren't you, fella?' Jackie saw the best in everybody, man and beast.

Boxer snorted again and pawed at the ground with his front hoof.

He raised his mug. 'Thanks for this.' He took a sip and then rested it on the fence. 'I've been thinking, how about we drive into town tonight and have a meal?'

'It's a bit extravagant, isn't it?'

'I thought it would be nice, you know, give you a break. It would be a chance for you to dress up for once, let your hair down, have some fun. It's been ages since we've done that.'

Poor Jackie, he never stopped thinking of her welfare. She sometimes thought his kindness and generosity were more than she deserved. There was a part of her that wished she could love him in the way that he obviously loved her, but she had had her heart broken irreparably once before and she was not going to go down that road again.

He took another sip of tea as he waited for her answer.

'All right then,' she said brightly. 'Let's do it. To hell with the expense.'

Jackie's face cracked into a broad smile as he winked at her. 'Good girl.'

Chrissie smiled at his enthusiasm and squeezed his arm. The years had been kind to him considering the hard work he had endured. He had aged in a rugged, craggy way that only came with being exposed to the elements in all weathers. His red hair was much lighter now, more strawberry blond in fact, but peppered through with the inevitable grey. He had remained in largely good health, the only evidence of the advancing years being apparent when he stood up from a crouching position, a manoeuvre he could not perform without groaning and clutching his back.

Once all the animals were fed, watered and safely secured for the night, Chrissie and Jackie climbed into their battered old van and headed into town. As they made their way down the deeply rutted farm track, the van rocked violently from side to side, which always made Chrissie giggle. Once out on the lane, the ride was smoother and she was able to let go of the dashboard and relax a little.

The lane was only single-track, but fortunately they rarely met anything coming the other way. As they rounded a bend, therefore, it was a complete surprise to see two cyclists heading straight for them. Jackie slammed on the brakes and the van skidded into the hedge. Chrissie put her hands over her ears as the hawthorn scraped along the window like nails down a blackboard.

'Christ almighty!' exclaimed Jackie, who never swore. 'I wasn't expecting that.'

The two cyclists, a couple in their thirties, held up their hands by way of apology as they dismounted their bikes and pushed them past the van.

The man was especially apologetic. 'Sorry, sir. We shouldn't have been riding two abreast.'

Jackie nodded as he put the car into first gear and continued on his way.

'That was unusual,' mused Chrissie. 'I wonder where they're going.'

'It was a bit odd,' agreed Jackie. 'He definitely wasn't from round here. I'd say he sounded American.'

38

After negotiating the rather treacherous uneven farm track, William and Tina eventually arrived at Briar Farm. The journey had taken much longer than expected. They had come as far as they could by bus and then cycled the rest of the way. The bus driver had taken some persuading to allow them to put the bikes on his bus, but had eventually relented. Although it was still early in the evening, they were much later than they had anticipated. They propped the bikes up against the fence and entered the yard. The sun was low in the sky and it cast a golden light over the farm buildings; there was still plenty of heat in it. Other than a few hens scratching round in the yard, the place was eerily deserted. William put his hands on his hips and surveyed the tiny farmhouse.

'It doesn't look as though anybody's home.' He ran his fingers through his hair as he beckoned Tina to the front door of the cottage. 'We'd better make sure.'

They both stood in front of the heavy door, hardly daring to breathe as William tentatively rapped on the wood. His heart was hammering in his chest and his mouth was suddenly bone dry. He had waited a lifetime for this moment. The door was so thick that his knuckles barely made a sound, but respectful as always, he waited a good few seconds before trying again.

'I don't think anyone's in,' declared Tina. 'What shall we do now?'

William wandered over to the front window and cupped his hands to peer through into the tiny front room. 'You're right. There's no one here. We'll just have to wait, I guess. Let's take a look around.'

They strolled over to the large barn at the far end of the farmyard and then stopped in their tracks as they heard a rustling sound coming from inside. William tapped on the door. 'Hello, is there anyone in there?'

They both jumped back in alarm at the sound of

327

dogs barking manically, throwing themselves at the huge door. They sounded so ferocious that William grabbed Tina's hand and they ran without a backward glance in the direction of the cottage.

'Well if there is anyone around, they sure know we're here now!' William's heart was fit to burst as he vaulted on to the stone wall that surrounded the little garden. He helped Tina up and they sat side by side pondering what to do.

'They can't be out all night,' concluded William. 'Not with all these animals to look after.' They could hear what they assumed to be pigs snuffling and grunting in another low barn, and there was a rather bad-tempered-looking horse in a nearby paddock.

Tina squinted at the slowly setting sun. 'At least it's a pleasant evening.'

She jumped off the wall and skipped over to the bikes, pulling a tartan thermos flask and a grease-proof-wrapped package from the basket on the front. She laid out a tea towel on the wall between them and opened the package.

'Oh good old Mrs Flanagan. Look, ginger cake!'

William looked at the dark, moist slab.

'I can't. I'm too nervous to eat.'

Tina had cut two slices and was about to take a bite when she changed her mind. 'You're right, maybe we should wait.'

William laughed. 'Don't be silly, you go ahead. I'll have mine a bit later.'

Tina adopted a serious tone. 'Are you all right, William?' It was most unlike him to refuse food. She put her hand on his knee and he covered it with his own and smiled.

'Are you kidding? After years of agonising and searching, not to mention a journey that has taken me across the Atlantic and across the Irish Sea and back again, I'm now finally going to meet my mother. Of course I'm all right. Nervous, yes, but excited too. I just know everything's going to be fine.'

Chrissie and Jackie had almost reached the outskirts of Tipperary Town, a journey that had taken nearly an hour in their rickety old van. The quiet country lanes now gave way to wider roads, and Jackie was able to speed up a little. 'Almost there,' he said, turning to Chrissie. 'You hungry?'

She smiled at him affectionately. 'Starving.'

'I thought we could go to the Cross Keys.'

Chrissie's eyes widened. 'The Cross Keys? We can't afford that.'

'Let me worry about that.' He reached over and patted her knee.

Chrissie reached up and touched his cheek gently, then suddenly clamped her hand over her mouth. 'Oh my God!'

Jackie instinctively pressed the brake. 'What is it?'

'The hens! I forgot to lock up the hens. How could I, after what happened?'

The previous month, a fox had stolen into the yard just before dusk and killed every last one of their little clutch of hens. The bloody carnage had shaken even Jackie, and he had gone into the barn and returned with a look of grim determination on his face and a rifle slung over his shoulder. The fox got away that time, but they had both resolved to be more vigilant in the future. The next day, Jackie went to the market and resolutely replaced all the slaughtered hens.

'We'll have to go back, Jackie, I'm so sorry.'

There wasn't a more patient man on this earth than Jackie Creevy. He looked at Chrissie kindly. 'Never mind, we'll try again sometime.'

'We will, Jackie, I promise.' She glanced across at him and studied his profile. He was clean-shaven and smelled of lemon soap. He was wearing a crisp white shirt that hardly ever saw the light of day and beige trousers that would be impractical on a day-to-day basis. 'I'm really sorry.'

'Stop apologising. I know you would never forgive yourself if something happened to those hens.'

She bit her lip and gazed out of the window as Jackie executed a three-point turn in the middle of the road.

'Don't worry, we should be back before dusk.' He looked across at her and smiled fondly. 'I'm sure there won't be any shocks waiting for us when we get home.'

39

The sun had dropped behind the mountains by the time Chrissie and Jackie arrived back at the farm, and Chrissie's heart was in her mouth as she climbed out of the van and looked around frantically for their little family of chickens. She found them over by the large barn, scratching away without a care in the world. She rounded them up and ushered them into their coop. Then she let the dogs out for their last run, refilled their water bowls and went to check on Boxer's trough. It was only then that she noticed that Jackie was over by the house talking to two strangers. She wondered who on earth they could be. They never received casual visitors. She was still carrying a metal pail as she made her way, slowly at first but then a little more quickly, towards the group. Jackie heard her coming and started towards her, holding out his hand. 'Chrissie...'

Chrissie felt her head begin to swim. She stopped a few feet short of the little group and they all stared at her. Her eyes struggled to focus through her tears and she opened her mouth to say something, but her voice was drowned out by the sudden crash of the metal pail as she let it fall to the ground.

She took another step forward and covered her mouth with her hands. Then she tentatively reached out to the young man who was gazing at her so closely and the years just melted away.

'Billy? Oh my God, Billy. I always knew you would come back.'

She ran to him and buried her head in his chest as her tears began to flow. Slowly he placed his arms around her and squeezed her gently. She pushed back a little and stared into his face. She thought how handsome he still looked, how the years had been kind to him, and as she cupped his face in her hands she searched for the scar above his left eyebrow. There was no scar, and the jolt she felt was like an electric shock. Of course this wasn't Billy. How could she have been so stupid?

Jackie placed his hands on her shoulders and turned her round. 'This isn't Billy,' he said gently.

She lowered her head. 'I know,' she whispered. 'I'm sorry.'

He tilted her chin so he could look at her face. 'This isn't Billy. But it is his son, *your* son. This is William.'

Chrissie felt her knees start to give way, and Jackie caught her under the arms. He turned her round and she saw the stranger properly for the first time. Her throat was tight and her voice a mere whisper. 'My God. My baby.'

Her legs could hold her no longer, and she collapsed to the ground. She buried her head in her hands and rocked gently back and forth. 'You found me. I can't believe you found me.'

Jackie turned to William. 'Let's get her inside.'

The cottage was both warm and welcoming and as guests, William and Tina took the comfy armchairs while Chrissie and Jackie sat on the hard straight-backed chairs. This house clearly was not used to entertaining visitors.

'I can't believe this, William. It's a miracle.' Chrissie touched his cheek again. 'You're really here?'

'Yes, I can't quite believe it myself. There were times when we thought we'd never find you.' He looked across at Tina. 'I couldn't have done it without this young lady.'

Chrissie stroked William's hand as though he were a long lost pet. 'I never forgot about you, William. Truly I didn't. I've tried to find you myself, but the nuns wouldn't tell me anything. How on earth did you find me?'

William leaned back in his chair. 'Well, it's a long story.'

He told her how he had his parents' blessing to travel to Ireland, and how he had visited the convent but the nuns there were unhelpful, to say the least. Then he told her of Nurse Grace Quinn, who had remembered her.

Chrissie's eyes widened. 'Grace is still there?'

'Yes, it was her who told me your real name; I had only known you as Bronagh up until then. She encouraged me to travel to Manchester to try and find your birth certificate.'

'Yes, we talked about my upbringing in Manchester. She was really very kind to me, to all the girls in fact. I don't think I could have endured that place without her.'

William continued. 'Anyway, I went to Manchester and that was where I met Tina.'

Chrissie glanced in her direction, wondering how she fitted into all this.

'I doubt I would have found you if it wasn't for this girl. I met her at the library where the records are held and found that she had already ordered a copy of your birth certificate.'

Chrissie addressed Tina. 'Whatever for?'

Tina glanced over at William, unsure what to say next. He reached into his jacket and pulled out Billy's letter. 'She wanted to trace you because she felt you ought to have this.' With a shaking hand he passed the letter over to his mother. She slowly unfolded it and stared down at the once-familiar but now long-forgotten writing. She turned to Jackie.

'Would you fetch me my glasses, please?'

Then, thirty-five years after she was meant to, she read the words that would have changed her life.

180 Gillbent Road
Manchester
4th September 1939
My darling Christina
*   I'm not very good at this sort of thing, as you know, but right now my heart is breaking and this is spurring me on. The way I treated you yesterday was unforgivable but please know that it was just the shock and no reflection of my feelings towards you. These past few months have been the happiest of my life. I know I've never told you this before but I love you, Chrissie, and if you let me I want to spend every day we have left together proving it to you. Your father tells me you don't want to see me anymore and I don't blame you, but it is not just about us now – there is the baby to consider I want to be a good father and a good husband. Yes, Chrissie, that is my clumsy way of proposing. Please say you will be my wife so we can raise our child together. The war may separate us physically but our emotional bond will be unbreakable.*
*   I need you to forgive me Chrissie. I love you.*
*   Forever yours, Billy xxx*

The cottage was deathly silent as she looked up. She folded the letter carefully and slid it back inside the envelope. Then she turned to Tina, her voice wavering with emotion.

'How did you come by this?'

Tina related her story. 'I couldn't understand

why he would write a letter like that and never post it. I just had to find out more.'

She told Chrissie how she had visited Billy's parents and how Alice Stirling remembered him writing the letter and going out to post it. Alice told me that he went round to see you the next day, but you had already been sent to Ireland. Your mother promised to contact you and let you know that he had called and wanted to be there for you.'

Chrissie stared straight ahead. 'She never did.' William shuffled uncomfortably. 'Well she didn't have a chance, did she?'

Chrissie turned and frowned. 'She should have tried a bit harder. I always knew she was terrified of my father, but to not tell something like this is unforgivable.'

William was confused. 'But she died...'

'I assumed she would be dead by now. I've tried to contact her over the years. She never even came to her own sister's funeral, you know, and she promised she would be there for me when you were born, but once I'd left Manchester, she just forgot all about me.'

William and Tina stared at each other.

William cleared his throat and spoke gently. 'Chrissie, your mother died just a couple of days after war broke out. She was hit by a car during the blackout. She died before I was born.'

'What? That can't be true. You mean she died shortly after I arrived here? My God, why didn't my father tell me?'

Everything fell into place then. Her mother had not abandoned her after all and her father had denied her the chance to say a proper farewell.

She breathed deeply through her nose and fought to control her anger. She did not want to embarrass her guests, but it was no good. The years of hatred and resentment towards her father bubbled up and boiled over as she erupted into a volcanic fury.

'God!' she screamed. 'I hate that man! How could anybody do that to their own daughter? Wasn't it enough that he kept me from being with Billy by sending me over here?'

The tears flowed unchecked and she wiped her nose with the back of her hand. Jackie cradled her in his arms, and she gave way to sobs that were so powerful she could hardly breathe.

40

William and Chrissie stepped outside for some fresh air. The light was fading now, but they strolled around the yard with Chrissie linking her arm through William's as she gazed up at the clear sky where the first few stars were beginning to twinkle.

'Do you want to tell me the rest of the story?' she asked.

'I want you to know everything. It's the least you deserve. Are you sure you're feeling strong enough?'

Chrissie sniffed. 'I've tried not to think about my mother all these years. It was her abandonment of me that I found so hard to accept. I knew my father was capable of anything, but not her. I really thought she loved me. Now I find out that she died just after I came to Ireland. It's incredible. How could any father keep that from his daughter?'

William shook his head. 'I don't know, Chrissie. It's beyond me.'

Chrissie stopped walking for a minute. 'Do you know if he's still alive?'

William shook his head. 'We don't know anything about him, I'm afraid. When Tina visited Wood Gardens, she found that all the old houses had been pulled down. That was where she met Maud Cutler. She was the one who told Tina that your mother had been killed in the blackout.'

Chrissie gave a small laugh. 'Maud Cutler. God, I haven't heard that name in years.'

William continued. 'Maud also told Tina your parents' names, so it was relatively easy for her to get hold of a copy of your birth certificate. Once we had that, and your mother's-maiden name, we came back to Tipperary Town and started asking around. Nobody could help us and it seemed that all our efforts had been in vain. We had even packed our bags. I was going home to America and Tina was going back to Manchester.' He stopped for a moment. 'God, I'm going to miss that girl.'

'So how did you find me?'

'Well, we went out for our last meal, and when we returned to Mrs Flanagan's, she had someone waiting in her front parlour who said he knew my mother.'

Chrissie's eyes widened. 'Who was it?'

'A guy named Pat. He calls round here apparently and takes your produce into town. He had overheard some people talking in one of the pubs we'd visited and he got in touch with Mrs Flanagan.'

'Pat, yes. He's been calling here for donkey's years, even before I arrived. Well would you believe it? Good old Pat!'

'So that's about it really. In a nutshell, that's how we came to be here.' William placed his arm protectively around his mother's shoulders.

Chrissie lowered her voice so that he struggled to hear. 'There is one more thing I need to ask.'

His heart quickened. He could guess what was coming.

'Do you know what happened to Billy?'

He stopped and turned to face her, and took both her hands in his. 'There is no easy way to say this. He was killed in action in 1940. I'm so sorry, Chrissie.'

She let go of his hands and turned away. She felt up her sleeve for her handkerchief and gently dabbed her eyes.

'I really loved him, you know.' She turned to face him again. 'All these years I've thought of him as a coward for not taking responsibility for his actions, for leaving me to fend for myself. If I had received his letter I would never have come to Ireland. We would have been together and I would have stayed in Manchester. I knew I could cope with anything if I had his support, but when my father told me that Billy had deserted me, I just knew I wouldn't be able to do it on my own. We could have been a

338

family, William. Maybe he wouldn't have been killed if he knew he had so much to come back to at the end of the war. Maybe he wasn't careful enough.' Her sobs echoed round the quiet farm-yard.

William wrapped her in his arms. 'Shh, there's no point in talking like that.'

'Why didn't he post that letter? It would have changed everything.'

William shrugged. 'We'll never know the answer to that, but he wrote it, didn't he? At least you know how he felt. That's all you have, and it will have to be enough.'

'This has all come as such a shock, William. I feel as though I'm going to wake up any second. Thank you so much for coming to find me. You have no idea how happy you've made me. I just wish your father could see you now. He would have been so proud. You are so like him. I'm sure he would have been a wonderful father.'

'That's just what his mother told Tina.' He reached inside his jacket pocket. 'Here, Alice Stirling gave her this.'

Chrissie took the old black-and-white photograph of Billy and bit down on her bottom lip as she gazed at it.

'He really was the most handsome man. Look at him in that uniform. What on earth did he see in me?'

'He loved you, Chrissie. You know that now.'

She passed the photograph back to William, but he put his palm up to refuse it.

'No, you keep it.'

'But it's the only picture you have of your father.'

339

William thought of Donald then, back in Vermont. The honest, hard-working lynchpin of the family, who had strived to give William the best home he could have hoped for. Donald was his father and he had plenty of photographs of him. His search for his biological parents was over, and although it had answered some of his questions and brought him a degree of peace, he would never take for granted the two people who had brought him up and made him the person he was today.

He pushed the photograph towards Chrissie. 'Please keep it.'

It was late in the evening by the time William and Tina announced that they really should be getting back.

'But it's dark. You can't cycle home now,' exclaimed Chrissie. 'You can stay here, in the barn.'

'In the barn?' asked Tina.

Jackie laughed. 'I slept in there for years. You'll be quite comfortable. I'll even bring you out a mug of cocoa.'

He exchanged a look with Chrissie, who smiled at the memory. What a day this had turned out to be. Her only son was home and what a fine young man he had become. The nuns had certainly placed him with kind, loving parents, she had to acknowledge that.

Later, lying in bed, Chrissie pulled the covers up to her chin. Even in the middle of summer her bedroom never got warm, and she needed the benefit of her flannel nightdress all year round. She picked up the cocoa Jackie had made and

340

took a sip. She could hear him downstairs now, scraping out the embers from the range ready for the morning. He still slept in the little bed in the corner, even though Chrissie had insisted countless times that he should take the bedroom. He wouldn't hear of it, of course. He was far too much of a gentleman.

She took Billy's photograph off her nightstand and stared at it again. It must have been taken only a matter of weeks after she had last seen him, but he looked much older. Maybe it was the uniform. She couldn't bear the thought that he had gone off to war without knowing what had happened to her and their baby. She picked up his letter again and read it through to the end, then pressed it to her nose, trying to detect any lingering scent of him that might remain. Eventually she folded the letter and tucked the photo inside.

'Oh Billy,' she sighed. 'I loved you so much.'

When she awoke the next morning, Chrissie's thoughts were muddled. She tried to focus on the events of the previous day and momentarily panicked when she concluded that it had after all been a dream. She sat up in bed and felt around in the gloom on her nightstand. She felt the crinkle of paper in her fingers and she pressed Billy's letter to her chest with a sigh of relief. All these years she had thought there must be something innately wrong with her. Why else would a man walk out on his lover and their child? Of course, the nuns hadn't helped, convincing her that it was all her fault. She had been made to feel worthless, and the degradation she had experienced still resonated to this day. She smoothed the letter as she read it again. She already knew the words by heart, but she would never tire of seeing them again in Billy's small, childlike handwriting. She had been worth loving after all. More than that, she herself felt able to love again. She had wasted nearly a whole lifetime grieving for her lost love, denying herself the opportunity of a relationship with another man. And that man had stood by her all these years, his devotion never wavering, his patience never ending. Her indulgence in her own misery could have cost them a chance of real happiness. It was time to put that right. She was ready.

She crept downstairs wrapped in a blanket, with thick socks protecting her feet from the achingly cold stone floor. Although it was still early, Jackie was already out of bed and had a pan of eggs and bacon sizzling on the range. The fire was lit and the kettle on the hob blew out a plume of steam, indicating that her morning cup of tea was almost ready. Jackie stood with his back to her, unaware of her presence, and she suddenly saw the little cottage in a different light. Of course it was still sparsely furnished, but instead of hessian sacks at the window, there were now little red gingham curtains. Jackie had exchanged some eggs for the few scraps of fabric and together they had stitched the curtains by the fireside. On the rough stone floor in front of the range was an old rug that he had picked up from a jumble sale. It meant she could attend to the cooking without the cold creeping up her legs. The smell of the bacon made her mouth water as Jackie forked it on to a plate. He carved himself a thick slice of the bread she had baked yesterday and dropped it into the frying pan to soak up the bacon fat.

Chrissie looked again around the little room, and for the first time she saw it for what it was — home. She crossed the floor, and very quietly, so as not to startle him, she placed her cheek against Jackie's back and wrapped her arms around him.

41

Tina's hands were brittle with cold as she forced her fingers to work the key into the lock. The temperatures were brutal, but the sky was clear and a heavy frost had covered the pavements, turning them into glistening sugar-coated slabs of concrete, which always reminded her of Nice biscuits. The door finally gave way and she almost fell into the shop. She picked up the pile of junk mail and free newspapers from behind the door and the pint of milk from the step, tutting as she noticed that the birds had pecked their way through the silver foil again in order to drink the heavy cream on the surface.

Once she had thawed out she settled herself on to the stool behind the counter, reached into her handbag and pulled out a long pale-blue envelope. Inside were several sheets of thin paper. She smiled to herself at the prospect of reading all William's news. It had been six months since they had gone their separate ways, but they had written to each other almost every week since then.

She was so absorbed in the letter that she jumped violently when the shop doorbell rang.

'Sorry, love,' said Graham. 'Didn't mean to startle you.'

'Don't worry, it's fine. I was just reading William's letter. Apparently it's minus fifteen there at the moment and forecast to get even colder. Imagine that!'

'Sounds grim, I must say.'

He sat down on the stool opposite and stared at Tina as she read. Her face was flushed and her mouth was pulled into a permanent grin.

'Aaah,' she said.

'What does he say?'

'He says he misses me very much and that he thinks about me every day.'

Graham looked up towards the ceiling. 'And do you feel the same?'

Tina sighed. 'I'm not going through this again, Graham. Of course I miss him. We grew very close while we were together in Ireland, but he lives three thousand miles away. We're just pen friends.'

'For now, but I'm worried you'll up sticks and go and join him.'

Tina laid down the letter. 'And would that be so bad?'

'For me, yes. I don't want to lose you.'

Tina took hold of both his hands. 'Graham, I love you very much and you are so important to me. You are a dear friend and my rock, but I'm not yours to lose.'

Graham looked sheepish. 'I know that. I just feel protective towards you, after all you've been through.'

Tina held her hand up to silence him. 'No, we don't revisit the past, remember?'

'Of course, but it's been almost a year since ... you know...'

'Since I lost the baby? I'm aware of that, Graham, thank you.' She was also aware that she was beginning to sound impatient. 'William makes me happy, OK? You want that, don't you?'

Graham nodded slowly. 'More than anything, Tina. You deserve it.'

'Good, now can I finish this letter?'

Graham slid off the stool. 'I'll go and open up then.'

Tina turned the page she was holding.

'Oh my God!' She clasped her hand to her chest.

'What is it?'

'Chrissie and Jackie have got married! A couple of weeks ago, in the chapel nearby, just the two of them. Isn't that romantic? William says he received a photo through the post and they both looked blissfully happy. Oh, I'm really pleased for them. Looks like she was finally able to let go of the memory of Billy and move on. She'll be fine now. Jackie's a wonderful man.' She had a peppery feeling in her nose and she sniffed noisily. 'Well fancy that!'

Graham stood behind her and placed his hands on her shoulders. She instinctively leaned back and he planted a firm kiss on the top of her head.

'Thanks, Graham.'

'What for?'

'For caring about me. Even though you're worse than a father, brother and probation officer rolled into one, I appreciate it.'

He laughed as he closed the door behind him and then blew her a kiss through the window.

Tina turned her attention back to William's letter. As she read the final paragraph, she almost fell off her stool. She felt her face and neck flush and the back of her neck prickled with heat. She was glad Graham was not there to witness her reaction.

In the run-up to Christmas, the shop was always busy, and today was no exception. Everybody needed to rummage out bargains these days, and Tina was doing a roaring trade. There were five or six customers in the shop, which made the small room especially crowded. People were bundled up in their thick winter coats, and at least three of them had unwieldy shopping trolleys with them. Tina squeezed through to put some more clothes out on the racks. An old man who came in from time to time was talking to another customer. He must have been in his eighties, but his voice was strong and loud, albeit slightly gravelly. He wore a trilby on his head, and heavy dark-rimmed spectacles, and although he stooped somewhat, Tina could tell he had once been very tall. He pulled a stained, greying handkerchief from his pocket and wiped his nose, then took off his glasses and rubbed his rheumy eyes. He hadn't shaved for a couple of days, and by the smell of him, he hadn't bathed for even longer. His large fingers, the size of bananas, were blue with cold, and he had several sores on the back of his hands. In spite of his size, he cut a forlorn figure, and Tina immediately felt sorry for him. He shuffled along, leaning heavily on his walking stick as he thumbed his way through the clothes.

'Are you looking for anything in particular?' Tina asked kindly.

He turned to face her, and she noticed that the whites of his faded blue eyes were now yellowed and his pupils were cloudy. 'Oh, you know, just having a look round. It gives me something to do.'

'Well let me know if I can be of any assistance.'

He nodded and turned his attention back to the rack of clothes. Tina picked up a pile of tatty old paperbacks and started stacking them on a nearby shelf. Next to her; the old man pulled a suit from the rack. He held it at arm's length and scrutinised it.

'My God!' he exclaimed to no one in particular. 'Have you still not sold this?'

42

He went to put it back on the rack and Tina carried on with her shelf-stacking. She was thinking about William's latest missive and how wonderful it was that Chrissie and Jackie had finally committed to each other. They had both had so much heartache in their lives and she was grateful that they could now live out the rest of their days happily together. That would not have happened had she not found the letter in that suit...

She paused for a second as she replayed in her mind what she had just seen, then she haphazardly flung the remaining paperbacks on to the shelf and turned to look for the old man. Although small, the shop was immensely cluttered, and it took her a few seconds to realise that he had left. She opened the door to an arctic gust and spotted him making his way carefully along the icy pavement.

'Excuse me!' she shouted. There was no response.

She braced herself against the chill, her thin satin blouse clinging to her skin as she picked her way along the pavement. As she approached him, she tried again.

'Excuse me.' This time he turned around, a look of puzzlement on his face. 'Sorry to bother you, but would you mind coming back to the shop a minute?'

The old man looked confused. 'Which shop?'

'My shop. The charity shop you've just been in.'

'You think I've stolen something? From a charity shop?'

Tina was taken aback. 'No, of course not, though you'd be surprised the levels to which some people will stoop. No, I was wondering if I might have a word.'

The old man looked doubtful.

'Please, it's important,' she urged.

'All right,' he said grudgingly, and she took hold of his elbow and guided him back to the shop.

Once inside, she invited him to take a seat and then waited until the customers had all left. Then she bolted the door and turned the sign round to 'Closed'.

'What's going on here?' asked the old man suspiciously.

'Don't worry, I'm not holding you prisoner. I just don't want to be disturbed.'

She sat opposite and clasped her hands together on the counter between them. She suddenly felt like a police officer interviewing a suspect, so she leant back in her chair and adopted a more casual approach.

'That suit over there, the one you held up before. You said you had donated it. Are you sure?'

The old man looked affronted. 'Of course I'm sure. I may be old and decrepit, but I can assure you I am not losing my mind.'

'Of course,' Tina apologised. 'I wonder, could you tell me how you came to be in possession of it?'

'Well, it was a long time ago, but it was made for me by a tailor on Deansgate. It was very expensive at the time, but it really is good quality. That was why I was surprised that no one had bought it.'

'So let me get this straight: the suit belonged to you?'

'That's what I said.'

Tina cleared her throat. 'Does the name Billy Stirling mean anything to you?'

The old man's eyes widened. 'What's this all about?'

'Please bear with me, Mr ... er, I'm sorry, I don't know your name.'

'It's Skinner. Dr Skinner.'

Tina's mouth fell open but no words came out.

'What's the matter?' asked Dr Skinner.

She rubbed her temples. 'I'm just trying to

piece things together.'

'You just asked if the name Billy Stirling means anything to me. I'm not sure why you want to know, but yes, I have the misfortune to know who you are talking about.'

'How do you know him?'

'Many years ago he used to court my daughter. That is, until he got her pregnant and I had to send her away. It was for her own good, but it ended up destroying my family. I lost my wife and daughter because of him, and now I have no one.'

The fragments began to fall into place. 'Dr Skinner, do you know anything about a letter addressed to your daughter? It was in the pocket of that suit and it was from Billy Stirling.'

Dr Skinner scoffed. 'Yes, I remember. It was when war broke out. He'd been pestering my daughter, and when I told him to sling his hook, he wouldn't listen, kept trying to get in touch with her. I had to keep them apart. He was no good for her, but she couldn't see that. I managed to stop them seeing each other, but then he goes and writes her a letter. I was on my way round to see him to make sure he understood he wasn't to contact Chrissie again and there he was on his way to post it. It was only good fortune that I managed to intercept him just in time. I offered to give her the letter myself and he agreed. He didn't trust me, though, said he would call round the next day to check I had given it to her. He never gave up, that lad. Of course, as soon as I got home, I made arrangements to send Chrissie away. I put the letter in my pocket and forgot all about it.' He shrugged. 'That's what the name Billy Stirling means to me.'

'You never read the letter, did you? I mean, it was still sealed when I found it.'

Dr Skinner shrugged again.

'I wonder if it would have made any difference if you had.'

'I doubt it.'

Tina thought about all the lives that had been ruined because of one selfish act. Billy had gone off to war without any hope; Chrissie had been deprived of her home and her mother's love and forced to give up her child. She remembered the anguish and guilt William had felt as he searched for his birth mother. And Jackie, who had waited patiently for the woman he adored to finally realise that what she had been looking for was right there all the time.

'Don't you think Chrissie had a right to see that letter?'

'Don't you think I had a right to protect my daughter?'

Tina ignored his question. 'You say you have no one. Don't you ever think about Chrissie and her baby? Don't you wonder what became of them?'

Dr Skinner cast his eyes downwards. 'I didn't think about them for many years. After my wife died, I threw myself into my work. It was mortifying for a man in my position to have such a wayward daughter. As the years passed, I forced myself to forget about her and the child.'

Tina stared defiantly at the old man's craggy features.

'I read the letter, Dr Skinner. I know it wasn't

meant for me, but I had to. I know where Chrissie lives and I know where your grandson lives too. I gave her the letter she should have read all those years ago. She couldn't understand why Billy had deserted her and none of us could understand why Billy never posted his letter. Well now we know, don't we? They could have been a family, they *should* have been a family, but your callous interference denied them that.'

If Dr Skinner was surprised by this news, he did not show it. He merely shrugged. 'Like I said before, it was for her own good.'

'Her own good? You have no idea of the heartache you have caused, have you? Your daughter despises you, Dr Skinner. You ruined the best years of her life. Thankfully, after reading Billy's letter, she has now found peace. She has been reunited with her son and is finally happy, despite your best efforts to deny her that.'

Dr Skinner took out his old handkerchief again and wiped his eyes. 'You weren't there, young lady. You have no idea what you are talking about. You are meddling in things you don't understand.'

Tina thought about how he had sent Chrissie away in disgrace, and the suffering she had endured in the convent. She had actually felt a physical pain when she learned the story of how William had been taken from his mother, for she knew only too well the sheer heartache of losing a child. And she thought of Billy. A fine young man who had seen the error of his ways and was willing to stand by the girl he loved and forge a stable family for them all. Billy, who was killed in action and never knew that he had fathered such a wonderful boy as William. It could all have been so different if the man sitting in front of her had done the right thing and given the letter to his daughter.

She stood up and took a deep breath.

'Dr Skinner, in all my life I have never come across a more vindictive man than you, and believe me, I know a bit about malicious bullies. Billy wrote that letter from the heart and it deserved to be read, but your self-centred actions altered the lives of so many people, including your own.'

Dr Skinner tried to clear his throat, but old age had made his voice croaky. He cast his hooded eyes downwards and whispered, 'How is she?'

'Chrissie? Oh, you care now, do you?'

'I've *always* cared. That is why I did what I did.'

As he stood up to leave, he sent his walking stick crashing to the floor. Tina bent down to retrieve it and placed it in his gnarled hand.

'She was my daughter, and in spite of what you might think, I did love her.'

Tina held the door open for him. 'Goodbye, Dr Skinner.'

After Dr Skinner had left, Tina picked up her handbag and brought out William's letter once more. She had read it over and over again, and the thin blue airmail paper was already worn, but the final paragraph still brought a huge smile to her face: *I have never been more in love with anybody in my life. I can't imagine spending the rest of my days without you. I will never love anyone like I love you. Please, Tina, come to America and be my wife.*

She half laughed, half cried as she clutched the letter to her heart.

Long ago, a young man on the threshold of the rest of his life wrote a similar letter to his sweetheart. Had he not done so, she wouldn't be standing here now looking forward to a future with the man she loved.

She looked towards the ceiling and tears pooled in her eyes.

'Thanks, Billy,' she whispered.

Epilogue

Present day

They were seated on the front porch now, on the swing seat overlooking the herb garden. The pungent scent of lavender wafted over on the warm breeze and Tina took a sip of her iced tea. Every time she tasted it, she smiled to herself. She never would have imagined a down-to-earth girl from the north of England drinking cold tea, without milk or sugar but with a slice of lemon of all things!

'That's a sad story, Grandma.' Ava noisily slurped the last of her home-made lemonade through a straw and rested the empty glass between her knees. Her little legs were too short to reach the floor, so she asked her grandmother to make the swing go. Tina immediately obliged and gently rocked the seat back and forth. Ava was right, it was a sad story, but Tina had long consoled herself with the fact that it had a happy

354

ending. After all, if Billy *had* posted his letter, she never would have met William. She had come to terms years ago with the fact that Chrissie's loss was her gain.

She glanced over at her husband now and felt the usual rush of affection that even after all these years made her heart pound and her cheeks flush. He caught her eye, then took his secateurs and snipped off a large pink rose. He inhaled its intoxicating scent for a second before he held it up in her direction. She couldn't hear his words from across the lawn, but there was no doubt about what he said.

I love you.

Acknowledgements

My sincere thanks must go to my family and friends, who have spurred me on all the way to the end and in particular to those who read early drafts and imparted their wisdom, knowledge and expertise. They include:

My husband Robert Hughes, my daughter Ellen, my son Cameron and my parents Audrey and Gordon Watkin.

My friends who gave up their time when they surely had better things to do: Yvonne Lyng, Kate Lowe, Grace Higgins and Helen Williams. Also special thanks to Wendy Bateman for her encouragement and infectious enthusiasm.

I am indebted to all the team at Headline but especially to Sherise Hobbs and Beth Eynon.

I am also grateful to my agent Anne Williams for guiding me through the whole publishing process and patiently answering my endless questions.

Finally, whilst St Bridget's Convent is entirely fictional, institutions such as this did exist and I would like to pay tribute to all the girls who suffered at the hands of such a cruel and heartless system. Chrissie's story reflects the suffering of over 30,000 girls, many of whom still bear the scars to this day.

K.H.

The publishers hope that this book has given you enjoyable reading. Large Print Books are especially designed to be as easy to see and hold as possible. If you wish a complete list of our books please ask at your local library or write directly to:

Magna Large Print Books
Magna House, Long Preston,
Skipton, North Yorkshire.
BD23 4ND

This Large Print Book for the partially sighted, who cannot read normal print, is published under the auspices of

THE ULVERSCROFT FOUNDATION

THE ULVERSCROFT FOUNDATION

... we hope that you have enjoyed this Large Print Book. Please think for a moment about those people who have worse eyesight problems than you ... and are unable to even read or enjoy Large Print, without great difficulty.

You can help them by sending a donation, large or small to:

**The Ulverscroft Foundation,
1, The Green, Bradgate Road,
Anstey, Leicestershire, LE7 7FU,
England.**
or request a copy of our brochure for more details.

The Foundation will use all your help to assist those people who are handicapped by various sight problems and need special attention.

Thank you very much for your help.